#TeenSheriff Evelyn Lassiter
By Lumen Reese

Hi Audrey!

Congrats on winning the give away!

Hope you enjoy the book.

Lumen Reese

Copyright © 2024 by Lumen Reese.
All rights reserved. No part of this book may be reproduced without permission. Certain copyrighted works are referenced within, mentioned in good faith in accordance with the fair use doctrine.
#TeenSheriff Evelyn Lassiter is a work of fiction. Any resemblance to persons living or dead is coincidental.

**Author's note:**
**This book is dedicated to the artists who best encapsulate my complicated relationship with my patriotism: visual artists Anthony Hurd & Noah Verrier, writer & tv show host Jon Stewart, musicians Cut Worms, Caroline Rose, The Walkmen, Courtney Marie Andrews, and especially the late, great John Prine and Johnny Cash.**
**It is also dedicated to Elon Musk, who represents for me everything that is wrong with America. Fuck that guy.**

Book cover by Alfred Obare (Behance)

ISBN: 978-1-952373-21-3 (Print)
978-1-952373-20-6 (Ebook)

**Follow the author on Goodreads, on Instagram**
**@ZoominLumen**
**Or, opt-in to her mailing list by emailing**
lumenreese@gmail.com **with 'join' in the subject line.**
**If you enjoy this book, please review! Reviews matter.**

Also by Lumen Reese:

**Science Fiction:**
Monarch Falls (The Four Quarters of Imagination #1)
Fire Fields (The Four Quarters of Imagination #2)
The Undesirables
The Bride Hunt of Elk Mountain
FAULT
Satan Hides the Hook (Spring 2025)

**Fantasy:**
Trial of the Lovebird Butcher
Monster Midwife
To You Shall All Flesh Come
Witch Wife (November 2024)

**Contemporary Young Adult:**
Claire Got Herself in Trouble

Chapter One

Once you turn about sixteen, grownups like to ask you what you plan to do with your life, as if you're equipped to be making that kind of decision. As if the world's not on fire. As if you're not already worried enough about everything else that they're piling on you. Homework, friends, nutrition, pregnancy, HPV, driving tests, Instagram, prude, slut, aging Madonna, whore, low-rise jeans, gap year, student loans, travel, Trump, Covid, online classes, AP courses, prom, Ukraine, Black Lives Matter, Palestine, fucking Elon Musk, national unrest (Taylor's Version) and so on, and so on.

They ask you what you plan to do, and they mean for the next few years. Usually college, or trade school. Something to get you off on the right foot. But if you're not sure, if you change your mind? A misstep these days comes with a hefty price tag. And to top all that off, even if you know what you want to do, every field is crowded and there's always someone better than you, someone with more followers, more hype around them. Someone a college would rather have than you. A person damn near needs an algorithm calculating their every move these days, to be a promising young woman. To stay one.

I had been dodging those kind of questions for a few years already, by the spring of 2023. Free-range parents can turn helicopter real quick, when they're as anxious about the dark and competitive world as anyone, and when their overachieving daughter starts floundering. Especially if they get the vibe that you're keeping secrets. Which I was, of course. All teenagers do. We're entitled to.

I was eighteen, nearing the end of my senior year of high school. And I had a plan. I'd had it for months, I'd worked on it diligently, to the detriment of school work. Nothing crazy, just a few b's and a c. I'd kept a tight lid, in case it went badly. Then I could let it go gracefully, pretend it never meant that much to me.

On a warm Tennessee Tuesday, I could hardly keep a lid on my excitement as I got up for the day. I finally had an answer for my parents, my grandparents, my teachers, my guidance counselor... and for any naysayer in the whole damn town.

Still in my pajamas, I went out before dawn to tend to my horse, Mabel. A brown and white mare, she chittered when I went into the little stable, nuzzled my hand and headbutted me as I fed and watered her, cleaned out her stall. She could roam the fenced-in pasture of our small side yard during the day, stretch her legs. I'd give her a little workout after school. I kissed her between the eyes, told her I loved her as I always did. She was getting old. So was I.

My blood was humming as I dressed. I'd laid my outfit out the night before, just like I did before every first day of school since kindergarten. Boots with a little heel, high-waisted corduroys with a little flair, a red, white and blue checkered blouse that tied in the front. Just a peep of tummy, not enough to get me dress-coded at school but enough to give confidence. Whether it all went the way I wanted or whether the day ended with me in trouble, it was better to look cute. I brushed my blonde hair, washed my face and did my eye makeup.

When I popped out into the kitchen, Dad was scrambling eggs. "Morning Eves. You look good." He had a look on his face as his eyes followed me to the fridge, he thought it was odd, wanted to say something else, maybe ask what the occasion was. Maybe he thought he ought to know, was racking his brain for something he had forgotten. Maybe I did too much, got up too early, was making him suspicious. But I had to be up when the 7:00 news came on.

"Don't I always?" I grabbed milk and caramel, taking a big Mason jar from the cupboard and filling it to the brim with ice then drizzling caramel, adding an inch of milk, heading for the Keurig. As the machine gurgled and the coffee started to stream out, perfuming the air, I stared at it intently.

If I made eye-contact with my father, it was over. There was practically steam coming out of my ears, my toe was tapping frantically on the kitchen tile. I could scream. I could burst. The clock said 6:45.

"Toast?" He had moved on.

"Please."

"One or two?"

"Mm… two." I stirred my coffee with a metal straw, the ice clinked, my jitters got a bit less jittery.

The floor tiles were white, but the kitchen was no white and grey HGTV cookie-cutter nightmare. No, Mom loved color, had clashing ones all over the house. The backsplash was mostly pink, with green accents that matched the cabinets. The counters were all butcher's block, different stains of wood layered. Where the kitchen turned into the living room, the floral wallpaper took over, straight out of the sixties. Mom said it never went out of style.

I was sat at the kitchen's serving bar when the slider to the back yard opened behind me. It made me jump, even though I knew it was my mother coming from the chicken coop. I made sure to jam my straw in my mouth as I looked at her over my shoulder, giving her a smile and a nod, sipping my drink so I didn't have to speak.

"Morning! You're up early." It made me cringe, but she had a basket on one arm and lifted it triumphantly. "Farm fresh butt-nuggets." She giggled after she said it, the way she did every morning.

Dad chuckled, too. A pity chuckle. I thought that the two of them not getting sick of each other after twenty years must be some kind of magic. Especially someone as cheesy as my mother, someone as humorless as my father.

"Toast, Honey?"

"Yes please. One piece." She put eggs into their container on the counter, tucked the basket back into its usual spot, washed her hands. "Ophelia's still not laying… I'm worried about her."

Dad put a plate of eggs and toast in front of me. "Maybe she just needs a break."

"Little spa day? Must be stressful being a chicken."

"All cooped up."

Mom giggled at Dad's cheesy jokes, too. He smiled proudly. He wouldn't even try if she weren't around. They kissed, she brought her hands up to stroke the sides of his neat, black beard. They stared into each other's eyes for a moment, then she blinked and came back to earth.

"Oh! Don't burn the eggs."

"Oops." He turned the stove off, plated the rest.

I had tucked into mine, although my stomach was in knots. I knew I would need the energy by the day's end, and I couldn't be any more suspicious. There was no saying grace in our family, no waiting for everyone to be seated. "Good eggs."

"Same as I always make 'em."

"Mm." The clock said 6:49. Eleven more minutes, I could do it. I tried to swallow and a big air bubble in my stomach rolled up my throat, making me wince, tap the place between my lungs, try to loosen something up. I had been shoveling eggs in too quickly.

"It's not a race, Evie," Mom admonished.

I nodded, put my fork down and held my jar of cold coffee again, in both hands. "Hungry…" I realized that my plan coming to fruition would be even sweeter if I could get them to start in on me, only to turn around and rub it in their faces. "Maybe I'll do something with food, like for work."

She brightened. "Like culinary school?"

It made Dad smile, too. He was the cook in the family, even eggs needed multiple seasonings, an acidic element, the texture had to be perfect. When I scrambled them in the pan once, he looked like he wanted to disown me. Of course he had shown me how to do it the right way, but I didn't have time for all that.

"Or like a food blogger. Or a line cook. I think the Shack is hiring one."

That sucked the wind out of their sails. Mom opened her mouth, glanced at Dad, sighed and said nothing. He buttered toast for himself, Mom having been served, his eggs probably quickly getting cold. His lips were a tight line hiding under his mustache. He avoided looking at her. My future was one of the only things they ever fought about. For the moment, Dad was winning, they were leaving me alone, had stopped bringing it up.

I loved my parents, and I knew they loved me. But I resented the pressure they put on me. Even when they didn't say it, it was there in the silence. I wanted to poke at it a little more. The clock said 6:53.

"Maybe not a cook. Too many Karens these days, I'd end up putting pubes in someone's food…"

Dad coughed up eggs. Mom frowned at me, said nothing.

I kept pushing. "I think I'd only want to cook if I could work for myself."

"Like starting a catering company?"

"Nah, sounds like a lot of work. Maybe I'll be one of those people who makes big batches of tamales and sells them out of the back of a mini van in grocery store parking lots. Or on the side of the highway."

I had overplayed my hand and Mom figured out what I was doing. She tucked a strand of wavy blonde hair behind her ear, smiling. "Sounds fun. I love tamales." She bit the corner of her piece of toast. Her smile made the corners of her eyes wrinkle, and I saw myself in twenty years standing in front of me, one of those scary moments where you're reminded that time marches on, coming for you in a long game of hide and seek, whether you're ready or not.

I tried to take comfort in the fact that if Mom was a window into my future, I'd be a babe until I was well past forty. Maybe it didn't matter if I ever figured out what to do with my life. I'd just marry someone who knew what they were doing. I hurt my own feelings as I thought it. Piled eggs onto my toast and made an egg sandwich. Dad saw me building it and got me a piece of cheese from the fridge without me asking. Mom slid me the hot sauce. The clock said 6:57.

"I'm gonna put the news on," I declared.

Mom made a face. "Why? I'm sad enough about Ophelia."

No way to be casual about it, really. We never had the tv on in the mornings. I just turned it on, the national news was wrapping up before the local news would go on; a story about polar bears dying out. I tried to deflect from Mom's question. "Maybe I'd like to be some kind of polar bear expert. That's it, it's perfect! Finally, I know what I -wait, no. Apparently they'll all be gone by the time I get anywhere." I kicked my feet up on the coffee table, bit into my egg sandwich. The layout was an open one, Dad could see the tv from where he stood on the kitchen-side of the serving bar. Mom had sat on the living room side, her back was to it, and to me.

I could hear her sigh at my comment. She took the bait, that time, and her voice was tight, though she tried to keep it cheery. "You could study regular bears. You could be a zookeeper. A marine biologist. You could train bears to play instruments and do acrobatics in a circus. You can do absolutely anything you put your mind to, if you just put your mind to something. Anything. You can always change it later, it's never too late to reinvent yourself. But for now, I wish you would just- just try something. And maybe you'll love it!"

Dad sighed, too. He wasn't happy that it was brought up. He chimed in, "Good money in bear training, I bet." He wasn't joking.

I said, "Maybe I'm just one of those people who never does anything. Like Boo Radley. I'll be a shut-in, I'll only go out at night, I'll become more of a legend than a person. People can hang their sins on me, and I'll be like Jesus."

Mom sighed again, but with humor in it. "You'd be the best damn shut-in the town ever saw, Sweetie."

The commercials ended and the logo for the seven o'clock news played. Two anchors at a desk recapped a few national stories of utmost importance. He was a decent looking older fellow. She was a pretty woman in her thirties, probably Botoxed weekly, little needles in her eyes and cheeks. She probably had to worry every day that she would be given the boot, replaced with a younger model.

That was the problem. Every job I really considered seemed to have some obvious downside. The Army? Death of course. Professional athlete? The diet. Actress, newscaster, influencer? The vanity. Academia? Death again. The medical field? Needles and stranger's buttholes. Prostitution, the same…

Dad was a contractor, and he liked it. I thought that wouldn't be so bad. But you typically needed more muscle than I had to work with. I was five-foot-three, and scrawny. Mom was a homemaker, raised chickens, gardened, and cleaned a few houses on weekdays while I was in school. It didn't make me respect her any less, but I didn't want to scrub people's toilets. They got by just fine, with our tiny house on a bit more than an acre long since paid off, and only the three of us to feed, plus Mabel.

The anchors wrapped up their summary, and a few minutes into their program, the man said the words that made me break out in a cold sweat. "Now to Trisha Topanga at Elviston Town Hall for a report on the local elections."

Trisha was another former local beauty queen, just a bit further down the line, with her brown hair permed and her crow's feet winning the war. She had to make up for it with a million-watt smile, they had to be veneers. "Thanks Ken! Like you said, I am here at Elviston Town Hall where -in a shocking turn of events- the county sheriff's race has been called before the polls have even opened. It seems that with every district reporting, there are more mail-in votes already tabulated in favor of a write-in candidate than can possibly remain among registered in-person voters. Elviston County's former, nine-term sheriff Dax Raegan has been ousted in favor of someone named Evelyn Lassiter, who, according to public records is only eighteen years old."

"Huh?" Dad had a mouthful of eggs. "Did I hear that right? Eves?"

Mom had wheeled around; I didn't look back yet, I couldn't. "Evie," her tone was sharper. "Is this a joke? What did you do?"

I had let the joy soar up in my chest for a minute, felt dizzy -couldn't believe we'd all pulled it off- but I had to get it together, had to spin it. I took a massive bite of my egg sandwich, my face had to be beet red and I thought the crunch of the toast and my noisy chewing would buy me a few seconds. I swallowed. Summoning all my strength, I looked back over my shoulder. Flashed a sheepish grin. "No, it's not a joke. You wanted me to try something…"

The explanation fell flat, clearly. Mom rolled her eyes, pushed her plate back and stood, hands going to her hips. "Explain yourself, right now." She might as well have called me 'young lady'. And she didn't look happy at having to pull out the firm voice. I wondered if in that moment she saw herself as her mother, the way I had just seen myself in her. I wondered if it hit different in middle age, maybe it was even worse.

"Okay, calm down." I had to put my jar of coffee down, couldn't tell if it was the thing that was sweating, or if it was my hands. I wiped my palms on my corduroys. "This idea came to me a few months ago, when I started seeing the yard signs to re-elect Raegan. And at the same time, we had someone come to the school talking about registering to vote, and everyone was like 'what's the point?' And at first I was like, 'yeah, right.' Cause I remembered how you two both went door to door for that guy Paige, two years ago, and then he got like twelve votes-."

"-Fourteen," Dad corrected me. He looked like he was still a bit sore about it.

"And that old bastard Raegan-."

"-Language!"

"-Raegan won with only a few hundred votes. He hasn't done anything good for the town in like more than a decade, he doesn't campaign, he just assumes he gets to stay sheriff because nobody was going to run against him. It just made me kind of mad. Nobody cares about local elections besides these old people who are completely entrenched in their views from when we were at war with Germany, like, the first time, you know what I mean? And meanwhile there are like eight-hundred people in the senior classes at my school, St. Albans, and Quest, plus we all know some people from Reed City, people who graduated last year, or have older siblings, or people from our college classes, and we all hate Raegan because of that thing with Harry Santiago, that wasn't right-."

Mom said, "So you wanted to get young people interested in voting, alright, but why not get them to vote for Paige? Why make it about yourself?"

"Well, okay… I didn't love all the pressure you guys have been putting on me, lately. I didn't want to have to decide my whole future, right now, and I thought this would look great on a college application, a lot better than a gap year." Their faces were not pleased. I quickly added, "It's something to do, it's money coming in! Plus it will get me in some papers, I could have colleges fighting over me for showing this kind of initiative and leadership. I'll do it for a year, maybe -or until they change the laws so I don't meet the requirements anymore- and then I'll resign and get all my classmates to vote for Paige in the next election."

Dad was smiling, but a disbelieving smile. "Well." It seemed like all he had to say. I could tell he was just a little proud of me, in an odd way.

"I don't like it," Mom said. "Eighteen-year-olds can't be sheriffs. That's all there is to it."

"They can, though," I corrected her, trying not to sound smug. "The requirements are set by the county, and ours haven't been changed since 1914. All they say is that a person has to be at least eighteen, has to have a high school diploma or equivalent, law enforcement experience, and win the majority vote."

"You haven't graduated yet!" She said it like it would be her trump card.

Again, I made sure to keep my voice small. "I got my GED in secret, back in February. I took the test the day I said I was helping set up for the Valentine's Dance. And you know I took that Criminal Justice course at the Career Tech Center last year, it included a ride along, and we were all considered 'junior deputies' for the day, which was just a patronizing participation trophy, really, but I figure it counts as law enforcement experience…"

The silence lingered as Mom, fuming, looked at Dad. His eyes seemed to ask her to consider, always the advocate for peace in the house.

He said, "We need to talk about this. You should go to school -assuming you're still going to school."

"-Of course she is!"

"-And we'll discuss it more this evening."

Mom shook her head, arms folded across her chest. Her pale cheeks were burning, her pretty mouth was a tight pinch. "No. No way. No daughter of mine is going to be a cop, carry a gun, deal with criminals, not while you're a teenager, not while you're living under our roof."

"Then I'll move out," I said, and it made her jaw drop. "-I'd rather not," I rushed to add, walking to the kitchen to put my plate in the sink, holding the rest of my egg sandwich. I chugged the rest of my iced coffee. "I'd rather stay here with you guys, really, while I figure things out... But I'm doing this. I'll have money coming in, enough to get a place of my own, if I have to. Or I'll stay with grandma…"

Chapter Two

I walked the one and a half miles to school, up the vintage ornateness of the little town's Main Street. My best friend Delilah Stokely met me at the corner of Main and Warner, and we walked the last half mile together, as always. She did a little dance, when she saw me coming, waiting at the cross walk.

"Oh my God! I can't believe we pulled it off. Hold up!" She grabbed my arm to stop me in front of the spinning red and white thing in front of the barber shop. "-I want the first selfie with the new sheriff. Smile!"

I crouched a little so that our faces were even. Delilah was shorter than me, and curvier. She had a pretty face and she was always nice to everyone, and everyone liked her. In many ways, she was my better half, and the only reason I had gotten so far was that I always tried to be like her. We beamed in our picture, and we took a few until we both looked good in one.

"Use our hashtags," I reminded, as we started walking again.

"Hashtag-Teen-Sheriff, hashtag 'get-out-and-vote', hashtag 'back-the-blue'. You look so cute, by the way."

"Have to, in case I end up on the news."

"Oh, you will. I have calls in to a few stations."

"You're amazing, you know? I never could have done this without you." When I came up with the idea, it seemed harebrained. Delilah was the one who made me think that it could be done, the more analytical of the two of us, the more organized. I wondered more than once if she shouldn't have been the one to be put up for the job, but she insisted it had to be me. I was taller, and blonde. And people wanted to follow people like me, she said. She had the brains and the charm, I had the backbone.

"Don't even worry about it, just follow through and make us proud."

Her words dug a barb of worry into me. I could be flakey, I did sometimes let people down, and she knew it. If I didn't make the news, if I didn't stand up for what everyone wanted me to, I would crush her. She worked so hard, we both did, organizing the students of our class, and other schools, too. All of it in secret. It was easy to get people excited but getting them to follow through, flogging them with text reminders to mail in their votes, talking one-on-one with those who needed the push, either worried about repercussions or just finding it too hard to believe that kids could make a difference… it had been tireless.

"I'll try," I said.

The high school was the newest building in town, opened only last year. It was utilitarian, grey stone and lots of glass, two stories, bench seats that were shaded by metal umbrellas outside of the cafeteria, not enough for everyone, usually just us popular ones got to eat outside. A few of our friends hung around before school started, the wealthier ones drinking Starbucks.

They started to clap as Delilah and I approached. I did a little twirl and then gave a bow, gesturing to Delilah and adding to the applause. She blushed, gave a little wave, she wasn't as confident as I was.

The others started chanting, "Sheriff! Sheriff! Sheriff!"

"Who wants a selfie with your new sheriff?"

"Yeah, me first." Scott Proffit tossed me something as he clambered, climbing over the table, whacking his head on the metal umbrella and making it waver like a gong.

I chuckled at the dollar store kid's cop badge he had thrown to me, and held it up, while Scott did the devil's horns, sticking his tongue out. He was very hard-headed, but he was a good guy.

"Remember our hashtags?"

"Yeah, I remember."

"Who's next?"

People had come running from inside when they saw me, underclassmen that I didn't know, still pimply, still short, still scared of their own shadows and more than a few not wearing their deodorant religiously yet.

"Tiktok with the new sheriff!" a boy with patchy facial hair got too excited and yelled at his phone camera -and directly into my ear. "Take over the town, woo! Black lives matter! Fuck the police!"

It made me freeze, smile disappearing, mouth open, I wasn't sure what to say. My parents talked about the dangers of rhetoric like that, and they were the smartest, most level-headed and conscientious people I knew. "Black lives do matter! Alright, that's enough," I ducked out of his shot. "All of you get to class, before I arrest you for truancy."

They chuckled and dispersed, a few asking, "Catch you later?"

"Selfies at lunch?"

"Of course, of course, my loyal constituents." I waved them off. Delilah and I split from the pack to head to AP English.

When the teacher Mrs. O'Connell saw us coming, she jumped out of her desk and came over, excitement on her face. She was young for a teacher, dainty and religious and pregnant more often than not. She was in her second trimester, showing and occasionally nauseous. "Evelyn, oh my gosh! I cannot believe it! What made you think of this, and what are your plans? Let's talk about it!"

The bell rang and I was able to beg off with a few words, but everyone was looking at me and she started the lesson with an open forum about my election. My classmates expressed with varying levels of excitement how it was cool that young people could actually make a difference, or that it was a position which only reached the county level and that we couldn't really make any difference at all. That led to me being asked to explain the role of a sheriff, to those who were unfamiliar.

"Well, your local cops are mostly responsible for the town they live and work in. Sheriffs cover the whole county, and they sometimes have to coordinate resources between towns, or communicate from one town to the next about developing situations, because a lot of systems are closed, they don't talk to each other. That's why Ted Bundy got away with it for so long, he kept moving."

"Man, Teddy would've been toast if he was in your jurisdiction!" That was Scott again, and the class laughed.

"Alright, class," Mrs. O'Connell took control back. "Let's not forget that there were real victims, who lost their lives. Evelyn -Sheriff Lassiter- what do you plan to do with your position?"

I sniffed loudly, squaring my shoulders in a show of bravado, then settling down into my desk and flicking my plastic badge before crossing my arms. "Clean up the town."

It earned a few giggles, and Mrs. O'Connell, still smiling, rolled her eyes. "Really, Evelyn?"

I felt sweat break out under my arms. "Really, I just didn't like the way Raegan swaggered around, acted like a bigshot but never did anything for the town. He treats some people differently than others. And so I just want to take things day by day, do my best to be fair, give everyone a fair shake." A lot of it was platitudes, but they nodded, seemed to accept it. I didn't know what else to say.

"Alright. Well, class, I guess it's time to get to work."

She started teaching, but not two minutes later, the door opened and Raegan and a deputy stepped in. I sat up straighter, feeling a kind of fear that only came from men in uniform. I felt it when my dad got pulled over, I felt it when I saw men in black body armor armed to the teeth picking up money from the bank. They had the authority, they had the might of others behind them, they could do what they wanted and get away with it.

Raegan pointed at me, then to the hallway. "Let's go," was all he said.

I glanced at Delilah. She looked panicked. I tried to smile, stood and started to go.

Mrs. O'Connell was a 'back the blue' sort, I knew where she lived and I had seen a sign on her lawn, but even she was uncomfortable. She sounded timid as she tried to speak up. "Evelyn has class, officers."

Raegan put on a smile. He was surely small-town handsome twenty years and sixty pounds ago. "She won't be gone long, Ma'am. Just need to chat with her."

I left my things on my desk and stepped out into the hallway. I made sure to get a look at the nametag of the other officer. His last name was Kipling, he was shorter than Raegan and similarly stocky, beer-bellied. He put his arm out, trying to hurry me across the hall and into the currently empty room where I had calculus classes later in the day. His hand touched my back and I shrugged him off, feeling rising discomfort.

"Don't touch me, thanks."

"Well sor-ry," he chimed musically, looking to Raegan for his agreement.

Raegan ignored him. He pulled the door closed behind us, and I didn't like it at all, crossing my arms over my chest.

"Can I help you gentlemen?"

"Save it, Missy," Raegan snapped. "You think you're real cute, don't you? What's your angle here?"

My heart was hammering in my chest. "Town needs a change in leadership." I tried to sound aloof.

"Is that so?" His face was pinched, he scratched stubble on his cheek and each individual hair crisply flicked back into place in the heavy silence of the room. "Are you trying to make a joke of my county and my officers, Missy?"

"You've done a pretty good job of that yourself."

He slammed a fist down on a desk and it made me jump halfway out of my skin.

"Whoa!"

"You little shits have no respect! You want everything handed to you, everyone's a winner! You think you can curl your hair and get your friends to follow you, and that makes you somebody!? You're about to learn how life works, Missy! I'm talking jailtime!"

I blustered, forcing my lips to stay in a haughty sneer. "What's the charge, *former* sheriff?"

"Obstruction, for starters! How about fraud?"

Kipling chimed in, "Tampering with an election."

I did what my mother taught me to do. What I had seen her do in grocery stores, doctor's offices, at school functions, whenever faced with a trumped up man. I forced down my fear, stood up taller, and I laughed at them. My loud cackle made Raegan spin away, then wheel back around, narrowly throwing himself into Kipling's way before the younger man could come at me.

"Hold it!"

"Little bitch!" He pointed a sausage finger at me over his friend's shoulder.

I jumped back, my laughter turned hysterical as it felt weirdly fueled by the fear surging through my veins; blood rushing to my legs to carry me away, fight or flight. Mom was right. Men did not like to be laughed at, especially ones like those, who stomped their feet to get respect.

Raegan kept his cool, he hissed out, "You don't know who you're screwing with, Missy. I was in the Army, I did a tour in the sandbox -Gulf War- and I know people. But that's okay… Laugh while you can."

I headed for the door, not turning my back on the two of them. "I've got class, former sheriff, Deputy Kipling… Raegan, you're definitely not on the force anymore. Kipling, I suggest that you get back to work, cause I'll be taking a hard look at the budget and the payroll once I'm in, later. I'll see you after school."

*

It was taco Tuesday in the cafeteria, and I was making mine into a taco salad when the principal found me in the lunch line. "Miss Lassiter, there are reporters waiting to speak with you outside. If you're okay with that."

"Sure." I took my tray to the tables in the little courtyard outside. A lot of my classmates were gathered round, and two reporters -a man and a woman- in suit jackets sat at the center table with Delilah, Scott, and a few of the others. They had saved a spot for me. A camera man stood back, getting the shot.

"Miss Lassiter?" The pretty dark-haired woman stood to shake my hand, while the brown haired, bearded and studious man did not. He only looked at me, took notes on a pad, and listened.

"Yes."

"I'm Alanna Malone, I'm from the Chattanooga Late Night news, we want to do a story on you."

"Wow, okay."

"Is it alright if we record you?"

"Can you not use shots of me eating? I only have like twenty minutes for lunch." And my appetite was legendary, I shoveled a bite in as soon as I was done talking.

"Sure, no problem. So why don't you tell us a little about why you decided to do this?"

I swallowed, rattled off the same stuff I had said earlier, and worried the whole time that people would hear it so many times that they realized what a phony I was, that there was nothing of substance behind my decision.

She asked how I pulled it off. I made sure to name Delilah and Scott and a few others who had helped me scare up votes, managing another bite as she found her next question.

"What do you have to say to anyone who might think that a teenager isn't suited for a job like this?"

"Well, if we can join the army and vote, we can enforce laws, right? Give me a chance. I think I can really bridge the gap between the young and the old in this town… the way that things should be and how they are."

"And with the reckoning that has been happening nationwide -following the very publicized wrongful deaths of Eric Garner, Breonna Taylor, and George Floyd- many have called for the entire institution of policing to be done away with. Are you one of those people?"

"Uh… We need change, definitely. I'm not sure how drastic that change needs to be… exactly, but I know that a lot of innocent people have died because of police. Now that I'm the sheriff of Elviston County, I plan to do what I can to make sure that kind of thing doesn't happen here."

"And what's your first act as sheriff going to be?"

I felt apprehension at revealing it out loud, in case there was a hang-up and I couldn't deliver. But I was too far in it. I barreled ahead. "Sheriff Raegan hung a flag up a couple years ago that says 'blue lives matter'. I'm going to replace it with one that says 'black lives matter', because there's no such thing as a blue life."

"That might anger some people." She doesn't phrase it as a question.

"Well, they can recall me or vote me out in two years. For now, I'm the sheriff, and I'm calling the shots."

"That's a good soundbite," Alanna Malone said. "And when are you planning on changing out the flags? We'd like to get it on video."

"After school. Around four."

"We'll be there. So nice to meet you, Evelyn." She shook my hand again, then the three adults stood and left.

I shoveled a big bite of taco salad in, checking the time. I had only a few minutes left to eat.

"Can we all come to the flag ceremony?"

"We should burn that old one."

"I don't think burning a flag is a good idea, my first day in office."

Scott said, "You're right. Wait for your second."

## Chapter Three

Scott drove a rusty old red Ford truck, so only Delilah and I could legally ride with him. He parked in the lot of the communal precinct-firehouse-town hall building, and we walked around to the front. The American flag flew high, at the top of a tall pole, and below it, another said 'blue lives matter'.

The news crew was waiting with a camera on a tripod, a white van parked on the street. The lady reporter waved to me, but didn't move to come over, just hung back and made sure that she liked the shot that her crew was getting. It made me instantly excited, standing taller, pushing out my chest. I had to remind myself that like most adults, they were only interested in me because they thought that they could get something from me. It would certainly pass.

A troop of four cops in uniform -one Raegan, one Kipling, and two other unexceptional men- came spilling from the mouth of the orange brick building. Raegan scowled, stalking over at the head of the pack. They did remind me of wolves, in a way.

Kipling tried to charge ahead, but Raegan caught hold of his shoulder and murmured to him, slowing his attack dog down. Raegan kept coming, swaggering step by step, and came to a stop a stone's throw from me, with the flag pole in between us. As he centered himself, he let his hand rest on his gun, holstered at his hip, and stared me down.

I looked at the knotted white rope wound around a pin at the bottom of the pole. "How does this work?" I whispered to my friends.

Scott jumped to my aid, beginning to undo the knot, squinting but very capable with his hands.

I stood aside, grinning. "You want your flag back, Former-Sheriff Raegan? You can take it when you go."

He said nothing in response, just glared and breathed heavily.

The flag slid down the pole.

As Scott lowered the flag he started to sing the national anthem. No sooner had he gotten out, "Oh say, can you see-?" than a few angry huffs and snorts came from the cops. Kipling's face went from a red but still mask to an ugly snarl. He glanced at Raegan, at the others, and he started to charge forward on stomping steps. Raegan snatched him by the collar and wrenched him around; he spun like a ballerina.

"You're just gonna let them!?"

"Not now, Dipshit!" Raegan was all too happy to get some of his frustration out.

Kipling's hand had gone to his gun, he turned and glared at us again and the sight made my guts twist.

"Let's everybody calm down." The man who came from the front door of the station and around the click of cops was average in height and build, but his voice drew everyone's attention. He was black, with a neat crew cut and an open face, carefully kept blank. He was Leo Paige, Deputy, who lost the last election two years ago. His eyes took me in for just a second, then stayed on Kipling, the clearer threat.

Scott had frozen, and looked at me.

"Keep going," I said.

His hands started moving one over the other once again, and both flags descended the pole. He sang, and his voice took on a tremor. "-The dawn's early light…"

I turned my back on the cops, although my body told me not to. Sweat had broken out under my arms and felt chilled in the spring breeze. I addressed the camera. "The people of Elviston made their voices heard. We're a good little community, we've got some old fashioned ways, but the majority of us are young and we aren't afraid of the hard work of making this town better. We believe that Black Lives matter, and that police should be held to a higher standard, even, than the rest of us. Because they -we- have a duty to protect all of our constituents. Our neighbors." It wasn't exactly off the cuff, but it sounded good and genuine, I thought.

Scott had unhooked the old Blue Lives Matter flag, it still caught the breeze as he held it out to me, by the corners. I passed him the folded new flag, took the old, and folded it up. "Here you go, Former Sheriff Raegan. Take it with you, when you go."

I crossed the short distance to them, although my hackles rose with each step. Kipling was still glaring, although Raegan had knocked his hand away from his gun. Paige stood a few feet back, separate from their group and mine, and watched silently. He had turned his back to the cameras, I noticed.

Raegan snatched the flag from me. His murmur was far too low for the news crew to detect, even if I were wearing a mic. "Keep piling up these disrespects, if you want to, little lady… I'll keep tabs."

I got the feeling that 'lady' subbed in for 'bitch' because the cameras were present, just in case. Or, maybe the old dog dig have some kind of southern pride. Either way I felt bolstered by his obvious hatred of me. I smiled sweetly.

"Well, you've got nothing but time, now. You spend it however you want to."

He turned to go inside, with the female reporter chasing after their group of four as they went. "Sheriff Raegan, anything to say?"

"No comment."

Kipling looked like he tried to turn around, but Raegan kept shoving him along.

"Keep moving. Don't give them anything."

Paige was looking at the Black Lives Matter flag as it ascended the pole. He muttered, "You couldn't have ironed it?"

I blinked and looked at it myself. The cheap fabric did hold a lot of wrinkles. I felt a twinge of guilt. "Oops. I guess I should have-."

He had already turned to go inside.

The lady reporter rushed to him, holding her microphone in his face. "Deputy Paige, would you care to comment?"

"No." He held the door wide and stopped, looking back at me.

I was between the door to the building and the flagpole. I waved for Scott and Delilah to come, and to hurry. I didn't want to go in alone. Not yet. They wouldn't realistically protect me much, but still, I wanted them there. It seemed that as much as I had considered the possibilities that winning the election presented, I had not actually thought about being alone with a bunch of cops, who hated me, potentially every day, for long stretches. I suddenly dreaded the future.

The lady reporter still hounded Paige, but she used her sweetest southern lilt. "Are you holding the door for Ms. Lassiter because she's your new boss, or because she's a girl?" Her tone did not belay the fact that she was fishing, trying to stir up trouble, because that was what her viewers would want. I reminded myself that she was not my friend.

Paige did not rise to the bait. "I'll hold the door for anyone. Excuse us, we're done here unless you have some genuine business, here. Thank you."

I had hurried into the cool entry hall, Scott and Delilah, too. Paige shut the door, shutting out the news crew.

The walls were glass in the front hall, showing a small cubicle for city business on the right, where a woman sat watching us. It opened to a larger bullpen area, the seat of the county Sheriff's office, also, essentially, the town police precinct. On the left was the tall garage space for the firetrucks, and on the second floor above it, the fire station, with sleeping quarters, kitchen, showers for on call firefighters, pole and all. We had toured the place freshman year, and I had gotten to spend a few days on the police side during my criminal justice course, last year.

The deputies had taken up their desks in the bullpen, and watched me through the glass, like I was a fox in the henhouse. Although I felt more like a hen in a fox's den.

I said, "Can we talk, uh… Deputy Paige?" I didn't want to call him 'Mr. Paige' although that was my first instinct. He was my elder, but I was his superior, I had to remind myself. And simple 'Paige' would come off wrong. Too familiar, and somehow also like I was talking down to him.

He didn't look at me, just took the lead up the hall and said, "I'll walk you in there, if that's what you want." He held the inner door for me.

I slunk in, Scott and Delilah came after, crowding close to me. I made sure to set my shoulders back, keep my head high as I walked through the bullpen, in between a half a dozen desks. There was a coffee station on a counter on the far wall, with cabinets above and below. Above, they had locks on them, I wondered if they were official forms and files, or just sugar and coffee filters, jars of pretzels and peanut butter. A fridge and vending machine stood in a little alcove I could see, across from what had to be a bathroom.

At the back of the building was an office for the Sheriff. The walls were glass, with blinds which were pulled up at the moment. Raegan stood behind what used to be his desk, packing up a few knickknacks into an empty file box. He glared at me, still chucking objects in. A signed baseball, a framed picture.

"Key's there."

A silver key sat on the edge of the dark, wooden desk. I pocketed it, then traced the gleaming finish of the wood. "This is nice. Is it mahogany?"

He didn't answer, yanked the top drawer out of the desk and dumped its little contents into the box. Receipts, a stapler, some change, a pack of cards. A paperclip tumbled out. I scooped it up and tossed it in.

The box full, the office a blank slate, Raegan took a second to stare at me. A bitter smile spread on his face, then he unclipped the sheriff's badge from the front of his shirt. He tossed it on the desk, making it skip once like a stone on a pond. Then he marched out of the office, through the bullpen. "I'll see you boys soon." He left the building.

The office was small, and with the four of us inside, it was crowded. The desk took up most of the space, with a few file cabinets on one wall, a mother's tongue plant on the other side in the square of light from the window at my back, and two chairs on the inside, glass wall.

Paige stepped out.

I settled down into the comfortable, brown leather office chair behind the desk. Picked up the six-pointed star of the badge, and spun it between my fingers.

Scott and Delilah got hyped again in the blink of an eye.

"Oh my God, that was insane!"

"We're gonna make the news. Could you believe that guy grabbed his gun!? I was terrified!"

I smiled but my heart felt heavy. "I should have ironed the flag. And I don't know where I go from here, guys…"

Their expressions flattened, being faced with my worries.

Delilah said, "We have a plan."

"It's a pretty vague plan. I don't know how to do this. Sensitivity training? Who do I call? Where am I getting the money? How do I even find the budget? Am I going to get any kind of training, here? Obviously Raegan isn't going to help me, and the last sheriff before him is dead."

"Ask that guy Paige to help you," Scott said.

"I feel shitty about asking him for help… It should have been his job. You saw him out there, he actually knows what he's doing."

"Too late to change it now."

"You should tell him how you're feeling, and that we can get people to vote for him, whenever you get kicked out or the next election happens. But you're the sheriff, right now."

"Right…"

"Should we go?"

I inhaled deeply. Exhaled and my breath came out shaking. "Yeah, you can get going. I guess I'll talk to Paige and get used to being here alone."

"Are you sure?"

"I've got homework but I can do it here, if you need me."

"I appreciate that. I'll be alright."

I didn't exactly believe it.

## Chapter Four

When the kids left, I once again asked Paige, "Can I talk to you, Deputy Paige?"

A few of the other officers looked at him with apprehensive, stern gazes. They sort of looked at him like they looked at me. He walked up the rows and closed the door behind him. He pulled one of the chairs from the wall up to the other side of the desk. I sat, too.

He sat watching me.

I started nervously. "So, my name is Evelyn Lassiter, first of all. We haven't been introduced."

"Leo Paige."

"I don't know if you remember, but my parents Vince and Marissa worked for your campaign, two years ago. They went door to door and manned a booth outside the Piggly Wiggly."

"Nice of them…" He kept his face and tone blank.

"I surprised them with this whole thing."

"You surprised a lot of people."

"Yeah... First of all, I'm sorry that you lost your election. You should have won. If you had, we wouldn't be here, now."

He tipped his head in acknowledgement.

"Secondly, I should have ironed that flag, and I'm sorry."

That made him smile a little, and still he said nothing.

"I did have good intentions, though, with this whole thing. I thought it would be good for me, but for the county, too. I got Raegan out of here, at least."

"There is that..."

"I know they're going to change the laws, or recall me as soon as they can. I might have a month, or two, I don't know. When there's another election, we'll get people to vote for you. My mom says I should have done that in the first place, and she might be right... but I didn't. It would have been a lot harder to get people my age excited about you than me. And I wanted to make a splash, I wanted the recognition. That's me being honest."

"Okay."

"As long as I'm sheriff, I need your help, please."

"And it's my duty to help you, as a deputy sheriff."

"Okay..." I sort of figured he wasn't amused by me, but I would take what I could get. "I'm thinking if I can only get one thing done, I'd like to put everyone through some sensitivity training, start requiring body cameras while on duty. I need to find money in the budget. Kipling's salary should cover it."

"We're already short staffed. If you fire Kipling everyone will be working overtime, that's no way to make friends."

"There have to be other qualified candidates."

"Yeah, cause cops are so popular, these days."

"Ah… Where should I start?" The question made me sound dumb, maybe. A little helpless.

"You need a gun. We can expedite a permit for you, but not without you putting in some range time with a trained instructor, which -luckily for you- I am. We should do that right away, if you want any chance of people taking you seriously."

"Right now?"

"Your parents expecting you home?"

"Nine o'clock curfew on school nights. Eleven on weekends."

"You know you need to put in plenty of hours here, preferably forty, or you could be charged with misappropriation of county funds. Although that's already a possibility."

I shrugged. I hadn't considered it.

"You plan to stay in school?"

"Yes, I want to."

"So, ten or twelve hour shifts Saturday and Sunday. Four hours after school every day? There needs to be a certain number of deputies on duty at a time, if someone calls in, you need to be here. I think you'd better plan on some call ins. You think you can keep that up?"

"Let's go shoot."

He drove us to a shooting range on the edge of town, asking surface-level questions about my experience with firearms. There was a coldness to him, he was walled off, perfunctory, as he explained protective gear to me in the end stall of the range. It was all indoors, the target that Paige hung up zipped on a line out to the far end of the building.

He drew his service weapon, an automatic gun, and as soon as it was in his hands, I found myself taking a step back, didn't hear his next words.

"What?"

He ejected the magazine and checked the chamber. "Unloaded. Take it, don't point it at anyone, even if it's not loaded."

I took it, but it felt wrong in my hands.

"Safety here. This is the grip, the barrel, the trigger. Don't put your finger on the trigger unless you're prepared to pull it. Magazine release here..." He went on with more specific names, the sights, the disassembly lever. He took it apart and showed me how the pieces fit back together. He reloaded.

"Ears on," he instructed.

I slid the protective earmuffs on.

He fired a few rounds, stopping to direct my vision to his stance. "Feet shoulder's width or a little wider. Slight crouch. If you want, you can put one foot back. It's important to be steady. Lean into it, a little. Arms out. You right handed?"

I had to watch his lips and listen closely to discern it all. I nodded.

"Alright, look here. High on the grip, wrap around, non-dominant hand comes up to support." He switched the safety back on, then offered it to me.

"That's it?" I gawked, horrified.

"That's it, take the gun."

"You're giving me a loaded gun, just like that? That doesn't seem right."

"You're learning. They're simple devices, you understand them, now it's time to give it a try."

I felt queasy, but I took the gun, ten times heavier in my hands with the bullets inside. I looked over at Paige, who stepped into my peripheral vision. I mimicked his stance. My hands shook as I raised the weapon. A few long seconds ticked by. I had the sights lined up, I actually felt my aim was fairly good, that if I fired, the bullet would find the center of the round target. But my finger would not squeeze the trigger.

Paige said, "You're alright. Pull the trigger."

"What if it misfires?"

"It won't misfire, I take care of my weapon."

I let a few more seconds go, inhaled, exhaled. I could feel him watching me and through the nervous knot in my stomach, the prickling fear at the back of my neck, I felt like a coward. I didn't like letting a man look down on me, judge me. I forced myself to pull the trigger and the gun exploded with the force of the bullet being projected. I yelped, jumped back from where I stood, but the thing was still in my hands, I splayed my fingers wide to keep them off the trigger. Doing everything I could not to chuck the gun away from me, I held it wide.

"Nope! No, no, no."

Paige's hand wrapped around mine and removed the gun. "Alright. You're okay, you shot the gun. It didn't backfire, it worked the way it was supposed to. You even hit the target."

"I can't."

"Why don't you watch me, then try again?"

"I can't. I'm not touching that thing."

"You shot a rifle, how is that different?"

"I don't know. I was young."

"And your father taught you. Maybe he could teach you how to shoot one of these, too. Or he could come with us next time, help you feel safer."

I didn't speak, but I knew it wasn't going to happen. Paige emptied the rest of his clip, every bullet seemed to hit the target, and as I watched his strong form, confident but not rigid, in control and not afraid, I wondered again if I had made a mistake, and what kind of world we lived in.

When the clip was empty, and Paige hit a button to bring the target whizzing up to us, all of the bullet holes were in a tight cluster except for one.

I pointed to the outlier. "That's mine, isn't it?"

He tried not to smile, nodded.

"Okay. Well, that was a failed experiment."

"Like anything, you've gotta work at it."

"I'll get a bb gun."

He made a face at me, but subtly.

"They can pack a punch. I saw my friend Scott get shot with one, once. It'll stun you."

He shook his head.

At the station, the three who had been hanging around earlier were gone. Two others had come in. They sat at their desks, working at their computers.

Apparently they had pulled someone over who had a warrant out for his arrest, and had detained the man. Paige introduced me to them, they did not give off much hostility, but were not welcoming, either.

"She sworn in, yet?"

"Not yet."

"She in the system?"

"No."

"I guess this paperwork will have to wait until tomorrow, then."

I sensed I should say, "Sorry."

"It happens," was the terse response I received.

Paige stepped back into my office with me, walked me through the procedure of booking the detainee and arranging transport for him. Then he got out forms for me to fill out, including my application for a permit to carry a firearm. There were separate systems for accessing criminal records, DMV records, even our payroll and timesheets. I had to setup logins for them all, as well as an extra security program on my phone. The process of swearing in could be done with any other officer present to witness, but not before I had a physical on file, so I had to get that scheduled for tomorrow at the latest.

He left me alone to wade through it all. His shift ended. I was starving as a few hours ticked by, but I did not want to order food to be delivered to the precinct, and I had very little in my savings. At eight, I finally clocked myself out, shut off the light in my new office, and started the walk home. I could have called home for a ride, but didn't want to do that, either.

It was ten to nine when I walked in the front door. There was teriyaki chicken, rice and broccoli all leftover in the fridge. I started inhaling it cold. Mom watched me from the couch, dad had probably already gone to bed.

She muted the tv. "Come sit with me."

I brought the food and obeyed.

"How was it?"

I sighed. "It's going to be really hard."

"Yeah?"

I shrugged. "I'm still going to do it. Paige is going to help me. I swapped the flags out."

"I saw it on the news. The other officers didn't look very happy with you. As your mother, it was very concerning… I don't like the thought of you working with a bunch of volatile gun-nuts on a power trip."

"They're not going to shoot me, Mom."

"I just don't think it's good for you to be surrounded by that kind of thing. And hanging out with a bunch of adults. You're young, you should be having fun, hanging out with people your own age, figuring out who you are and what you want to be, not carrying a gun-."

"-It's not like that anymore. We don't have that luxury."

She looked at me for a long moment. "Dad thinks you need to be allowed to do this. I guess we can't stop you. But I want you to get your diploma, and I don't want your other responsibilities falling through the cracks. I took care of Mabel, today, but I'm not making a habit of it-."

It made me wince. I hadn't exactly thought about Mabel, I hadn't even remembered to ask mom to exercise and feed her, she had just done it.

"-Which means you need to come home after school, then head to the station? Do you really think this is worth what you'll get out of it? You made the news, what more do you even stand to gain?"

"I don't know... Make a little money. Put everyone through some sensitivity training, at least. Might have to crowdfund it, apparently, I can't just fire someone right away. Thanks for taking care of Mabel today, but I've got it from here. I'll have to do short workouts in the morning and the afternoon... I bet Scott will give me a ride home after school and then to the precinct. Or maybe I get a cruiser I can use..." I circled back to something she had said, and that had been nagging at me; something I wanted to confess to my mother. "And I probably won't even carry a gun. I shot one today, Paige was trying to teach me, but it was scary. I don't like them. It's not like it's going to be dangerous, there hasn't been a serious crime in this town in years."

I was to eat my words, of course.

Chapter Five

I felt more tired the next morning than I ever had in my life. Physically, I felt fine, but summoning the strength to drag myself out of bed was tough. The idea of putting on makeup, picking an outfit, knowing that people would look at me and talk to me -and from sunup to sundown, no less- was draining. I could do it though, because I had to.

I smiled in the mirror as I brushed my hair. "Sheriff Evelyn. Day two. I got this."

Dad was cooking apple pancakes.

I grabbed one off of the stack and rolled it up, munching through it as I walked out to Mabel's little stable. She chittered as I entered. "Oh Hello!" I spoke around the last big mouthful of my pancake. "Did you miss me? I missed you, Pretty Girl. I'm sorry I was busy last night. Let's go for a quick trot, okay?"

After I gave her a workout, brushed and fed her, I went back in and inhaled another pancake with butter and syrup. Dad asked how my first day of work had gone, and I gave him the abridged version. Like Mom had, he expressed concern but told me that he believed in me. Mom came in from the chicken coop, locked eyes with him, and shook her head sadly. Ophelia was still not laying.

"Pancakes," he said, by way of condolences.

"Yum."

School was less eventful. I still felt eyes on me all the time, there were still a few selfie-seekers, but no news crews, no teachers hosting discussions about me. The day dragged on. I realized I was not looking forward to going to the station. I fantasized through my English class about going home and staying there. How I could waste the evening on dumb videos. Would they really go to the trouble to bring me up on charges of wasting county funds, or whatever? I doubted it.

I had already asked Scott to drive me home and then to work. He waited for me in the parking lot with a smile. I climbed into the truck and we cruised the few miles to my house. With the windows down and my hair blowing, I felt better. But as soon as I stepped in the door, the comfort and familiarity of home doubled my anxiety and unwillingness to leave again.

Scott came with me to tend to Mabel. He stroked her snout and said, "So I can give you rides every day except Mondays, cause I've got wrestling practice. You can get your mom, or maybe Delilah's mom to get you home and to work, right?"

"Yeah, I'll figure it out, or I'll walk. I really appreciate you helping me out when you can."

"Just doing my part."

When we passed back through the house, Mom had a brown bagged meal prepped for me, and had filled my water bottle. Her pretty face was purposefully stoic, but I stopped to look at her a minute as I collected the dinner. "Thank you."

She couldn't help but to soften, and nod.

Off we went for a physical. Scott waited in the lobby of the hospital while I went in, got my blood pressure taken, heart and lungs listened to, spine examined. The doctor signed off on my being fit for duty, and I made it to work at 5:00.

I asked Scott if he wanted to go into the station with me, but he shook his head, uncharacteristically sheepish. Maybe the encounter with Kipling scared him more than he initially let on.

"You'll be fine," he said. "Kick some lazy cop ass. I'll see you tomorrow."

"Okay, thanks again."

"Of course."

My own nerves were a tangled mess as I walked inside. I deflated even more when I saw that Paige was not in. I introduced myself to one of the two men in the bullpen, who I hadn't met. Deputy Spencer. He looked impatient, but shook my hand and said it was nice to meet me.

I copied and uploaded the form from the doctor. Then I sat at my desk and wondered what to do next. I checked my watch against the station's computer system, set it to an exact match. Waited. Looked out at the bullpen. Spencer and Holloway both seemed to know exactly what they were doing.

Movement caught my eye and relief flooded through me when I realized it was Paige walking in. I automatically surged to my feet and went out to meet him.

"Hey. Physical was good, form is uploaded. Can we do the swearing in, now?"

"Yes, give me one minute." He had something wrapped in plastic under his arm.

"Okay…"

He had a brief exchange with Holloway and Spencer, then gestured for me to go back to my office and followed.

"Where's that form? For the swearing in."

I scanned a few piles, found it, slid it to him across the desk. As I did that, he set down the package of tan shirts he was carrying, wrapped in plastic.

"Uniforms for you. Extra small. Not surprised they still had plenty of those in storage." He held out his hand. "Give me your star."

"My-?" I realized he meant the badge and unclipped it, slapping it down on his palm, which was a shade of pink, unlike the rest of his dark skin. "Why the badge?"

"Would you rather a bible?"

"No."

"Alright, left hand on the badge, raise your right."

I did as he said.

"Repeat after me: I do solemnly swear that I will perform with fidelity-."

"I do solemnly swear that I will perform with fidelity…"

"-The duties of the office to which I have been elected-."

"The duties of the office to which I have been elected…"

"-And which I am about to assume."

"And to which I am about to assume." I pulled my hand back, but he was not done, shook his head. I jolted back into the proper position.

"-I do solemnly swear to support the constitutions of Tennessee and the United States-."

"I do solemnly swear to support the constitutions of Tennessee and the United States…"

"And to faithfully perform the duties of the office of sheriff for Elviston County, Tennessee."

"And to faithfully perform the duties of the office of sheriff for Elviston County, Tennessee."

"This is real shit, now, Evelyn." He offered me my badge back with a stern look. "Take it seriously."

"Okay. I will."

I pinned the star back on. He leaned over the desk and signed the form, then slid it to me. I did the same, dating it.

Paige surveyed me. I was still wearing my own clothes, a blouse with a collar and dark jeans. "Change your shirt, then come out. We're taking a detainee to the courthouse."

"Awesome. Can I drive?"

He blinked, stopped in the doorway. "Can you?"

"Yeah, I've got my license."

"I'll drive until further notice."

"Okay."

The cruisers were tan colored, small SUVs with 'Elviston County Sheriff's Department' on the sides, lights on the top. As I climbed in the passenger side, I looked over my shoulder and saw the detainee through the metal mesh dividing the front from the back. He was a greasy looking man with dark hair, in his forties.

"What are you in for?" I asked.

He stared at me. "What is this, take your daughter to work day?"

Paige slid into the driver's seat.

The detainee snorted. "Never mind, that ain't your daddy…"

"I'm the new Sheriff," I declared, trying to sound confident.

Staring with a vacant expression for a moment, the detainee then cracked a smile and devolved into laughter. I felt a twinge of embarrassment, reached out and flipped on the loud, whooping sirens. I remembered how from my ride along, a year ago.

"No." Paige switched them off. "Emergencies only."

"Come on."

"People are going to laugh at you. Get used to it. If you let them get to you, you'll only look stupid and reinforce what they think. So sit with it. And buckle up."

The cackling went on in the backseat as we pulled out onto the road. After a riotous minute, the detainee brought up a handcuffed hand, which jingled, and wiped a tear from his cheek. "Oh man. Thank you. I needed that. They're hiring little girls to be sheriffs now. You're the future of law enforcement. It truly is the end of days, for our country…"

I read his papers while he was whooping and laughing. "You're one to talk about the future of the country, you didn't pay your child support for more than three years?"

He scoffed, indignant. "I didn't want 'em. She gets a choice, why shouldn't I get a choice?"

"You certainly made a few choices. That's why you're here."

"Land of choices, America," Paige chimed in, with - I thought- a hint of sarcasm. He didn't have to elaborate; his ancestors didn't have much choice, even just a generation or two back.

We didn't talk the rest of the way. I was not used to not having music on in the car. I had nothing to do but sit with my thoughts and watch the buildings of downtown, the park, the cars pass by. The car's scanner patched in a few times, with other deputies answering the calls through the low static. Paige clearly kept an ear open, with his eyes on the road. His professionalism and calm impressed me once again.

At the courthouse, we both stepped out. He instructed me, "Just stay behind me." Then he opened the back door and guided the detainee out.

Someone met us at a grey metal door at the back of the utilitarian white brick building. Through a plain hall with track lighting, we trooped, and deposited our detainee in a barred cell with a bunk, sink and toilet.

He dismissed us, leaning on the bars. "Man screw you guys."

Paige filled out the necessary paperwork, with me leaning over him as he did. He explained anything I didn't understand, then took copies for our records.

"Now what?" I said, when we were back in the car.

"Patrol. Take any calls that are close by, or serious in nature."

"We can go anywhere in the county?"

"Yes."

"We're responsible for the whole county."

"Yes. Sort of."

Paige instructed me on running plate numbers on the little laptop in the cruiser. It sat on a little shelf that swiveled over my seat and over the dash. We drove around, with me running plates just to get the hang of it, nothing flagging in our system.

After an hour, a car went screaming past us on the highway, at least ten, maybe fifteen miles over the speed limit. Paige reached down to flip the switch, the lights started to flash, reflecting on the tan hood, and the siren blared.

"Oh shit!" I exclaimed, and sat up straighter in my seat. "I didn't get the plate."

"That's alright, here we go."

He steered us around cars pulling off to the shoulder, stepping on the gas, the engine revving as we picked up speed. In a few short seconds, we had caught up to the rusty, blue nineties sedan. It kept on cruising and for a moment my mind flashed to a high speed chase, to bullets firing across two lanes of traffic, spike strips, tires blowing, the sedan rolling, a spectacular explosion of metal and glass on the yellow striped black tar.

The sedan pulled over, parked.

Instructing me on every step, Paige said, "Lights on, sirens off. Got the plate?"

"Yes…" I was waiting for the system to load. "Registered to Dwight Walters."

"No warrants, multiple speeding tickets and moving violations. Come on, stay behind me. Watch and learn."

"Yes!" I unbuckled and bounded out of the car, one step behind him, heart pounding.

## Chapter Six

Paige took us back to the station after a couple hours of learning the ropes, which was good because I had left the sack lunch Mom had packed for me. I inhaled a peanut butter and jelly sandwich, carrot sticks and dip, and some pretzels all while watching some informative and mandatory videos. After filling out a few more papers, my four hours were done. I clocked out and walked up the aisle in the bullpen.

"Goodnight," I said to Paige.

Outside, the sky was dimming. The night was cool and windless, crickets chirped. It felt pleasant enough, but the path stretched out in front of me -the two miles home- seemed immense. I stood for a minute, mustering the courage to take the first step. I could have keeled over in the parking lot.

The door opened behind me, making me jump aside.

Paige had his keys in hand, gestured. "I'll give you a ride."

I exhaled. "Thank you."

"No problem."

I checked in with Mom and Dad although it felt like having my teeth pulled. I could still smell the Mexican food they had cooked for dinner lingering in the kitchen. I was asleep before my head hit the pillow.

My phone's alarm woke me and I couldn't do anything but snooze it. Those next ten minutes, I lingered between unsatisfying sleep and being unable to face the relentlessness of another day.

Dad knocked on my door and I groaned.

Mabel needed me, and that got me moving.

Back inside, I scrubbed myself down. I had slept in makeup, and my skin was angry at me. I elected to go without for a day or two, not to mention, I was running late. Dad pushed an egg sandwich into my hands as I headed for the door.

"Thank-." I licked the hot sauce that started rolling down to my wrist. "-You."

"I'll drive you to school. I've hardly seen you this week."

"Oh. Cool, thanks. Can we pick Delilah up on the way?"

"Sure."

He opened the door for me and we piled into the truck. On the way, he asked only, "You doing alright?"

I said yes around a mouthful of egg. "Tired though."

"I was the same when I got my first job. You'll get used to it. We'll help you out how we can."

I slid over when Dad stopped at the corner in front of the barber shop. Delilah slid in.

"Hey Mr. Lassiter, thanks for the ride."

"No problem."

"Ready for the Stats test?"

I wasn't, even remotely, but for my father's benefit I said, "Yeah, totally."

But we were in the middle of English when the door opened and a uniformed officer appeared. It was Paige.

Mrs. O'Connell was instantly excited. "Officer, how can we help you?"

He gave her a smile, but addressed me; everyone knew why he was there. "Duty calls, Sheriff."

I looked at Mrs. O'Connell, she was my teacher, she was nice to me and I respected her. But I was also a sheriff. I couldn't exactly ask permission to do my job. "I guess I have to go, Mrs. O'Connell."

She was cheerful. "Okay! Be safe and kick some butt!"

"I'll take notes for you," Delilah said.

"Thanks." I was going to miss the Stats test, but that wasn't the worst thing in the world. I could get my hours at the station in, and have the evening to myself. Mom and Dad would not be happy about me missing school, but I desperately needed the night to study and rest.

As soon as I shut the door behind me and stood in the empty hall of checkered tile and blue lockers with Paige, I said, "This could not have come at a better time! What's up?"

"There's been a murder," he said.

My stomach dropped. I stopped in place. Paige kept going, his footsteps echoing. I snapped out of it and ran to catch up. "A murder? Where?"

"Outside of town."

"Who?"

"Don't know yet, that's kind of our job to find out."

"Right…"

In the cruiser, he reached over to the glovebox, taking from it a stack of three small notepads. He unwrapped it and tossed me one. "Take notes. Everything we do in a day, especially with something as serious as this. You need to be able to look back and find any little detail. It could make or break a case. Got it?"

I had seen him taking his own notes, and not thought to get myself a pad. I was a bit touched by it. "Got it."

\*

It was a dirt two-track road, in the wooded area off of the highway that led out of Elviston and down to the lake one way, to the system of factories on large plots of land the other way. A beat up, old Chevy sedan -dark blue where it wasn't rusted- had one tire on the grassy slope, sitting at an angle. A local police cruiser was already on the scene, we had to park behind it and walk past it, through the weeds. The tree cover overhead was thick, blocking out much of the spring sun.

A uniformed local cop was interviewing a woman dressed for hiking, knee-deep in the undergrowth.

Paige walked up and addressed the man. "Excuse me. Paige, Sheriff's Department. Need you to call in another unit, set up a perimeter and get plate numbers of all passing cars out on the main road, can you do that?"

"Yes, Sir."

"Ma'am." He tipped his head, excusing us.

"She found it?" I guessed, hurrying after him.

Paige peered in the open window of the Chevy. "Found him."

And there he was, my first dead body. A scrawny man, in his thirties or forties, unkempt brown hair, holes in his shirt. A big blood splotch around the right side of his ribs, old, dried. His skin was translucent white, with blue veins showing through and a sheen of grease on top. His eyes were unhealthy, the whites were yellowish. The irises were pale.

I couldn't help myself, I leaned closer. In the reflection of his pupils, I could almost see the eternity he was looking into. It made the hair stand up on the back of my neck, a chill skitter down my spine.

He smelled. He had been dead a day or two, I'd guess. The whole shitty car reeked of cigarettes and sweat. I reckoned no one had been missing the dead man, nobody had been looking. If the amateur photographer geocacher hipster hadn't been doing her nature walk, the body would have gone unfound for days more, weeks.

"Okay…" I moved around the car, taking it in, looking for clues. Clues, like they look for on CSI, Criminal Minds, all that jazz. I tried to keep moving. The truth is, my mind was spinning, I was looking but not really seeing, not taking anything else in. I felt the dead man's presence, I felt like he was watching me even though he just kept staring forward. I felt strangely shy in his presence.

Paige was taking notes on a small pad. His face was blank as usual. Only his slightly pursed lips betrayed that he was deep in through.

When he looked up at me, I looked away in a hurry.

"What do you see?"

I took a deep breath. "Not much," I admitted, keeping my voice low. I didn't want the local cop or the witness hearing me. "Probably bled out?"

"Not enough blood."

He was right, of course. There didn't look to be any other blood pooling in the car, except for what was staining the dead man's shirt, and there was no way it was enough to kill him. I forced myself to look into the corpse's eyes again. They were strange, aside from being haunting.

"He looks sick."

"He's certainly not well."

I blinked and looked up at him again. "Is that a joke?"

He shrugged. Closed his pad. "Coroner's here. He's also licensed as a crime scene photographer."

The black van had pulled up behind our cruiser. A short, fit man with a camera around his neck and a clipboard in his hand struggled up the slope, through the weeds, and over to us.

He was breathing heavily. "Hey, Paige, what do we got?"

"First off, Elmer, this is Evelyn Lassiter. She's the new sheriff. Evelyn, this is Elmer Fisher."

"How do you do?" Elmer had an odd way about him, big eyes, probably a touch of the 'tism about him. He thought fast and spoke faster. "What do we got?"

"One body," Paige said. "You tell me…"

"How am I supposed to get it out of here? Can't roll a stretcher through these weeds. Can't you tow the whole car out?"

"I don't want to have to block the road, or disturb the crime scene. We'll help you lift the stretcher."

"Hm. Step back, please."

We each trudged a few feet off of the path and watched as Elmer started taking pictures of the crime scene, dozens of photos, from every angle. He was meticulous. Paige took a few more notes, squinting as he looked down at the scene. Tapped his pen on the pad and pursed his lips again.

I stood on my tiptoes and leaned closer, trying to get a look at his notes.

He swiveled away from me, closing the pad, looking at me with indignation.

"Jeez, sorry, I didn't know we were in competition."

"I want you to make your own observations, not cheat off my test."

"I had a test in my AP Statistics class today…"

"Dead body," he reminded me. He seemed irritated at having to put me through my paces, not the most patient person and I knew he was helping me because he felt obligated.

"Right. I really don't know." I thought that there was something he wanted me to notice, to say. "Give me a hint?"

"Nope."

"Come on, I'm only a kid."

"Don't pull that on me, and don't let anyone else hear you say it." He shook his head, but then he relented. "There's blood on the shirt, but I didn't see a hole in it."

"He put someone else's bloody shirt on?"

"Or he put his own shirt back on after the injury occurred."

"He had somewhere to be? Got it treated, but then didn't go home or clean himself up…"

"Or an old wound opened back up."

"Why would that happen?"

"He looks sick. Some illnesses cause slow healing, like Leukemia. Maybe he's on blood thinners. Maybe he stressed the wound, in a fight or with physical activity. Could just be an infection."

"That would explain the smell."

"That's normal decomposition smell." He said it matter-of-factly, but also with an ease I aspired to. He dropped down the slope once again, joining Elmer at the driver's side door. "Can I get a pair of gloves from you?"

He pulled them on and went around to the passenger's side, opening the glove box, pulling out the registration. He waved for me to join him, and I dropped clumsily down onto the two-track.

"Want me to run it?"

"Yes. Gloves."

"Elmer, can I-?"

The coroner was crouched, just staring at the body, thinking. He offered me a glove across the car without looking up at me. I had to bend down and in to reach it, and the smell surged up my nose like water, making me gag.

"You're okay, go run the name."

I did so, blinking my watering eyes. Shut in the cruiser, I caught my breath, tried to let the tension out. If Mom and Dad could see me investigating a murder, what would they think? And what would my classmates think? Would they be impressed, or would they be horrified and realize that what we had all done was foolish?

The registration was in the name 'Frank Gillespie' and the mugshot which came up with the report of his past drug conviction matched the dead man in the driver's seat. I wrote down the info.

Elmer and Paige walked by the cruiser, struggling to carry a heavy looking gurney with the wheels folded up underneath it.

Paige grunted out, "Shouldn't you have an assistant?"

"Nobody wants to work."

"County doesn't pay enough, you mean."

Hearing it made me realize that I didn't know yet what my salary was. I climbed out of the car and followed them. "Hey Paige, what am I making?"

"Scale starts at sixty."

My hand shot to my chest, I stopped in his tracks. "Sixty thousand dollars?"

"Per year. You won't be here that long."

"That's still five grand a month. I'm gonna make five grand if I'm here a month!?"

"If you do the job." He didn't sound excited for me. "Steady?" He was talking to Elmer, then, who was rocking the gurney where it was parked to make sure it wouldn't tip.

"Yeah, grab the legs."

Paige pulled on a second glove before touching the body, but then the two men transferred it over onto the stretcher. They caught their breath and wiped sweat from their brows. Elmer started to strap the body down.

"Hold on," Paige said. He lifted the dead man's shirt up, waving for me to come closer.

I leaned over, burying my nose in the collar of my shirt.

The corpse's pasty abdomen with sparse, dark hair and flaky dried red blood on it was skin and bone. The wound was between two ribs, just a small hole. A peek of red meet showed at the center of the hole, with the skin pulled in around it by a few black stitches.

I said, "It looks like a bullet hole."

Paige agreed for once. "Yeah. Help me turn him."

I blinked, my stomach dropped, but he was talking to Elmer, who understood and helped lift the corpse, rolling it to one side. Another wound on the back, just a bit bigger.

Paige said, "Exit wound. The stitches look professional, to me."

"Yeah."

"Registration?"

I looked at the napkin. "Frank Gillespie. Charged with possession three years ago. It's him." I nodded to the corpse.

"Nothing recent, though?"

"No...?" I didn't follow his train of thought.

"Like a police report indicating he was shot, and pressed charges."

"Oh. Duh. No."

"Alright, let's see if he was treated at any hospital in the county in the last couple of days."

Elmer asked, "You gonna help me with this, or not?" He zipped up the black body bag.

"Right. Jeff!"

The local officer hurried over, and together the three men carried the stretcher and the corpse along the rough forested ground, past both cruisers and down the short embankment. I ran ahead and opened the van's back door for them. "Good work Gentlemen!"

Paige asked Jeff, "You got this? Wait for the tow?"

"Yeah, go ahead."

We did rounds of the county hospitals, asking first if Frank Gillespie was treated, and when told that he was not, asked for anyone who may have been admitted without giving a name, or a fake name. Checking security footage against each of their admissions, we ruled them out one by one. A few hours passed like that.

Mom called and left a message not very gently asking why I wasn't in school. I texted her back, explaining, but I knew I'd hear more about it when I went home.

Paige swung us through a gas station and we ate a late lunch parked on the side of the building. I had a piece of pizza, a taquito and a slushy. Paige had a turkey sandwich and a zero-sugar Gatorade. I could tell that he was thinking as he chewed, from the look on his face.

"If our victim wasn't treated in a hospital, where was he treated?"

"And why wasn't his being shot reported?"

"Probably he was in the process of committing a crime when it happened. Trespassing, stealing stuff to fence, drug deal gone wrong. But where did he get stitched up?"

"Pharmacists are doctors," I said. "Or a veterinarian."

"Sure. Let's look into that next."

He started the cruiser, took us back to Elviston, to the two pharmacies, first. I mostly watched as he asked the purveyors questions, although I tried to listen closely for any inconsistencies in their answers, any nervousness in their voices. I didn't think I picked up on anything, and Paige seemed to be in agreement, spending only a few minutes at each place.

We walked back out to the cruiser and he asked me, then, "Is there a vet in this town?"

I realized then that he couldn't have grown up in Elviston, where it hadn't occurred to me before. If he had, I would know him a little more, would know someone in his family, some of their dirty laundry. "Not an animal guy?"

He blinked, didn't answer, just stared at me over the hood.

"Okay, geez. The vet's on Sumac. His name is Dennis Wright. He's an Aquarius."

We had each popped open our doors, and as we slid into our seats, he sighed. "Why do you think I need to know the man's sign? Why do you know the man's sign? This is not an episode of The Dating Game."

"Okay." I buckled up, smiling to myself. "Sorry. What the Hell is The Dating Game? Like Love is Blind for old people?"

## Chapter Seven

"Dennis Wright, D.V.M, Aquarius, bibliophile, Gators fan, at your service." Dennis rattled it all off as he shook Paige's hand, then mine, and his huge teeth shined out of his beaming mouth. He narrowed his eyes as he placed me. "Evelyn, that's right. How's that old nag of yours?"

"She's good, no more abscesses. Thanks."

"What can I do for you upstanding officers of the law?"

We were all standing in the man's little office, gathered around his cluttered desk. No air conditioning and a little stuffy. The screened window in the back only let in a gentle sigh of a warm spring breeze. Paige led the conversation.

"What kind of animals do you treat here?"

"Oh the usuals. Cats, dogs, birds, rabbits, rodents. I've got a client with an African spurred tortoise. Over fifty years old -the tortoise not the client- and as Miss Evelyn knows, I'll make house calls to see horses, cows, goats and sheep. Don't care much for snakes and lizards, but if the situation demands, I'll do my duty. I'm an Aquarius, you know."

"We know… Your training, is it pretty similar to medical school?"

"Somewhat. There's some overlap between people and animals. We're all just big sacks of meat in the end, if we've got two arms and two legs or four paws, hooves. Diagnoses and treatment protocols, stuff like that…" Dennis was still smiling with big teeth.

"First aid?"

"Sure. Disinfectant, sutures, bandages, the works."

"Gunshot?"

"Gunshot," Dennis repeated, then his eyes drifted up to the ceiling, thinking. "Are you asking how would I treat a gunshot wound?"

"Have you?"

"Nnno." He dragged out the word, shaking his head. "-Geez, it's hot. We haven't had a spring like this since I was -I don't know- since my youngest was still at home, probably. Ten or twelve years."

"Had a dispute with two neighbors on the south side of town, about two years ago. One of them shot the other's dog. Since you're the only vet in town, I thought they might have brought the dog to you."

"Oh! Dogs, yes, I did treat the dog. Gorgeous shepherd, walks with a limp now but not too worse for wear. I thought you meant human gunshot victims, for some reason. You being a cop, I guess."

"Right. You didn't treat a human gunshot victim, in the last few days? Named Frank Gillespie?"

"No." A clipped answer, that time, a head shake and a lingering silence.

Paige took a note. "Treating a willing human patient, that's not a crime I'm interested in, if it even is one in the first place. Practicing without a medical license, maybe? Anyway, if you did treat Frank Gillespie's gunshot wound, you'd be helping us in our investigation to tell us so. It would be the smart thing to do."

I could see Dennis considering for a moment. Then he smiled, shaking his head. "No, sorry, I don't know anyone by that name."

"Alright, sorry to bother you, then."

"Have a nice day," I said, following Paige out through the waiting room where two dogs were straining at their leashes, wanting to play with each other. Paige danced between them, not amused, and I stopped to give them each a pet, having to hurry to catch him outside.

"He was lying," I declared, sliding into the cruiser.

"Yup. I told him he didn't have anything to be afraid of, from a legal standpoint. Not where we were concerned... So why won't he talk?"

I considered. "He wasn't just patching up someone who walked in needing help. They're in cahoots? Dennis doesn't seem like the type to be in cahoots."

"Don't say cahoots. I want to get a warrant for his appointment book, trace his movements over the last few days outside of work, too. Find out when he patched up Gillespie, then maybe we can find out why. Not sure if we can, though... A hunch isn't enough."

The day was ticking by. School would be letting out soon.

"How long do you think we'll be at this? My horse needs exercise."

"It's a full-time job, and it's your number one priority now."

"Right. Okay. I'll ask my mom to handle it."

More like *beg* her to handle it.

Her reply was almost instantaneous, that she would handle it for now and we would talk about it later.

"Maybe we don't need a warrant. He has a receptionist or two, let's go through them."

"I know a girl who works there on weekends." She was in my grade, although we weren't close.

"Call her."

I scoffed. "Nobody calls anymore. Why don't I just send her a fax?"

"Okay." He rolled his eyes and I saw a hint of a smile, just for a second.

"A singing telegram. A homing pigeon…"

I sent her a message, but got no immediate reply.

Paige said, "What can we do in the meantime?" He knew the answer and was prodding me again, trying to get me to think and take the lead.

"I don't know… Ask around about Dennis. Try to figure out what his involvement could be."

"Possibilities including…?"

"He either has something to lose or something to gain. Threats? Or debts. Or a habit he's funding."

"Could be. Didn't strike me as a junkie. Maybe a drinker."

"I don't think so." I didn't know Dennis very well, but I knew that he took pride in what he did, kept regular hours, had been married for years and had raised a few kids who were pretty well thought of around town.

"Start asking around. Let's go to the bar."

While he drove us there, I fired off a few more texts. To Mom and Dad, to Delilah and Scott asking them to ask their parents. In a small town, it was very hard to keep secrets. Everybody knew everybody. If Dennis was in some trouble, somebody knew it, it was just a matter of finding out who. I felt guilty asking Scott to ask his mom, knowing that she frequented the bar in town. I put him and Delilah in a group text, hoping he wouldn't feel singled out or ashamed.

The bar was called The Ex Wife. It was a dank hole on Main Street, open from 2pm to 2am. Dim overhead lighting illuminated stained red carpet and warped chair rails separating from the walls. The fryer in the tiny kitchen behind the bar made the whole place smell like grease when in use. The cook put a basket of onion rings in the serving window and rang a bell as we walked in.

"Order up."

A couple of young adults were in a booth by the front window. I noticed that they straightened up, looked anxious when we entered the room. A few others, scattered around, looked like they had been in their seats at interior tables and stools at the bar unmoving for years. They hunched over their drinks, eyes on the tv watching keno numbers get drawn. Their eyes were unafraid, completely unmoved as they glanced over at us, then went back to the tv.

The bartender returned from running the onion rings to the young people. "Can I help you?"

"Step over here and talk to us, please…" Paige gestured and the man came around the bar, away from the customers. "We're wondering if you know the town's veterinarian Dennis Wright?"

"Doesn't sound familiar."

I was already pulling up his Facebook account to show the man a picture. "This is him."

The bartender considered, he didn't seem uncooperative. He shrugged in the end. "He's not a regular. I can't say he's never been here."

"Okay, can you ask your coworkers? Other bartenders?"

"I can try, they might be sleeping…"

"Please. Here, take my card. Let us know if they answer you, or you can have them reach out to me directly. Thank you."

With that, we returned to the car. Paige turned it on and cranked the AC, but he didn't put the car in gear. We sat in silence for a minute. I could tell that he was deep in thought. After a minute, he asked, "Anything from the masses?"

I checked the phone. Mom said that she knew nothing about the vet's personal life. Delilah said the same for her parents. Nothing from Scott or Dad. The clock showed half past three. I wondered when I would get to go home. Because of the extra hours I had worked today, I could skip an evening shift, tomorrow… or work a few extra hours -all day, from dusk until dawn- Saturday and have Sunday off entirely.

"Nothing useful."

Paige ran Dennis Wright through the system, searched his wife and kids' names, as well. None had any prior criminal charges brought against them, although his daughter Sybil was named in three reports, those incidents leading to charges of drunk and disorderly conduct, resisting arrest, and assault. In each report, the accused was her boyfriend, Rodney Bean. The assault charge was later dropped.

"I remember you," Paige said, more to himself than to me or the image of Rodney on the screen. He blinked and looked at me. "He's a real loser."

"You don't say..." I would have guessed as much from his crazy-eyed and scowling mugshot. I checked my notes. "Sybil Wright is also the owner of a car which passed through the checkpoint you had set up on the road where Frank Gillespie's body was found. I bet Rodney was the one driving, though."

"It's the road which leads from central Elviston to most of the factories outside of town. Could be a coincidence... Let's keep asking around, check the restaurants with liquor licenses." He went to turn the key in the ignition, but I stopped him.

"Wait. Let's sit here a few more minutes."

"Why?"

I checked my phone. "Just a few minutes..." I felt warm blood rushing into my cheeks, I did not want to explain.

Paige read my embarrassment and did not pry any further. He ran some more names through the system; the girls who worked the desk at the vet's, Dennis

Wright's older brother. He didn't seem to find any of it interesting.

When Scott's red truck pulled up in front of the bar, I sat up straighter. Paige was aware of my body language, looked up, putting the pieces together.

"Stay here," I told him, and hopped out of the cruiser.

Scott's mom Penny was climbing out of the passenger side of his truck. Her jeans were tight and bedazzled, her top was low-cut. She said something to him while she bent over to check her hair in the side-view mirror. As I approached from behind them, I noticed Scott's eyes found me in the rear-view.

"Hi, Ms. Proffit."

She took a second to place me. "Oh, Evelyn! Hi, how are you? I'm just getting a jump on the weekend! Ha ha." Her chain-smoker chuckle was a rasp in her chest.

I glanced at Scott, his face was knowing, he gave me a nod. He had asked her what I wanted to know, he had answers. I skipped asking her anything, myself. "Oh, you know. Just here on business, saw you and Scott and wanted to say hello. I'm the sheriff, now."

She blinked in shock, took in my uniform, the cruiser. "You don't say? That's amazing, aren't you Scott's age?"

"Yeah, he helped with my campaign. The whole class pulled together, it's like a protest."

She started for the bar's door, saying hurriedly, "That's fantastic, Sweetie! Give 'em Hell! Bye, Scotty! Bye Evelyn."

"See you later."

"Bye…"

She disappeared inside.

I leaned in the passenger window of Scott's truck. He was leaning, looking relaxed, but his eyes were locked on the quaint old buildings of Main Street around us. I could tell that he was embarrassed. I wanted to tell him that he didn't need to be, but didn't think it would help.

"What's up?" I asked, instead.

"I asked her if she's seen the vet around, but we don't really know him, so she couldn't be sure. She said she thought he looked familiar, that he might have been around like a month ago, around her birthday weekend."

"Oh. That's good, I guess… We should probably talk to her."

He sighed, pulled his phone out. "You don't have to. I had her send me all the pictures from that weekend." He flipped through them quickly, looking for one in particular. There were a lot; if it was a Saturday, and her birthday weekend, nonetheless, she probably started early and finished late. "This is him, right?"

In the photo, Penny was in the middle of two other middle-aged women. She wore a sparkly crown and a sash that said 'birthday girl'. They all held drinks and were standing before the bar's front window, showing the dark street and string of lights in a tree behind them. In one of the booths, sitting alone, hunched over a glass of dark alcohol, was Dennis Wright with a long face.

"Yeah. I think that is him, and it has a timestamp, too. This is great, Scott. This is very helpful. Thank you."

It lets him smile, look like himself again. "No problem. You can deputize me anytime, I can protect and serve."

"I'll keep it in mind. Send me that?"

"Yeah."

"Alright, get home safe."

"You too."

"See you tomorrow."

I walked back to the cruiser, grinning. "The vet was here. Back in March. We've got photographic proof, date and time-stamped. He was there pretty early, looks like 6:45."

"Okay… Let's see if anything noteworthy happened that night."

He checked reports from that night and singled one out immediately. "Hit and run of a parked car, owner didn't see the perpetrator. It was on Sheffield Street, which is… not on the way from the bar to Wright's house, or his office."

"His daughter's house?" I was twitchy in my seat, adjusting, sitting up higher. My heart was starting to pound. We were doing it! Investigating. Running down a lead.

Paige typed, hit enter. He seemed to have a good map of the town's layout in his mind. "Yes. It's all circumstantial, but it looks like we've got something." He had noticed my excitement and was warning me not to get carried away.

"He was drunk, and he drove to his daughter's house -either she needed help or he just worked up the nerve that night to confront her loser boyfriend- and he hit a parked car on the way. How does this relate back to him patching up Frank Gillespie and lying to us about it?"

"You tell me."

I took a shot in the dark. "Frank knew about Dennis driving under the influence, he offered to provide an alibi in exchange for help with his wound."

"How would he know?"

"Maybe he knows Rodney Bean, they look like they run in the same circles. He heard about a confrontation, and a couple of damaged cars, and put the pieces together."

"It's a thought…" He was doubtful.

I could see the gears turning in his brain again. "What are you thinking?"

"Wright's not scared of an insurance claim. He's scared of being charged. Fleeing the scene of a crime, maybe, it's a misdemeanor… So is a first offense DUI, but he'd be more likely looking at jailtime, putting them together."

"He might be ashamed, too. His reputation could be at stake." And saying it, I felt just a little sorry for him. No prior offenses. One mistake, maybe made in the heat of the moment, because his daughter needed him…

"I don't think Frank Gillespie would be able to hold this over Wright's head."

There was something that he wasn't saying.

I prodded him. "And?"

He started the cruiser. "A cop could, that's what I'm thinking. And that wound looked like a gunshot, but there was no report of anything like that, recently. It stinks. Like someone is trying to cover something up."

"Are we going to talk to the daughter?"

"Yeah, that's where we're going."

Chapter Eight

The trailer where Sybil Wright and Rodney Bean lived was rundown, just outside of town, at the end of a long, dirt drive. The lot had a few patchy spots of brown grass, held a few broken down cars. When we parked in the driveway, Paige told me to wait.

He was serious, as always. "The most dangerous calls for a cop to go on are domestic disputes. I already checked, and neither of these two has a gun registered in their name, but that doesn't mean that there isn't one present. We know they're volatile-."

"-We know he's volatile," I interjected.

He waved a hand. "If she has lived in a volatile environment for years, we're going to assume that she's volatile, too. For our safety. We're going to keep our eyes open. And you're going to follow my lead. Alright?"

"Alright."

We approached the house.

Sybil Wright must have noticed us pulling into the yard. She met us at the door. She was a tall woman, not slender, with nice skin and nice black hair. Her face had a slight puffiness to it; maybe she had been crying. When she spoke, I saw that she had her father's big teeth.

"Can I help you?"

"Deputy Sheriff Leo Paige, Sheriff Evelyn Lassiter, with the Elviston County Sheriff's Department. We'd like to talk to you about an ongoing investigation. Is there anyone else in the home?"

"No…"

"Is Rodney Bean around?"

"No, he's at work… Would you like to come inside?"

"Alright, yes Ma'am."

He took the lead, stepping inside.

The living room was comfortably arranged, with matching furniture, a big tv. I followed Paige's eyes as they looked up the hall to where the bedroom and bathroom must be. As Sybil moved into the kitchen, taking down glasses, we followed, gathering around the serving bar.

"Would you like some iced tea, or water?"

"Water would be nice, thank you."

I let his answer stand for both of us, let him nudge me to stand on the inside, near the back wall. He kept his back to me, facing the rest of the house with one hand on his belt, near his holstered gun.

"What's this about?"

Paige took a drink before answering. He wiped his mouth with his thumb and index finger, gathering his thoughts. I wondered if he was considering what to reveal, and what to hold back, if anything.

"Your father seems to be in some legal trouble. Do you know anything about that?"

She blinked, shocked. "No, what kind of trouble? Is he alright?"

"He's alright." Paige nodded, looking at her, reading her reactions. "A body was found this morning, off Highway 31. We have-." His phone buzzed in his pocket, he reached for it to silence it. "Sorry about that. - We have reason to believe that your father had interacted with the victim recently, and is trying to hide it. Can you think of any reason why he might feel the need to do that?"

She looked confused, and considered the question seriously for a long moment. "No, I don't know. My father never has anything to hide, he's an upstanding citizen, he always has been... Who's the victim?"

"His name was Frank Gillespie."

Her face showed no recognition that I could see. She shook her head again. "I really don't know."

"Has your father been acting any differently, lately?"

"I haven't noticed anything, no."

"And you see him often?"

"Every Sunday. I have brunch with my mom and dad and my brothers after church."

Paige checked his notebook. "Do you remember where you were on the evening of March 18$^{th}$?"

"Home, probably. I have Lupus, I'm usually home. March 18$^{th}$..." She went to a calendar on the fridge, flipped the page back. "It was a Saturday. Rodney plays cards with friends on Saturdays, so I would have just been home alone."

"And your father didn't come over, that night?"

"No. I don't really have people over. When we get together, it's at their house."

Paige took notes. "I think that's all the questions we had for you. Sheriff, did you have anything?"

For a second, I forgot that I was the sheriff, that he was talking to me. "Rodney plays cards on Saturdays? For how long?" I was thinking of a window in which Dennis might have tried to come over, to convince his daughter to leave; come home. I was also thinking of a future window where we could come back to talk to Sybil ourselves; or a way that we could catch Rodney up, to get him away from her and keep him away. A card game presumably meant illegal gambling with unsavory characters, at least to me.

"He heads over after his shift ends at the factory, which is at five. They're usually done about nine."

"And where does this game happen?"

She hesitated, wondering if she should reveal it. Seemingly innocuous information, but if the cops wanted it, she shouldn't. I saw the moment that the decision was made on her face, and I thought I saw that in that moment that she thought 'fuck it'. She wanted him gone? "It's at the sex shop, in town." Ah. Contempt. "The owner is a friend of Rodney's, and the other guys. I don't like it, I don't like any of them."

"Thank you for the water." I downed my glass.

Paige said, "You should encourage your father to come to us. If he can help us in our investigation, we can help him with whatever he's facing. If he waits too long, there will be nothing that I can do. Can I leave my card with you?"

He offered a card across the counter, and she started to reach up to take it, reflexively. But as her arm stretched out, the sleeve of her Henley shirt rode up, showing a bruise wrapped around her wrist. She froze, clammed up, tugged the sleeve down.

The sight of it sent a shock through me, like I had been hit with a bucket of ice water. I glanced at Paige, my fight or flight instinct had curiously been triggered, and it seemed, on some level, I trusted him to lead. I wanted to know what he wanted to do.

His face was blank, as always. Unsurprised. Unbothered. Uncaring. When she pulled back, he tucked the card away.

Sybil said, "I shouldn't, actually. I can remember your name to mention you to my father. If I think of anything, I can find your number or call the precinct."

"Ask for one of us. Paige and Lassiter."

I felt the need to add, "If you need us, we'll be here."

Paige stayed alert as we left the trailer. Once we were back in the cruiser, he sighed and relaxed into the driver's seat. I was still rigid, my stomach was in knots. It didn't feel right to leave.

He said, "So on the night in question, Wright meant to come here, while his daughter's boyfriend wouldn't be around. She says he didn't make it here, but we can't take her word for it."

"He wanted to help her. She needs help…"

"Don't do that." His tone was firm. "If she asks for help, we'll give it to her. You can't make someone leave if they're not ready to. Trust me."

He waited for me to tip my head in acceptance. But I didn't feel any better, I would probably think of Sybil all night, for days, even. I would worry about her. I wondered if there were many things that Paige carried around all the time, if you just got desensitized to it.

Taking out his phone, he checked his messages. "Autopsy is done." He called and I could hear the ringing on the other end, then the answer.

"County Coroner's office, Elmer Fisher speaking."

"It's Leo Paige, what have you found?"

The next reply was impossible for me to make out. Paige took notes, answering each fact he was presented with. "Uh-huh. Yup. Yup. Yup. Thank you." He hung up and read the facts off to me. "Estimated time of death was between midnight and 2am yesterday morning. The wound was definitely a gunshot, there was residue, but no major organs were hit. The gunshot happened within the past two to three days. Cause of death was not blood loss, probable drug overdose. A tox screen won't come back until tomorrow at the earliest, it has to go to the lab in Chattanooga."

It was interesting to me, but I was mostly thinking about whether it meant I got to go home. I tried to focus. "Should we go to Dennis Wright again? Maybe he would cooperate if he knows that the wound isn't what killed Gillespie, and that we're starting to put the pieces together."

"Not yet."

I was curious what he was thinking. He was the only person I had to learn from. "Is that just a judgement call?"

"Yeah. We'll give him time to worry. When we go to him next, we should have something solid."

"So what now?"

He checked the time on his phone. "I think we wait for the tox screen, hopefully it gives us a new avenue. You want to go home." It wasn't a question.

I shrugged. "Yeah. I should study." Hopefully I would be allowed to make up my Stats test.

"Alright. I'll take you home."

The sun was still out, but hanging low over the trees at the back of our property, when Paige pulled up to the little house. I saw curtains move in the window, then Mom came hurrying out. I was out of the car by then.

"I know, I'm sorry-."

"-Leo!" She sailed right by me and went to stand by the driver's side, smiling big and leaning on the window. "Hi! Remember me?"

"Of course, How are you, Marissa? And how's Vince?"

"Well, this one-," she jerked a thumb in my direction, "-kind of putting us through the ringer, lately."

"I can imagine."

"But we feel so much better knowing that when she's on duty, she's with you. Thank you so much for taking her under your wing."

"Just doing my duty."

"Anyway, we were wondering if you and your wife would come to dinner, just so we can show our appreciation. Saturday or Sunday?"

I had joined her and he looked at me before answering.

"We can do that, sure. We'd love that. I'm supposed to have Sunday off, I think Kathy can make it work, too. And Evelyn, of course."

"Of course. I'm so excited. Maybe six?"

"Sounds like a plan. Should we bring something?"

"Just your appetites."

"Alright, see you then."

She tapped the door twice in the usual fashion to send him on his way.

Inside, Dad was cooking pork chops.

I lingered at the kitchen bar, with Sybil still bruises and reaching across her own in the back of my mind. "Do we need to talk?"

"Oh yeah," Mom said, gesturing to the seat. She went to stand by Dad. She sighed. "Evie-."

I shut my eyes so she wouldn't see me roll them.

"-When we begrudgingly agreed to this, it was with the understanding that you would still be going to school."

"There was a murder, Mom! Or, no, it didn't end up being a murder, but there was a dead person."

"I don't care if there were ten dead people. You're our daughter, you're eighteen. I don't want you missing any more school. The dead people can wait until three-thirty."

"They can't though. If I don't do the job I swore an oath to do, I could get in serious trouble. -But I promise, I promise I won't miss any more school for anything less than an actual murder. Okay?"

She made a face, not completely satisfied.

Dad chimed in, "I called the school. You're going in early tomorrow to make up that test you missed. Seven-fifteen."

"Okay."

"I'll drive you." He started plating up pork chops, mashed potatoes and asparagus.

"Thanks. And Mom, thanks for taking care of Mabel today. It shouldn't happen again."

"Okay, you're welcome." She came to sit by me, while Dad stood.

I took a bite. "Mm. Good, Dad."

"Thanks. So how did the guy die? Or can you not talk about ongoing investigations?"

"Um…" I mulled it over. "Probably an overdose. But don't spread it around."

Mom asked, "Any family?"

"No, none at all."

"That's sad… Leo said yes to dinner. Sunday at six."

"Should I make spaghetti?"

"How about lasagna?"

"That sounds good," I chimed in, "but it's a little weird, you wanting to have dinner with my coworker."

"We knew him first, Evie."

"Mm-hm…" I scarfed my food. I wanted to check on Mabel, then I had to shower, hit the books, get to bed early. I tried to swallow too big of a mouthful and coughed.

Dad said, "Remember to breathe, Eves."

"Mm-hm."

That night I dreamed that I was in an all girls' school in Japan, where I didn't speak the language or know anyone. Japanese girls made fun of me and giggled when I walked by. The toilets were too computerized and complicated, I couldn't figure out how to flush. I woke up to my ringing alarm and felt anxious and heavy.

It was Friday. One more day of school, a few hours of work afterward, one long, long day of work the next day, and I could have a day off Sunday. I threw on an outfit, worked my way through a plate of eggs. Mom was outside longer than usual on the egg hunt. When she came back in, that morning, her eyes were red. Ophelia the chicken had died.

At school I took the test, thinking I did okay. Before the regular school day started, I went outside to wait for Delilah at the courtyard. When I was watching people walk up the path from Main Street, a Frappuccino materialized next to my head.

I spun, jolting to my feet. "Oh my God! For me?"

Delilah had two, and offered me one. "I thought you could use it."

"You're an angel, thank you!"

"So what happened yesterday?"

I sipped, considering how much I could or should tell her. "Um… I'm not supposed to talk about it."

She looked a bit surprised, but then she shrugged. "I get it. You have to follow the rules."

"What's new with you?"

She pulled up a picture of the square she had finished last night of her web comic. She had almost a thousand followers, and I was proud.

"Looks nice," I praised.

Mrs. O'Connell was always Delilah's biggest fan, had urged her to publish her comic, last year. When the two of us walked into her room, she stood.

"There she is! What happened yesterday, Sheriff?"

"Oh, I can't talk about it, sorry. Delilah has a new panel…"

"Oh, good! Can I see?"

Lunch was pizza. Doughy, salty, square pieces. Side salad, an orange. Chocolate milk.

Scott sat down with Delilah and I. "Sheriffs drink chocolate milk?"

"This one does."

"Fair enough. We have to drop Mom off on the way, today."

"Of course. You've gotta do what you've gotta do."

Delilah knew what that meant, and looked down and away. He noticed and looked away, too. None of us who knew Scott and his mom would judge him, but I thought sometimes we assumed that he assumed that we were judging him, which made us feel awkward and not know how to act, and we would just end up coming off like we were dancing around some horrible embarrassing crime that he, himself had committed. But to say out loud 'It's not your fault, we don't think any less of you' would be absurd, would draw attention to him that he didn't want from our other, less in-the-know and less understanding friends.

I thought it was funny how sometimes I could sit at a table with nine people crowded around, and feel like there was really just the three of us. There were friends, and then there were friends, you know?

The second half of the day flew by, and although I was not dreading going to work as much as I had the first and second days, I wasn't exactly looking forward to it either. I was used to having a lot more free time, I felt like I could hardly catch my breath.

After school, Scott took us out of the way to pick his mother up. I slid into the middle of the bench seat as she climbed into the truck. Her perfume and hairspray filled the air in the cab, and I forced a smile and made small talk as we drove the couple of miles back into town. She climbed out at the bar, always cheerful. We went on to my house. Scott came in with me again, helped tend to Mabel, fed her an apple.

Mom was not home, but had bagged me a sandwich and some snacks to take to work. I changed into my uniform and we hopped back in the truck.

When we pulled into the lot, Paige was pulling in, in a cruiser with the windows down. He had probably been on patrol for a few hours already. I started to cross to him, but he climbed out of the SUV and headed for the door of the department, waving for me to come along.

"What's up?"

"Frank Gillespie's tox screen came back. He overdosed on a new, designer drug. It's referred to as

Blue 82. It first showed up in Elviston county a few months ago-." He opened the door for me. "At a party where two teenagers from Reed City overdosed. One of them died, the other has permanent brain damage. Another boy was charged with distribution-leading-to-death for supplying them."

"Harry Santiago," I said, and Paige looked surprised. "I remember that whole thing. He went to school with us until two years ago when his family moved. He's a year older than me. We had a class together when I was a freshman… I didn't know him that well, but a lot of people in my school said that he was framed." And they blamed Sheriff Raegan for how the whole thing went. It was a key part of my platform when I was running my underground whisper campaign. I didn't say that part out loud.

"The problem is that the stuff Frank Gillespie overdosed on is identical to what those kids overdosed on a couple months ago. The makeup is exactly the same, down to one one-thousandth of a percent. If it were a different batch, it's very unlikely that the composition would be that similar."

"It could have just come from the same supplier. One huge batch, six months ago, it could be a coincidence." But as I said it, it did not ring true.

"Awfully big coincidence…"

We had moved through the bullpen, and down the hallway with the vending machines, break room and bathroom. At the end was another door, which opened to a narrow stone staircase, leading down. A locked metal door barred entrance to the room in the basement. Paige had a key, and once again held the door for me.

Free standing racks filled the space, which had to stretch the entire length of the building. Letters labeled sections, each was filled with evidence boxes, mostly white but some which looked older were brown with black lids, breaking at the seams, water stained, mildewing. The air had a dank smell.

Paige took a book down from a shelf on the nearest wall. There was a small desk where he flipped through it until he found what he wanted. "Logged by Campbell… L-27."

I stood back while he went and got the box, bringing it back, flipping the lid off. He took a pair of disposable gloves from the top drawer of the desk, and moved evidence in bags out of the way. A flannel plastered with vomit I could smell through the bag, the normal bile smell but a chemical smell over it. A compact mirror. A razor blade. A few playing cards with specks of blood on them.

"Where'd the blood come from?" I asked.

"It wasn't my case, but I heard that the boy who died started hemorrhaging from the eyes."

"Eugh."

"No drugs."

"You sure?"

"It was almost a pound. It would be hard to miss."

"It wouldn't have been incinerated, or something?"

"Nope."

"Auctioned to fund the department's annual ski trip?"

"Nope."

"And only deputies could have gotten in here?"

"Yup."

"And you think that only a cop could have held the DUI and the hit and run over Dennis Wright's head?"

"I didn't say 'only a cop'… but probably a cop, yes. Put it all together, it's pretty damning. We need to pull all the boxes around this one, all the other ones related to the case, make sure the drugs weren't misplaced. I need some time to think about all of this… It should get handed over to the Internal Affairs Bureau, but that would mean stepping back while we're still shooting in the dark, and trusting it to a bunch of suits in Chattanooga, no less… For now, it can't leave this room."

I nodded, feeling a thrill take hold of me. A secret. A conspiracy, we were creeping up on. Someone innocent in the clutches of it… "So, boxes?"

"Yeah, go and start pulling them, I'll read them off to you."

"You've got it." I'd probably jump off a cliff if he told me to, if I thought it would help the case.

Chapter Nine

The evidence boxes turned up nothing, just ate up most of the evening. Paige took us out on patrol, sticking around Elviston, dropped me off before heading home, himself. I fell into bed, had more vivid and anxious dreams. When I woke up in the early morning, I realized why I had been having the nightmares, why I had been so tired and hungry. I had started my period, which always took me by surprise, even though I suddenly realized I had been having cramps the day before. I thought maybe I'd just had too much coffee, not enough water.

The bad news was that it would get worse before it got better. The good news was that if I made it through a couple more days, it would get easier, I would have more energy.

I tried to get back to sleep, but it seemed no good. And so around four-thirty, I dragged myself out of bed. The sooner I went to work, I reckoned, the sooner I could go home. I needed fourteen hours.

I brewed a doubly large iced coffee, borrowing one of Mom and Dad's travel mugs. Plenty of ice, plenty of caramel. As I sipped it, I painted over the orange tip of the bb gun I had bought, with black nail polish. It otherwise looked like a normal handgun. Made a piece of toast even though I didn't have any desire to eat. Packed a chicken salad sandwich, carrots and dip, some strawberries, a snack cake. I tried to be quiet, but Dad must have heard me rustling around.

He came out, rubbing his eyes. "Why are you up so early?"

"Can't sleep. If I go to work now, I might be home for dinner."

"Okay… I'll drive you."

"You don't have to." Although I'd get to work a lot sooner if he did.

"It's alright, just let me pee first."

At the station, the two deputies who had worked the night shift were filling out paperwork. Heart and Stanton. They let me know that a detainee would need to be taken to the county jail once I pushed the papers through and had someone to ride with me. I thanked them and headed to my office. It was just after five in the morning. I didn't expect Paige until eight.

And so I reviewed my notes on the Gillespie death, from the morning that the body was found. I sipped my iced coffee and considered. I wanted to come up with something to suggest to Paige. I wanted to figure out our next move, on my own. So I sipped and asked myself, 'What would Paige do?'

We seemed to know that there was a connection between someone in the sheriff's department and a man with a prior drug conviction, recently shot. The shooting was not reported, the wound was treated by a presumably blackmailed veterinarian. The next question that came to my mind would be: Who shot Frank Gillespie? The answer to that would lead to realizations about the nature of the coverup, the endgame of the conspiracy.

When Paige showed up at eight, I hurried to tap on the window of my office and waved for him to come in. Most of my coffee was gone by then, I was buzzing.

"Hey, good morning. I've been thinking. I think we should hold a press conference asking for any information about the shooting. I don't see how it would clue anybody in to our suspicions about a deputy being involved... our body had a bullet hole in it, we ought to know why. Besides a press conference, we might track down known associates of Frank Gillespie's, see if anyone knew anything. I've got a list of names and addresses here, people he did time with, people he worked with who were also addicts or convicts, ex-girlfriend. What do you say?"

He found that a little funny, but I thought he was a little impressed, too. It was probably nothing he hadn't already considered, but at least I was thinking about it, too. He said, "Nobody is going to care enough to host a press conference for this. But you can issue a statement to the local news."

"Alright."

"And let's go see Harry Santiago, get his side of the story. Unless we wanted to take Raegan's word for it in his report…"

"Go see him in prison, you mean?"

"He's at the county jail awaiting trial."

"Oh! That reminds me, there's a detainee who needs to be taken over there."

"Let's go."

"Sweet."

"Got your notepad?"

"Yes." I slung my backpack onto my shoulder.

Paige did a double-take, stared at it.

"What?"

He shook his head, said nothing, and we went to collect the detainee.

On the drive over, my painkillers started to wear off, and I took another with the last of my iced coffee. I started to feel warm and cracked a window, which messed up my hair. When I pulled down the visor to check my reflection, I wished that I hadn't. I had blemishes on my forehead, bags under my eyes. I looked pale and so much older than I usually did. I hoped it was just the PMS and not a permanent gift from the new job.

After handing over the detainee and filling out the paperwork, we requested to see Harry Santiago. Corrections officers put us in an interview room, with a simple desk and a few chairs. We waited for the prisoner to be brought up.

Paige suddenly thought of something and fished in his pockets. "Do you have any change? Or a single?"

"I have plenty of money, in my handy dandy backpack!" I patted the front flap.

"Good, go back to the vending machine. Get a soda or a candy bar for the kid. Whatever you think he would like."

I sort of scoffed. "You think he's gonna snitch for a bag of Skittles?"

"I think he's gonna be hesitant to trust a sheriff and a sheriff's deputy after what he's been through. So it won't hurt to butter him up a little."

I agreed, so I got Harry a bag of barbeque Fritos and a Coke. When I returned to the interview room, the gangly young man had already been brought in. He had a face more blemished than mine, with sad, apprehensive eyes and a boyish attempt at a mustache that only made him look younger. He wore a blue uniform with 'Elviston County' on the back, and was not handcuffed.

Paige said, "This is sheriff Evelyn Lassiter."

"Hi Harry." I sat down opposite him, while Paige stayed standing. "We had a class together, a couple of years ago."

"I remember…"

I smiled, but I didn't know what else to say. "I'm uh… I just took over as Sheriff. A lot of people at school thought that it wasn't fair that you were charged the way you were. They said that you sold some pot, but never any of the hard stuff, that Sheriff Raegan pinned those overdoses on you because it was the easy thing to do. Paige and I have found something, some new evidence that might shed some new light on your case. If you'll tell us about what happened that night, we'll do what we can for you."

Harry watched me as I spoke, barely blinking, not showing any emotion. When he spoke, his voice was hardly above a whisper, I had to strain to hear.

"Teenage sheriff. Pretty, blonde, white sheriff. You ran a popularity contest and won. Just my luck... If I could win a popularity contest, I wouldn't be here, now."

Paige prompted, "Tell us about it." He had his notepad ready.

Harry popped open the bag of Fritos first. Put one in his mouth and chewed, slowly. Then he opened the Coke and washed it down. It started to irritate me, but I knew that his family was poor, from the way that he used to dress you could just tell. And I had always heard that the food in jails was terrible. He chugged half the soda and when he came up for air, his face showed just a hint of pleasure.

"Alright. So, yeah, I sold a few joints sometimes, to kids at school. My family needed the money, my Mom can't work, the disability and food stamps don't go far enough… But I also liked that being a connection got me into parties, made it easier to talk to people, to girls. I'm not good at talking to people." He glanced at me as he said it, and I felt myself blush. He hurried on. "I never bought or sold anything but marijuana. I had offers. I turned them down. Nobody really cares about weed these days. I thought even if I got caught holding, they'll probably expunge records for first time offenders when it gets legalized. I never carried more than half an ounce, it would have been a misdemeanor, I could still get most jobs or go to college. I'm good with computers, I wanted to do something with cyber tech..." It was clear from his tone that he no longer thought it was possible.

We waited for him to go on.

"So that night... January, there was snow on the ground. I thought it was weird that they were partying at the boathouse at the marina. It's just a pavilion, you know? No walls. Marcus Campbell, he was the one who invited me-."

I glanced at Paige. Campbell was the name of one of our deputies, the one who logged the evidence from that evening. I didn't remember a Campbell being among those who overdosed or were arrested that night, and I didn't know if Deputy Campbell had a son. Paige gave a subtle tilt of his head to show that I was onto something, but we let Harry keep going.

"Him and Joe Handler were kind of my friends, they had invited me to parties before, and would even try to help me talk to Katie Shipparol. Which never went well, but I thought we were cool. I asked if they wanted me to hook them up, they said no, just come. Which I thought was weird, but Katie was a maybe, and I really wanted to think they really liked me. So I went.

"It was cold, dark, but they had some string lights hung. We could see our breath as we passed around a half a bottle of Absolut. I hate that stuff, it was the first thing I ever got drunk off of, and I threw up like twenty times that night, and just haven't ever drank it, since. So when they passed it to me, I just pretended to drink."

Paige chimed in, "Who else was there?"

"It was me, Marcus, Joe. Monica Fell, she was always a bitch to me, but she was dating Joe… And there were three boys there from Reed City, they were all on the football team, and they were friends with Marcus and Joe. Their names were Ian, Will, and Hiram. And there was a girl from their school, too. They called her Missy, but I don't know if that was short for Melissa, or just a nickname."

I was sure that there hadn't been that many people charged. I took notes of all the names, the location, the Absolut, everything. I wanted my notes to be as thorough -or more- than Paige's.

"We passed the vodka around the picnic table once, everyone was just talking about stupid shit. Then Joe brought out his backpack and he had a big brick of this blue shit. He cut it open with a pocket knife. Monica got out her compact, and he scooped a little out. We had heard about that blue shit, it made me nervous right away. I asked them where they got it -you always need to know where your stuff comes from, I know that much about the hard stuff… All the football players, and Monica had court-ordered community service to get an underage drinking charge expunged. The guy who runs the marina will give double hours because it's hard to find somebody to clean trash off the bank in the winter. That's where they found it, washed up. They didn't even know what it was. I told them they shouldn't do it, but some people -it's the ones who have everything, in my opinion, the ones whose parents give them everything-some of them develop this insatiable hunger for self-destruction…"

He paused for a long moment, picking at a hangnail. Probably thinking about how unfair life could be. I thought I had a good grip on it, then, just by observing and trying to internalize, but understanding something from the outside and experiencing it were two different things.

Harry went on. "Everybody else did a few lines, hitting it hard. They called me a pussy, tried to get me to join in, but I wouldn't. I drove, my Mom would kill me. I wasn't having fun, I wanted to leave, but I was starting to think I'd have to take a few of them home. The Absolut ran out, it was after midnight, I was freezing…" He started to sound far away. "Then Hiram started to have a seizure, everybody freaked out, some of them thought he was messing with them, cause he was a joker like that. The girls ran off, like on foot. I called 911. Marcus and Joe took off in his car. Ian and Will were tripping pretty hard, Will tried to leave but he couldn't walk straight, he just laid down in the snow, babbling. By the time the ambulance showed up, Ian was puking and bleeding from his eyes. Hiram wasn't breathing, I was doing CPR, I felt one of his ribs break but I knew I had to keep going."

Harry's voice crept up an octave, betraying the horror he felt looking back on the moment. His lip quivered and he sucked in a deep breath, cleared his throat to try to stabilize himself. I wondered if he had been terrified, the whole time he had been in jail. For his safety and his future and his family's sake. There was a pit in my stomach, imagining myself in Harry's position. I was cool with Marcus and Joe, not friends exactly. I made out with Marcus in a closet, junior year... It seemed like so long ago. He took me on my first date, but we decided not to go steady, no hard feelings. I'd really had a crush on his older brother more than him, who was off at college.

If they had invited me to hangout at the marina some night, I might have gone, just depending on if I had anything better to do. I wouldn't have put anything up my nose, but I might have sipped some Absolut, if I knew that I had a sober ride home. I sure liked to think that I wouldn't have left three boys hallucinating, puking, seizing, just like Harry hadn't. I couldn't be sure, though.

Harry brushed away a tear before it could fall. He crossed his arms over his chest, trying to look tough. "Now Hiram's in a coma, Ian died, but that's not the worst part. My sister, Inez, she's sixteen. She's been missing for three weeks. I wasn't there, I wasn't bringing in money, protecting my family, like I'm supposed to. And she must have either felt like she had to start bringing in money, or else she wanted to help me, somehow, and stuck her nose where it didn't belong. She was always tough like that, stubborn, smart... it's my fault that she's gone."

"It's not..." I said it, but he didn't respond, didn't even seem to register my words.

He went on, with a sad finality. "Will is only seventeen, he'll get a deal and testify that I brought the drugs, cause that's what the cops want him to do."

"Not if we have anything to say about it," I said, and Paige's eyebrow raised. He said nothing, so I prompted Harry, "Anything else? Any little detail could help us."

"Who were the police on the scene that night?" Paige asked.

"I remember Sheriff Raegan, I think two others, but I don't know their names."

Paige made a note, then pulled out his phone. He pulled up a picture of most of the Sheriff's department in jerseys, on a baseball diamond. "Can you point them out?"

Harry studied the photo for a long time, zooming in on faces, looking at them all. "I think this guy." Kipling, that figured. "And him." Campbell. Which we could have figured, but it was nice to have it confirmed. I made notes because Paige made notes.

"You think you can help me?" Harry's voice did not sound hopeful. More like a wild shot in the dark. "Trial date's set for the beginning of June…" A little over a month away, right around graduation, and when school let out. "I can take a plea deal, they're offering seven years with good behavior and I'd have a felony for the rest of my life… So I'd rather not do that."

"You're not guilty, not with what you're charged with," I said. "We're going to figure this out."

I noticed Paige's pursed lips. Maybe I shouldn't have said that.

Harry said, "I need to get out of here. Mom can hardly get out of the house, so I don't know how she's taking care of herself… maybe my cousin can help a little, but it can't be enough. And I need to look for my sister. If she's still alive -maybe she's in trouble, I don't know- but I do know some places she might go. If she's not alive, I need to know that, too. So that she can rest in peace. So that Mom can grieve."

I felt sick with how much had happened to Harry and his family. I reached out and caught his hand in one of mine, an impulsive decision, and he blinked in shock, but didn't try to take his hand back. "Tell me where to start looking, and I'll do everything I can to find Inez, and keep her safe."

Harry looked at me, his brow pulled down suspiciously. He looked at Paige. He looked unhappy with the prospects before him; trust us or do nothing. "Take this down…"

He gave me everything he had. Names of friends, anyone Inez might have turned to, abandoned buildings in Reed City he wanted me to check. When I thought he was done, I stood, but he spoke once more.

"Jason Geraci. You should check with him. Inez knew him. Decent guy. He's an associate of mine." The way that he said it, I knew he had just broken a cardinal rule among drug dealers. He had given us his connection, and for nothing in return, nonetheless… It told me how desperate he was to help his sister.

Paige said, "Contact us if anything else comes back to you, don't talk to any other deputies. I won't give you my card, you wouldn't want to take it anyway… just call your mom and have her call us, and we'll be in touch. We'll go see her now, introduce ourselves."

Corrections officers came for Harry, and Paige and I walked back to the car. He waited until we made it to the garage to say what was on his mind.

"You shouldn't have gotten his hopes up."

"What do you mean? He's innocent, we're going to prove it."

"And what if we can't?"

I stopped at the passenger side while he went around. "We have to."

"It's been a couple of months, the evidence has been tampered with, the other witnesses have no reason to come forward."

"The evidence has been tampered with, isn't that enough?"

"Maybe. They still have a pattern of behavior from Santiago, witnesses willing to swear that he sold them drugs, and he was at the scene of the crime. He's legally an adult and he was partying with a bunch of minors."

I didn't like the sudden sinking feeling, the realization that I may let the kid down. If he were let down by regular cops, that was kind of one thing. But if I took over as sheriff, mostly to make a point, and let down an innocent kid immediately?

We climbed into the car. I asked, "Marcus Campbell, that's Deputy Campbell's son?"

"Nephew, I think. Campbell's not married, never mentioned any kids."

"Let's go talk to Ms. Santiago."

## Chapter Ten

The Santiagos lived in a rundown rented trailer behind their landlord's nicer trailer set back from the road on the outskirts of Reed City. A long, dirt driveway took us back into the trees. A wooden wheelchair ramp looked relatively newly made from unfinished wood and led up to the front door. We wound our way up it, knocked.

A woman's voice called from within, "Just a minute!"

And it was more than a minute that we waited, while we could faintly hear the sounds of movement inside. A mechanical whir grew closer, then the door opened, just an inch. An eye peaked out. Then the whir retreated. "Come inside."

I stepped in. The air inside was oppressive, had a smell of bitter medicine of some sort. The lights were dim, the television was not on in the living room.

Imelda Santiago was a big woman, at least four hundred pounds, in an electric wheelchair. She had very long hair, shiny and black, in a braid that reached all the way down to coil in her lap. She swayed in her chair as she drove it backward over the trailer's uneven floor, probably rotting below the door where wet shoes had been kicked off for more than thirty years and soaked through the green carpet.

"Harry told me you were coming." She spoke with an accent, I thought maybe Columbian. "Have a seat, please. I can get you some water or hot tea, if you'd like?"

There was only a floral loveseat to sit on, so we sat next to each other. "No, thank you Ma'am."

"Are you going to help my children?" Her voice shook with helplessness, her face hardened a moment later and told me that she expected very little.

"I hope so," I said. But then I looked to Paige, not necessarily trusting myself to ask the right questions, to take something so important on, myself.

Paige just said, "Tell us about Inez."

The girl's mother sighed, she smiled as she thought of her daughter. "Inez is my little girl. She has such a good heart. She's very smart for her age. She always makes sure I have my medications when I can't get out of bed. She wants to be a doctor, although she says that she might settle for nursing school. Harry always looked out for Inez. When he was taken to jail, we were lost. Inez went missing about two weeks later. That was at the beginning of the month. The last day I saw her was the 5$^{th}$. She went to school, she seemed normal, or close to it. We were getting back into the swing of things, she was talking about getting a job after school, to help make ends meet, since Harry was gone... She didn't come home."

I said, "I'm sorry... this must be really difficult for you. Harry gave us some names, Inez's friends and his associates, who she might have gone to. Can you look it over, tell us anyone else you can think of?"

She took my notebook, squinted in the low light. "This is a good list. Harry would know better than me, they were very close. She can't remember their father, she was too young when he died. Harry was the only man in her life."

"Inez hasn't been in contact at all, since the 5$^{th}$?"

"No, nothing. Nobody has seen her." The woman wiped a tear away before it could fall. Her nails were painted. I got the impression that she had a lot of time, a huge void to fill with both of her children having been ripped away from her.

"Was there anything taken from the house?"

"Some food was missing. Bread and peanut butter. Beef jerky."

Paige, I guess, felt the need to ask, "Is there any chance that Inez just ran away?"

Imelda scowled at him, her dark eyes were fierce. "She is a good girl, she cares about her family, and school, and her future. She stays away from drugs. She is *not* a runaway, and you are not going to write her off as one!"

Paige nodded, took notes. "I'm sorry I had to ask, Ms. Santiago."

"We're not trying to write Inez off. I told Harry that we would do everything we could to find her, and we're looking into his case, too."

"That's why Inez is gone," Imelda said. "Mark my words. I know my girl. She was looking into the corruption in your sheriff's department, and she got too close. Something bad happened to her. I hope that I'm wrong… I'm tired. If I could get out and look for her, myself, I would. But I can't. Is there anything else?"

It was still fairly early in the day, but I didn't know what was wrong with Imelda. We might have taken a lot out of her with our conversation. I saw a glimpse of Harry and Inez's lives, and I was sad for the two of them. "Is there anything I can do for you, before we go? Have you eaten?"

She waved me away. "Just lock the door on your way out. Find my girl. Get my boy out of jail."

We locked the door and left. Settling back into the car, Paige said, "Most of Frank Gillespie's associates are here in Reed City."

I didn't like the idea of pushing Inez to the side, but Frank Gillespie was dead, and she was only missing. "I'll start finding addresses for those kids on the way."

The first two associates of Frank Gillespie's that we tried to locate were not at home, had been fired from their place of work. The third sat in the living room of his trailer, completely visible through thin curtains, and flipped us off, refusing to come to the door.

The fourth was a woman, a former girlfriend of Gillespie's. Another trailer, in Reed City, in a trailer park. The yard was nice, with little ceramic mushrooms and gnomes decorating the flowerbeds of perennial plants emerging from red mulch. A wind chime tinkled as she opened the screen door.

"Hello?"

"Dora Melvin?"

She looked apprehensive but clear headed. She bore the old scars on her face of a meth addict who had picked at her skin, but none were fresh. I knew she had had run-ins with law enforcement in the past, but nothing for the last couple of years.

"Yes. How can I help you?"

I spoke up. "We have some questions for you about Frank Gillespie. May we come inside?"

She made a face, distaste at the mention of the man. Then she looked at me with a hint of confusion. She must not keep up with local elections. She nodded.

As we stepped in, I gestured and mouthed to Paige to let me take the lead on this one. He nodded.

The inside was cutely decorated like the outside, although the cabinets and counters were dated, probably from the nineties. The couch that she guided us to was covered in plastic. A few baby toys littered the floor.

"The baby's napping. What do you need to know about Frank?"

I had made a list of questions to ask, but I didn't need to consult it yet. "You're aware that Mr. Gillespie passed away a few days ago?"

"Yes, I had heard. No great loss."

"When was the last time that you saw him?"

"Back in the fall, October. I ran into him at Walmart. He wanted to catch up, but I wasn't interested. I was eight months pregnant and twelve months sober."

"You didn't keep in touch with him at all?"

"No. We still have a few mutual friends, I knew that he was still dealing."

"What did he deal?"

"Just about anything under the sun."

I noted it. "Designer drugs like Blue 82?"

"I haven't heard of that, but if there was money to be made, sure."

I checked my list. "You hadn't heard anything about him having a disagreement with anyone, ripping anyone off?"

"No, and that doesn't sound like Frank to me. He considered himself a gentleman. He kept his associates happy, was always invited to parties, card games, cook outs…"

Sybil Wright had mentioned Rodney having a weekly card game. I glanced at Paige. He made a face, barely enough for me to register. He doubted what Dora was saying. He didn't say anything, so I kept on.

"You wouldn't be willing to give us the name of any of those associates?"

"Wouldn't be smart. Not the kind of thing people do around here."

"Of course…" I was lost as to what to say next. How to convince a woman with a baby to put herself in danger in the name of a lousy criminal-ex-boyfriend and a boy she didn't know. Or probably didn't know. I wondered whether -if I even could convince her- it would be the right thing to do.

Paige said, "If you can point us in the right direction with a name or even just a location, we can leave you out of it."

She considered, looking anxious. Finally, she shook her head. "I can't. I'm not a part of that anymore. Please go."

"Thank you for your time."

"Yes, thank you." I hurried after him and out the door, waiting until we were shut in the car to gripe, "What was that? You just gave up?"

"She asked us to leave. She hasn't been involved with that for over a year. We can find another way to Gillespie's associates."

"You got an idea?"

"Let's mull it over while we eat."

We had been driving around. It was not quite noon, but -as always- I could eat. Half of my day was gone, and I had hardly noticed the time passing, but my body felt heavy. I needed another coffee, or some sugar. I got a paper cup of half hot chocolate, half coffee at a gas station while Paige filled the tank.

He parked at the edge of the parking lot with the radar gun on, and we munched through sandwiches in silence. Like me, he had brought a sack lunch. His was turkey and Swiss. Cars rolled by, but nothing very fast.

After I finished my sandwich, and was munching through carrots and dip, I asked, "Whatcha thinking?"

"A pound of a new designer drug washing up on the shore of the Tennessee…"

"Kids could have been lying about where they got it."

"But who would give a teenager a pound of hard drugs? They couldn't have bought it, street value would have been probably ten thousand or more. None of their parents are leaving something like that lying around. Drugs on the shore means they were being moved by the river. The sheriff's department has a boat, it's in a slip in the marina. Let's borrow a drug dog from the state police and take a drive over there."

"We can do that?"

"Usually different law enforcement factions want to play nicely with each other. And you are the sheriff. We'll wait until later, when Campbell and Kipling are done for the day. In the meantime, let's hit up the kids from the party at the marina that night…"

"My people."

"You know them?"

"The three from my school, yeah."

"How well?" He clearly didn't like the sound of it.

"Not that well. Not like 'conflict of interest' level."

He drove in silence for a minute, but wasn't satisfied. "You considered when you took this job that you might need to enforce the law in ways that put you at odds with your classmates? With your friends?"

"Mm," I grumbled, shrugged. But honestly, it made me queasy.

It was the two still alive from Reed City first. Will Sacco was our first stop. He lived in an old brick home on a cul-de-sac, a black wrought iron gate around the property, and he was in the front yard playing with a golden retriever when we pulled up. As soon as he saw the cruiser, he took the dog inside.

We approached but before we could knock, the door opened and a graying man, handsome and fit for his age, looked out. "You're here about Will's case?"

"We're here in regards to Harry Santiago, who-."

"-I'll stop you there. I'm gonna have to ask you to leave my property. We obviously can't discuss that."

I was irritated, but Paige took it in stride.

"Alright, thank you for your time." The door closed in our face. "We had to figure we weren't getting much out of them. They have to protect their son."

Melissa Arlington's family lived in a big colonial-styled new build in a housing development. It was a picturesque home for a picturesque black family. When we were invited into the home by a helicopter mom, twin girls of about ten ran to check us out. She dismissed them to the backyard, then called Melissa down.

She was a tall and athletic looking girl, seventeen, good skin for her age and a carefully teased cloud of hair. She looked straight-laced at first glance, wore a cross; it was either a good mask or she had made a radical change since the night of the party. I guess losing two friends would do that to a kid.

She sat on a blue sofa, while Paige and I sat across in matching armchairs. Her mom hovered behind her, nervous, and she looked at me with a lot of apprehension, maybe even disdain. I was definitely letting Paige take the lead.

"Maybe we shouldn't be doing this without a lawyer present..." She clearly knew about the night in question; the girl had not been mentioned in Raegan's report, so I had wondered if we would be springing it on her. Clearly her daughter had told her.

Paige said, "There's no need for that, Mrs. Arlington, we're not here to arrest your daughter, we have no interest in that. There would be no way for us to confirm if there were drugs in her system on that night, or to assign any responsibility to her for what happened to the others. This is about Harry Santiago. We think he's an innocent boy getting hung out to dry because he was the only one who stayed when things went badly. And his mother can't afford a lawyer for him."

I saw guilt flash across Melissa's face. She looked down at her folded hands. Her mother was still not convinced.

"I have to worry about my own child."

"Ma'am, I give you my word we aren't interested in charging your daughter. The sheriff agrees with me-."

I nodded.

"-That matters like this -as far as children are concerned- are best dealt with at the family level. I think that you would agree though that there's an important lesson to be taught about taking responsibility, and rising to the challenges God gives when we have the chance to help someone."

Mrs. Arlington nodded, put her hands on her daughter's shoulders. "Tell them the truth." I noticed that she wore a cross, too. I hadn't seen it because I had been too afraid to look at her, because of how she was looking at me. Paige had clearly seen it.

"Tell us about that night," I prompted, trying to be gentle, understanding.

Melissa looked at me, nodded, pursing her lips. Thinking back. Her voice came out flat, far away. "I just wanted to hang out with my friends on a Saturday night. I wish we had just gone to Applebee's... But Hiram and Ian wanted to go to the marina to hang out with Joe and Marcus. Monica and Harry were there, too. I didn't know them as well, but it was fun at first. Ian brought cheap vodka. Joe whipped out a big brick of blue stuff, wrapped in plastic and tape. He had a pocketknife, and sliced it open. I was nervous the second I saw that huge thing of drugs, I was thinking 'that's not supposed to be here'... Then I was thinking 'I'm not supposed to be here'..."

Her mom put her hands on her daughter's shoulders.

Melissa went on. "I should have trusted that instinct. They asked for a mirror, I gave them my compact. I didn't want to tell them not to do it, be like their nagging mom. Nobody paid any attention to me until last year. I didn't want to go back to that. It's like you don't even exist..." Her face was turned down, but she looked up at me and said very pointedly, "*You* wouldn't understand."

It was true, I had always had friends. I thought I could handle not having *everyone* like me, but what would I do not to lose Delilah and Scott?

"Anyway, they started putting it up their noses, line by line... The guys were all hitting it hard, I was surprised. -Hiram volunteers at the animal shelter every weekend. Or, volunteered... Ian organized a blood drive at the school, after his sister had an accident and needed a transfusion. Do you know that someone in the United States needs a blood transfusion every two seconds?"

She looked between us like she really expected an answer. I shrugged, nodded. "That's amazing, I wouldn't have guessed that."

She sighed. "It doesn't change what they did, or what happened. I just don't want that to be all that they are to you people."

"That's not all that they were to us," I assured her. "We want to make sure that this doesn't happen to other people's kids."

Paige added, "Do you know where the drugs came from?"

"Joe said that he and Marcus found it on the riverbank when they were doing their community service."

We each made a note of it.

I said, "They were doing the drug, then what?"

"Hiram started shaking and spitting up. It was horrible. I just ran, I was so scared. I got to the park across the road and Monica was there with me. I called my mom and she took us home. The next day, I saw on Facebook that the cops had shown up to the scene, that Ian died and Hiram was on life support. That a dealer was in custody. I didn't realize that it was that Harry kid until much later. When I did, I figured that Joe and Marcus had made up the stuff about finding the drugs, to cover for Harry."

I couldn't help but to ask, "Where would Harry have gotten a pound of a new, designer drug?"

She blinked, her tone came out haughty. "I don't know. Wherever he got the pot he sold?"

"Is there anything else that you can think of, that might be relevant? Did Sheriff -former Sheriff Raegan ask you anything else?" Paige glanced at me apologetically at the slip up.

Melissa said, "I never talked to Sheriff Raegan."

"Never? Or anyone else from the sheriff's office?"

"No, nobody ever came to talk to me. I figured the others left me out of it. It wasn't my fault."

"No…" I looked at Paige, wondering if there were something else I should be asking.

He considered, pursing his lips. "I'd like to leave my card with you, in case you remember anything else. You can give me a call anytime. Or you can IM Evelyn online."

"Sure."

"Thank you, officers."

Mrs. Arlington showed us out. We sat in the car on their drive, while I pulled up the next address for the first person on the list that the Santiago's had given us. I saw the curtains move in an upper window of the Arlington house, and a beautiful little girl looked down at us. I waved to her. Paige was thinking. He seemed perturbed.

"This is getting serious. He didn't even go through the motions of proper procedure on this case. It's either incredible laziness, or it's corruption. Either way, I'm going to have to look over his old case files. He has put murderers behind bars. A serial rapist."

"Raegan? In this county?"

"Yup. I guess it's your problem for now, but if you wanted to ignore it until the recall, I wouldn't blame you."

It didn't sound like something that I was supposed to agree with. "No... But let's focus on Harry and Inez Santiago while it's fresh." We had been to see all of Frank Gillespie's known associates, and each of the kids from the party at the marina that were located in Reed City. The ones from Elviston would have to wait.

He said, "I don't think you should get your hopes up. Even if we find Inez, it might not do any good. If she's stubborn, she would probably just run away again."

"You might be right. But there's a chance she was taken, or she might have started this but now she's in over her head..."

He nodded, put the car in drive, backed onto the road.

## Chapter Eleven

Multiple stops to the homes of Reed City students proved fruitless. For the most part, they lived in nicer parts of town than the Santiagos. For the most part, their families were patient and happy to help by answering our questions. Most provided their opinions that Inez was a sweet and smart girl, who would not have run away. They said that it was so unfortunate that Harry had gotten into trouble, that they didn't know him personally but knew that the two were close; they were sure that her disappearance was his fault, somehow.

One of her friends told us that Inez had just been hired to wait tables on weekends at a local diner. I consulted my notes and saw that Harry had washed dishes there until his arrest. We drove over. It was a retro place, gleaming chrome and glass and red vinyl. A jukebox on the back wall playing the original version of 'Dancing in the Street'.

The waitresses wore yellow dresses and white aprons.

The manager was named Roy Brighton. He was a white man in his forties, with a sensitive face, beginning to grey in his dark beard. He sat down with us at a booth in the back, asking the waitress to bring us some waters.

"Inez used to come in with her brother, after school. He would wash dishes during the dinner shift, she would do her homework, or study. A few of my workers have to bring their kids to work with them, never a teenager before, but she was no trouble. I'd give her a piece of pie. Strawberry rhubarb was her favorite. -Is her favorite. When she asked me for a job, I was happy to help. I had her on the schedule the day that she went missing. I knew right away that something was wrong, she wouldn't have missed her first shift if she could help it, certainly not without calling."

I asked, "How long have you known Inez?"

He considered. "Five years."

"Harry worked here since he was fourteen?"

Brighton looked nervous, shrugged. "Their family needed the money."

Paige asked, "Did Inez ever talk to you about Harry's arrest?"

"Only about how sad it had made her, that it put her family in a tough position…"

"Nothing about the deputies who investigated the case? Former Sheriff Raegan?"

"No, nothing about him."

"Did Inez come to you for help? For a place to stay?"

Brighton blinked in shock. "No."

I wasn't surprised, Paige had asked even the teenagers we had questioned the same question, in the same, harsh tone.

"If she had, what would you have said?"

I glanced over. That was new.

The man hesitated. "Well I would want to help, but I wouldn't want her scaring her mother like this."

It rang true to me, I studied Paige and he seemed to be in agreement.

"Do you have any idea where she might be, or who she might have gone to?"

"No, I'm sorry. I wish I did."

Our next stops were a pair of teachers who Harry knew to be close to Inez. Each seemed saddened by the girl's disappearance just like Brighton, and each lived in a place too small to house a spare kid, anyway.

"Teachers are so underpaid," I remarked, as we walked back to the car for what felt like the hundredth time that Saturday.

"Yup."

Each one, Paige had asked with the same intensity, 'Did Inez come to you?' and when they said, 'no', he had asked, 'What would you say if she had?' They had each stammered something about obeying the law even if it was hard or it hurt to do so.

Last on Harry's list of people Inez might have turned to was his connection, Jason Geraci. He lived in a condo in a red brick development, with nicely manicured hedges and curbs and a scenic walkway around a little pond out back. It seemed that selling drugs kept him living comfortably. When he opened the door, a delicious smell wafted out past him; he was a fit Italian man in his mid or late twenties, he was wiping his hands with a towel as he took in the sight of us.

"Can I help you, officers?"

"We'd like to speak to you about Inez Santiago."

He made a face I couldn't quite read; he was not surprised, he was not smiling, he was not afraid or irritated. "Come in. I was just making a polenta, there's plenty to go around. Meal prep, you know."

We stepped into the chic living room, followed him through the open floor plan to the kitchen. He was scooping polenta into black containers, slicing chicken breast to go on top. "Hungry?"

"No, thank you," I said, although it smelled delicious. "So a source informs us that you know the Santiagos."

"You mean Harry told you." He didn't seem to care.

"Tell us about Inez, how you know her, how long, when did you last see her and how did she seem to you?"

"How do I know her… through her brother, he's an acquaintance. He brought her to a couple little get togethers I had, watch parties for Stranger Things, classic Ms. Pac-Man tournaments, thinks like that. My sister is around her age. How long? Just the last maybe… year and a half or two years. Last time I saw her, I drove her to county to see Harry, that was around the end of last month, Saturday. How did she seem? Sad. But not resigned. She's never been very talkative. I wasn't surprised when she went missing. I'm not really worried about her. She's smart. Savvy."

Paige asked, "Did Inez come to you for help?"

He kept boxing up his polenta and chicken, his tone and expression showed nothing. "No, she did not."

"If she did, what would you do?"

"Alert the proper authorities about the presence of a teenage runaway. Of course." He closed the fridge and leaned on it, crossing his arms. "Anything else?"

I decided to throw a Hail Mary. "I'm sure you don't like law enforcement. I don't either, that's why I got myself elected to be sheriff, and to get Raegan out of office, out of power. I knew Harry from school. I told him I would do what I could to look into his case, and that I would find Inez and help her if I could. You can deduce from the fact that he sent us here that he trusts us to do that. So if you know anything about Inez's whereabouts, or where she might have gone, you should tell us, now."

"I don't know anything."

Paige was not satisfied. "We can make your life difficult. Follow you around, track down your connections, make them think you're talking to us. Get you audited."

Jason shrugged. "Won't do you any good. You can see yourselves out, now. And for the record, I really hope Inez is okay. But if she doesn't want you to find her, you won't."

His words rang true. Paige and I were silent as we buckled in, back in the cruiser. I didn't think we would be following up on any of the threats, it would indeed be a waste of time. And we had exhausted Harry's list of likely accomplices for the girl. The last thing that we could do was to drive around and peak inside of the abandoned buildings he had noted. None looked to be broken into or have any other evidence that someone had stayed there. I felt numb. I was going to fail to find her. I couldn't let it go, but there was nothing else that I could do, for the time being. I would keep her in the back of my mind, revisit her daily.

"So back to Elviston, then? The other kids from the party at the marina?" Back to Harry's case; he was the one that we could maybe help, right now.

"Yup."

"Maybe we should do a press conference for Inez, ask for any tips."

"It's not a terrible idea, since we've got nothing else to go on. But that sort of thing usually just brings out the crazies, and a bunch of mistaken sightings, and wastes a lot of the department's time."

Joe Handler's rum-soaked father turned us away. Didn't say a word, just stared at me for a few long seconds, then looked at Paige, snorted a derisive snort, and shut the door in our faces.

Marcus seemed to be home alone. He answered the door in blue checkered pajama pants, a grey Fall Out Boy shirt. He looked good, tall and broad in the shoulders, narrow in the hips. A swimmer's body, but he played just about every sport. Brown hair askew over his forehead. Dimples for days. His older brother was somehow even cuter.

He smirked, crossing his arms in the doorway. "Uh-oh. 5-0's here. Come to arrest me? Cause I have a permit for these." He flexed a bicep.

I said, "We came to talk about what happened at the marina, back in January."

He considered, making a confused face. "You mean when I was doing my community service to get that drinking charge expunged?"

"The night that Ian McMahon died and Hiram Walsh overdosed and slipped into a coma."

Another face, an amused one. "I don't know anything about that, I wasn't there."

"We have multiple witnesses that say that you were."

"That doesn't sound like me. And who says so? A couple of drug users, and drug dealers?"

Paige tried to redirect. "It wouldn't be feasible to charge you at this point, no tox screen, no way to say for sure that you used, no responsibility for the two who overdosed, being that you were still seventeen on the night in question-."

"-And that I wasn't there."

Paige sensed that the conversation would lead nowhere. He offered his card. "In case you change your mind."

"I don't need it."

Still, he held it out. "Scared the guilt will get to you?"

Marcus smiled, took the card, waved it at us. "Goodbye Deputy Paige. Goodbye Sheriff Evelyn... you can come back anytime, but leave your dog in the pen."

Monica Fell and her family had moved to Tallahassee in March, and we weren't about to drive down there to interview her. We had killed a few more hours. I still had my snack cake in my backpack, and munched through it, causing Paige to look over at me.

"Watch the crumbs."

I mumbled an affirmative, dug for my painkillers and water bottle. I was tired. Full-body, limbs heavy, head buzzy, eyes sleepy tired all over. I hoped Mom and Dad were cooking something good for dinner, that I could be home while it was still somewhat warm on the stove.

But we had one more thing to check off our lists, had to do it before I could consider the day done. "Drug dog?"

Chapter Twelve

The nearest state police precinct was in Chattanooga, a half an hour from where we were on the far side of town, then twenty minutes back to a cute residential street in Elviston.

Paige explained, "We're gonna stop and take my car. Can't be sure that someone isn't monitoring the trackers in the cruisers, and it's better not to attract too much attention."

"Kinda taking that chance, either way, aren't we?"

"Yeah. I'm gonna change my shirt, do you have anything else you could wear?"

"Uh, I've got a camisole on under this."

"I'll find you something, my wife won't mind. Come inside, she wants to meet you. Bring the dog."

I jumped out and eagerly hooked a leash to the German Shepard's collar. He was a beautiful dog, as disciplined as a Marine and named Kevin for some reason. Giving him a few pets, I led him to the front door. It was a blue two-story house, white shutters and picket fence, slightly tacky metal sunflowers hung around the wooden door.

"Honey, I'm home," Paige called, his usual monotone.

As I stepped into the pleasantly cool and sun-drenched kitchen, I could hear computer keys tapping at a frantic pace. It let up and a very petite, pretty black woman appeared from around the corner. Her hair was in braids, she wore blue eyeshadow that made her amber irises pop and matched her blue blouse.

"Already? Oh hello! You must be Evelyn." She had stood on her toes to kiss Paige, he had presented his cheek, glancing uncomfortably over at me.

"Evelyn Lassiter," I introduced myself, shaking her hand.

"Kathy Paige, nice to meet you."

"Nice to meet you, too."

"And who's this?" She knelt and gave the dog some scratches.

"That's Kevin, our newest deputy."

Paige had gone further into the house, disappearing around the corner. When he returned, he wore a white polo, and held up small pink one.

"Can Evelyn borrow this? I don't want to run her home just to change. We have one more stop to make before the day is done."

Kathy scoffed, crossing her arms. "Not my favorite polo!"

"Uh-huh," Paige responded to her thick sarcasm with a tiny smile, tossed the shirt to me. "Bathroom's that way."

I figured the polo was not much her style, maybe it had been a gift from him so that they could match. When I re-emerged, I heard him explaining.

"We're doing some snooping at the department's slip at the marina."

"Incognito," she murmured.

"I'll take her home afterward, so maybe an hour."

"Okay… I'll start dinner. Be careful."

I heard a kiss and emerged, just for him to immediately step back, putting space between them. "Twins!" I exclaimed, striking a pose in my cute polo. "Come on, Kev! Nice to meet you, Kathy, and I'll see you at dinner, tomorrow?"

"Yes, can't wait."

On the way out, the dog pulled on its leash, sniffing shrubs around the front of the house. It lifted its leg to pee. Paige frowned, crossed his arms. He clearly wasn't a dog person. Maybe not an animal person in general.

"What do you want me to do? He's gotta go!"

I tried to lead the dog back to the car, but he had other business to do, and squatted on Paige's lawn. I groaned.

Paige went back inside and got some paper towels and a bag, wordlessly handing them to me, then pointing to the blue garbage bin by the curb. He went and got into the car. My face was warm.

"I'm your boss, you know!" But was I going to order him to clean up dog shit? Of course not, and he knew it.

When I put the dog in the backseat of Paige's small Chevy SUV, got in the passenger seat, he offered me hand sanitizer. I accepted, and we started for the marina.

The sky was still bright blue overhead, but out to the west the sun was sinking, dyeing the sky orange and gold. We passed the park where Melissa and Monica had run and been picked up, pulled into the lot of the marina. There were a few other vehicles in the lot, but nobody was walking around.

It was the very end of April, and mostly fair, but the air was cooling as the sun sank, the breeze was chilly. A bit early for boating, but not for those devoted to the lifestyle. We walked from the lot across a stretch of grass and to the wooden pier. I looked up and down at boats of various sizes and colors in slips. The dog sniffed the boards of the pier, tugged at the leash at a red and white boat called the Anna Rose.

Paige led the way, keeping his eyes peeled. The pavilion where the teens had partied that night in January was on the water's edge, at the center of the long pier. Thick wooden legs stretched down into the darkening water, a cement patch with few picnic tables, no walls, a black metal roof. We had to walk past it to get to the Sheriff's department's slip on the far end. Paige slowed as we passed, we took it in, but there was nothing left for us there, evidence-wise.

The department's boat was mostly white, with a tan stripe on the sides, Elviston County Sheriff's Department written in black letters. It was one of the bigger boats in the marina, had a main deck which could hold probably ten or twelve, a covered lower deck, and a small second deck where the gleaming metal wheel and red and blue lights were stationed. We stepped onboard, having to coax Kevin for a moment, but he made the hop and wagged his tail, then went straight to sniffing. He sniffed all around the main deck, where bench seating wrapped around the back and all opened to storage underneath. Nothing inside but the usual boat and police equipment, strings of buoys for cordoning off stretches of water, life vests and flashlights, signal flags. In one bench, a metal device and wound chains, probably for dragging the river for bodies. I shuddered at the sight of it.

Kevin did not alert on the main deck. We took him upstairs, to do a quick scan of the upper, and he gave us nothing there. Paige had to duck his head to go below deck. It was a tight room, just a sitting area that could also be a single bunk on each side, a mini fridge, a bathroom no bigger than a telephone booth.

Kevin sniffed around, jumped up onto one of the bunks, nuzzled the fake-wooden wall panel, and alerted, bowing down on his front paws and pointing with his nose, very decidedly. His tail wagged; he was happy to be doing his job.

Paige snapped his fingers and ordered the dog down. He felt around the panel, which had slats every six inches or so, and tapped on it. It sounded hollow.

"Let me." I passed him the leash, felt around the seams, got my fingernails under it and pulled. It popped loose. The hole in the wall showed a cavern a foot deep and two feet high, curved with the white fiberglass of the hull. Plenty of room to smuggle drugs. The light showed no traces visible to the naked eye, but the dog seemed sure, and it was good enough for me.

"We're on to something…"

Paige looked perturbed, and said nothing. He made a note in his little notebook and so I hurried to do the same. I wasn't thinking about next steps; it had been a long thirteen hours and I was thinking lustfully about dinner, a shower, and my bed.

He pulled out his wallet and produced from a pocket in it a tiny black thing, round, no bigger than a quarter. "This is a tracker. So that we'll know where the boat goes, if someone does take it again." He tucked it in between two cushions on the bench seat.

I checked the time on my phone. "It's after seven. The card game will be started at the sex shop."

He nodded. "Let's get the dog back to the State Police, then we can take a look. Either way, we have to go back to the station before I take you home. I have an idea. It's going to be tedious."

"I expect nothing less."

I was sad to say goodbye to Kevin, but as we pulled back into Elviston, to a stretch of squat little buildings a block behind Main Street, I felt a new surge of energy. I was almost home, and we were onto something. The sex shop had a nondescript sign and some neon of a pair of lips glowing red in the window, the blinds were pulled, we couldn't see inside. But we did watch the door for a bit, took notes of all the plates in the little parking lot around the back, one parked on the street out front. We ran them through the system, six names came back including Rodney Bean. Four more men and one woman, who was the owner of the shop. Two of the men had records; Cameron Wall had a simple assault charge from when he was eighteen, Daniel Reiter had a slew of drug charges, an assault with a deadly weapon and had been caught holding an unregistered weapon while on parole.

"Reiter looks good," Paige said. "Campbell was the one who arrested him for the gun charge -his last arrest- and it ended up dismissed. Maybe that's when they brought him in."

"I think we should stay on Rodney Bean, I think he's involved."

"You want him to be involved, you have no reason to think that he actually is."

"He's an entitled asshole. Entitled assholes always want something for nothing, easy money, don't care who they hurt."

"And if we find drugs on him, we can lock him up and make sure that he doesn't hurt his girlfriend for a while."

"Added bonus."

"We can't bust this card game and we can't pick them all off afterward without letting anyone who might be interested know that we're chasing down this Blue 82 source in connection with the Harry Santiago case. If we're wrong here, they're going to be ten times harder to catch. So we can pick one, and follow him, and do a routine traffic stop. Reiter or Bean?"

He wanted me to say Reiter, because he thought it was the logical thing to do, that my girlish emotion was clouding my judgement. "Rodney."

As luck would have it, Rodney was the first person to leave. His long shifts at the factory probably meant that he was tired, and when he pulled out onto the road, he did so in a wide swing that seemed to us a bit reckless. Paige hit the gas. We surged out from where we were tucked away. I flicked on the cruiser's lights and the siren blared out in the night. I felt a surge of adrenaline.

Rodney Bean pulled over on a residential street.

Paige reminded me, "Stay behind me, keep your eyes open. Watch him for any sudden movements. If I say 'get down' you get down."

"Okay."

We walked the distance to Rodney's car. Paige was shining a light in the back window, the backseat, finally at Rodney himself, who squinted out and already had his license and registration in his hand, stuck out the window between two grimy fingers.

"Problem, officers?"

"You took a very wide turn back there, Sir. Been drinking tonight?"

"No, Sir."

"Sure smells like you have. Go ahead and step out of the car for me."

A belligerent sigh. "I didn't do anything."

But he did climb out.

"Go ahead and blow into this for me, until it beeps."

I shifted my weight back and forth, looked up and down the dark street. I still found it a bit creepy to be out at night. I wasn't afraid of the dark, exactly, just didn't like how quiet it was. The breathalyzer beeped.

Paige read. "Point one-two. Over the legal limit."

"That's bullshit."

"Put your hands on the car. Do you have anything sharp on you that might hurt me?"

"No." Rodney was irate, he didn't raise his voice but it was clear from his tone. He started breathing heavier as Paige patted him down, removed a wallet from the front pocket of the dingy denim vest that he wore, a lighter, a pack of cigarettes. He skimmed down Rodney's scrawny torso, patted his pants pockets. Something crinkled. "You've got no right to search me," Rodney growled out, "I'm barely over the limit, I didn't hurt anybody."

The crinkly plastic bag that came out of his pocket was blue in the streetlight. I felt a surge of joy, I couldn't fight the smile that broke out on my face as I looked at Paige.

"Alright, you're coming to the station with us." He brought out the cuffs and as he steered Rodney Bean to our cruiser, tucked him in the backseat, I kept one step behind them, shined a light on them so that a passing car knew to give us a wide berth.

When the door was closed and Bean was sealed inside, I couldn't help but to whisper, "I knew it! I told you so!" I punched the air a few times, mimicking the stance of a prize fighter, "YES! YES! YES!"

Paige said nothing, shook his head and climbed in the cruiser. At the station we booked Rodney Bean, those were new forms for me. I got to read him his Miranda Rights on charges of driving under the influence and possession of a controlled substance.

Paige and I stood in the hallway between the fire department's side and the sheriff's station. He said,

"He's not talking now, we'll see how he feels after he sits a couple nights. I'll try him on Monday morning."

"And let me know?"

"Yup."

"Are we done for the day?"

"Just have to grab something."

I went in with Paige, saw one deputy at his desk, searched my brain for his name and ID. Stanton? Stanley? Not any of our prime suspects, but who knew? It made the hairs on the back of my neck stand up. Would I feel safe around any of my coworkers, going forward?

We went to the hallway closet. It was really more of a small room, shelves wrapping around, one single lightbulb swaying on a long wire. Boxes and boxes and boxes.

"It's not evidence," I worked out.

"Receipts and expense reports. Seven years' worth. I say that we go back six months at first, maybe a year after that. Grab a box."

We loaded boxes into his trunk. He grabbed the last one, I shut the closet door behind him, then said, "I think I left the light on in my office." I didn't realize it was odd, at first, but of course I wouldn't have left it on. I dipped in, felt for the switch, then saw the paper on my desk.

It was a drawing, not unskilled, of a voluptuous woman oozing out of a skimpy red string bikini. The face was drawn in the style of an anime girl, biting a lip and blushing, but it was clearly supposed to be me. There was a sheriff's badge pinned to one boob.

I stalked into the room and snatched the paper up. Anger rose like water up my throat, like I was physically choking on it. The crinkling paper shook in my fist, I whirled, looking to the bullpen for someone to blame, but that guy Stanton was the only one, sitting with his back to me, and my anger popped and deflated all at once. He wasn't a likely suspect, and even if he was, Mom had taught me never to let my goat get got, that it was what they wanted. I wasn't the one who flew off the handle, I was the one who laughed at the one who flew off the handle.

I simmered down, shaking all over, feeling sick, feeling my eyes burn. The tears came, and I let them, but only for a second. Then I put the drawing on the desk, smoothed the crinkles out of it, folded it neatly, and stuck it in my pocket. I shut off the light and walked out.

"Goodnight," I said to Stanton.

"Goodnight," he said back.

When I climbed into Paige's car, the traitorous dome light came on. He saw my red eyes, or noticed how I didn't look over at him, just pulled my seatbelt on with my gaze trained forward. In the second before the light dimmed, I saw his face flash irritation; he didn't want to have to deal with it, didn't want to say anything.

"What happened?"

"It's nothing." I heard my voice come out quivering, the tears threatened to bubble up again. I shook my head like a wet dog, made a guttural sound. "Bla-ha-la-la-la-ugh. Let's go! Good work today, Deputy."

He nodded, started the car, and drove me home.

On the way I felt myself get kind of numb. I asked, "What are we looking for in the expenses?"

"The cruisers are all diesel, the boat is regular gasoline, so we find any expenses for gas for the boat. And you can check in the system, see if the expenses were logged accurately. I have a feeling that they won't have been."

"Narrowing down our suspects. And then what?"

"I'm not sure… maybe we try to work backward, check with local and state police along the river for cases involving Blue-82 and connect the dots."

"Sounds smart. So we'll start on that, first thing Monday."

"And there's one more thing…" But he didn't continue, seemed very hesitant.

"What?"

"Tomorrow is Sunday, so Raegan will be at First Methodist for mass at 9am. He'll rub elbows with a bunch of town leaders, plus old lady busybodies, teachers, doctors, bartenders, then they'll all go to the Corner Café afterward for pancakes and cheap eggs benedict with that awful powdered hollandaise-."

"-I like their hollandaise."

"You ever had the real thing?"

"Only once, cause it's such a pain to make, so the powdered stuff is a decent alternative-."

"-The point is that being Sheriff is a political job. It's social. You should try to fit the role that they want you to."

"You think that will stop them from recalling me?"

"Not exactly, but even if you get recalled, you don't want to leave a bad taste in people's mouths. This is your hometown, after all. You know these people."

"And I never cared what they thought before, so why start now?"

"Think about it. There's already an 'us versus them' mentality between the old and the young. They write each other off and never try to find any common ground, isn't that kind of why you did this whole thing? I've been to services a few times, it's not so bad. Kathy and I can take you, if your parents don't want to."

"Okay, I'll think about it."

He was pulling up the drive of my house. Through the windows I could see lights on in the living room, the kitchen. My parents might still be having dinner, or they might have finished and sat down to watch a movie. I felt warm at the thought, I was more glad than ever before to have them. A part of me longed for a time when I could have pretended to be asleep in the backseat, had my father carry me inside and put me in bed. Then the next morning I could have woken up without a care in the world, and had them to decide everything I'd need or want or get to do in a day. It sounded so peaceful.

"Thanks," I said to Paige, and climbed out of his car.

Mom met me at the door, waved to Paige as he was still backing down the drive. "Alright, Evie?" She scratched her fingernails in a pattern on my back.

I must have looked like Hell. "Yeah, Mom."

"I made a roast, it's still warm."

"Carrots and potatoes?"

"Of course."

She shut the door behind us, and I paused in the entryway, turned back to her and threw my arms around her. "Thank God."

"Long day?" Her hand cupped the back of my head, she sifted her fingers gently through my hair, the same color as hers, and as soft as satin.

"Mm-hm."

"Tomorrow will be kinder. Come eat."

But she didn't break the hug until I did.

"Hey Eves," Dad called from the couch, sipping a beer.

"Hey Dad. What's on?"

"That new one with Jennifer Lawrence."

"Ooh, she's hot." I went to fill a plate with roast, pepperoncini peppers, potatoes, and sweet baby carrots stewed in meat juice. I sat on the couch between my parents, kicking my feet up. For a few minutes I ate and we watched in silence. But I could hardly keep my eyes open any longer, once I had cleaned my plate I said goodnight, went to shower. I could barely hold the hair dryer or a toothbrush up long enough to get the jobs done, but then I collapsed into bed and fell asleep in sixty seconds.

Chapter Thirteen

Having gone to bed before nine o'clock, I woke up early again, just after six. I hadn't set an alarm, and the sky was lightening but the light shining in my window was still the silver of twilight. I laid awake for a few minutes, cozy, comfy, contemplating the gluttonous day of laziness which could lay before me.

But in the back of my mind, I knew that Paige was right. There was an aspect of my job which demanded being of the people, and for the people. Although I was beginning to hope that they would recall me, I didn't want to give them any excuse. I'd make them look me in the eyes and say 'peace be with you' or whatever the hell they said in church. And Mom and Dad had been doing plenty to help me, so I climbed out of bed and went out to tend to Mabel. I felt guilty that I had hardly seen her, yesterday. I should have stopped for a chat after dinner.

She snickered happily as I fed her and rubbed her down. We went for a trot a few times around the side yard, it wasn't big but it did the job. When I put her back in her stable, I kissed her snout, promised to visit again in the evening.

I went inside and started making raspberry pancakes from the blue box of Jiffy muffin mix. I liked that the 'berries' usually still had some crunch and grit to them even after they were cooked. Dad was too proud, of course, but grandma used to make them on Sunday mornings when I was little, and would spend the night on Saturdays. So they tasted like childhood, like innocence. Mom felt the same, and bought them for us.

I threw some sausage links in another pan, sipped my usual iced coffee, and started another mugful when I heard someone stir in the hallway, move into the bathroom.

Mom was pleasantly surprised. "You're cooking?"

"Yeah, good morning. Thanks for taking care of Mabel again yesterday."

"You're welcome."

"Paige thinks I should go to church, today. The methodist one, I guess it's all the rage. For appearances, you know?"

"Appearances?" She didn't like the sound of it, was very against organized religion as a general rule. A new-age hippy, she was against almost anything organized.

"Yeah, well I think he's right. These are my constituents. Even the ones who didn't vote for me, and want to recall me, they should be able to meet me if they want to, feel like they can talk to me. And Raegan will definitely be there, he always is."

"-Oh, and that makes him holy!" she scoffed.

"Paige said him and Kathy could take me if you guys didn't want to go, but I should let them know as soon as possible."

She frowned. "No, if you think you need to go, I'll take you. I'm sure Dad will want to go, too. Just to support you. We're a nice family. If you want to charm people, we'll charm the pants right off of them."

"Great. Thanks." I gave her a plate.

She smiled at the sight of the pancakes. "Jiffy?"

"You know it."

She quickly took a bite, then hummed. "Mm. Crunchy."

I found the box and held it out to her. "You know they're not raspberries, they're actually apples?"

"Really?"

\*

The Lassiter family cleaned up alright. Dad wore a button down tucked into jeans, a black belt and boots. Mom wore a modest pink dress, white kitten heels. She looked gorgeous. I debated my own outfit for a long while, asked Mom's opinion.

She came in and frowned critically at the two I had laid out on the bed. "I don't think you should go with a skirt or a dress."

"Okay." She was right. I wanted to play the part they wanted but I didn't want to look weak. "So this?" A pair of slacks and a collared pink blouse.

But Mom made a face and shook her head. "It's not very 'you'. What about your corduroys?"

"Not clean."

"Jeans then."

"Think so?"

"Sure."

We took the truck, parked in a crowded lot. Apparently our early wasn't early enough. Paige and Kathy sat waiting in his car, climbed out when they saw us and everyone exchanged hellos. She was stylish in a blue and green dress with a swirling design, peacock feather earrings and less eye makeup to balance the look. He wore a salmon colored button down and tan pants, shiny black dress shoes.

As we walked in, the pastor and his wife were shaking hands. They knew my parents, and they knew of me, were delighted that we had decided to join them. I smiled and nodded and shuffled along as quickly as I could.

Pews were already crowded. There were some big hats and a lot of pastel colors, and dozens of eyes suddenly on me. I felt sweat prickle under my arms, it was warm inside the old church. I saw Mrs. O'Connell, her husband and two young children. I saw Dennis Wright, a woman I presumed was his wife, a younger man with his teeth who had to be one of the sons, wife and baby all gathered together. I saw Delilah and her parents, she came to stand with me and made me feel better as plenty of people that I didn't know came ambling over.

The first to reach me was a woman in her fifties with dyed blonde hair. "Hello, you're new! I'm Jeannie LeDoux, and you are?"

"Evelyn Lassiter, I'm the new sheriff."

"Oh! That's right, I heard about you…" Her tone took a noticeable downward shift. "So is it all for a laugh, or what?"

"No Ma'am," I answered. "I want to get people thinking about what they really expect from their law enforcement, and what they've been getting the past few years."

Mrs. O'Connell was making her way over. "Evelyn! Hi! I've never seen you here before!"

"Not a churchgoer, huh?" Jeannie surmised.

"Not previously, no."

"Evelyn's one of my students, Jean. She's very clever, and isn't it so neat what she's doing? Getting kids invested in voting, and trying to bridge the gap between young people and law enforcement? It doesn't have to be so bitter and adversarial, don't you think?"

"Well… That's something to think about, I suppose."

"Sure! I think Ben Townsend wants you-." She pointed and steered the lady away, going with her. "You two enjoy the service, good to see you!"

A few women in their thirties, all dressed nicely in floral dresses and heels, suddenly surrounded me.

"Hi there, Evelyn, isn't it?"

"The new sheriff?"

"We're from the Friends of First Methodist, we do community outreach for the church like charitable fundraisers, potlucks, community. Maybe you've heard of us?"

"Oh, yeah, I think so."

"I'm Marge, this is Sophie, Annette and Louanne. Evelyn, I'm sure you can agree how important charity and fostering community are."

"-We'd love to have you at a meeting, if you could spare the time!"

"You know," I started, thinking of how best to beg off, "I have so much on my plate until graduation at the end of next month. After that, I could probably make time."

"Well, we'll be looking forward to that. Sheriff Raegan always made time for us, so we hope you will too."

I hadn't spotted Raegan, yet. Peering over the crowd, I noticed eyes quickly diverting from me, people trying not to stare. A good looking man in mid or late twenties came over to me, next. He had dark hair gelled slick, wore a suit vest with matching slacks and wing tipped shoes.

"Haven't seen you around," he said, hands in pockets. "I'm Todd Brooks. And you are?"

"Evelyn Lassiter, Elviston County Sheriff."

He looked amused. "That's right. Little Hellraiser, aren't you?" He whispered, like he was trying to get in on the secret, or just delighted by the profanity in the holy place.

I smiled, although I didn't like him, thought he was trying too hard and didn't ring true at all. Shook my head. "I'm just trying to make my home a better place."

"Alright, fair play... I'm gonna be keeping my eye on you, Evelyn. I expect great things."

"Alright…" I really didn't know what to say to that. Was he trying to flirt with me, or make me uncomfortable, or both? I moved away. Delilah had been nearby and had apparently been watching.

"Who was that?"

"He said his name was Todd Brooks. You don't know him?"

"No… He'd be cute if he wasn't named Todd."

I hadn't brought my notebook, but I made a mental note to run him through the system later.

A commotion by the door drew my attention. Raegan had come in, making an entrance, with people flocking over. He was shaking hands and accepting condolences at a remarkable speed. His graying hair was smoothed, his jean legs had a crease and his black shirt with pearl buttons tucked into a leather belt with a big, brass buckle. He looked genial, although his eyes narrowed when he saw me, his smile did not falter.

Paige appeared at my side. "Let's go say hello."

"Yeah?"

"Yeah."

As we made our way over, the pastor and his wife made their way further inside the church. I guessed we had only a couple of minutes to finish mingling and find our seats.

People parted for Paige and I to get to Raegan, they seemed eager to witness the confrontation. There was so little to do in small towns, interpersonal conflicts became something everyone felt entitled to, frothed at the mouth for.

Paige offered his hand. "Raegan."

"Paige." They shook, a macho thing with white and pink knuckles. "Miss Lassiter."

I shook the old bull's hand, next. He didn't squeeze me hard, barely glanced at me. "You look well," I said, not sure what else to say. "Keeping busy?"

"Not retiring just yet." He didn't ask how I was handling things, or if he could do anything to help.

Part of me wanted to imply something about his suspected involvement in the drug theft and distribution, or his mishandling -intentional or not- of the Harry Santiago case. It seemed like the kind of thing people did in movies. But Paige had not, and I had to take my cues from him. If they didn't yet know that we were looking at them, that was for the best.

My parents had mingled, said hello to friends and clients, and found their way over to me. "We should sit down."

I was glad to stop preening and being nice for people. Most of the time I had the energy for it, but not lately. "Enjoy the service," I said to Raegan.

He nodded. "And you enjoy your day off, Sheriff." His tone was bright but I heard a hint of simmering hate underneath.

When we all settled into pews, we sat with Paige and Kathy, near the back. I tuned in and out of the service, happy to be able to just sit and stare, thinking about other things. People fanned themselves with bibles. At certain times, the entire congregation seemed to know when to say, "Amen." And in those moments, I couldn't help but to feel that it was eerie, a kind of hive-mind.

I had never thought much of religious people. Didn't care much for their opinions. Maybe I never gave them a fair shake because I figured that they wouldn't give me one, if they were to get to know me. If they knew that I didn't go to church, or hated cops, or kissed so many boys that a few girls accidentally slipped in... Even though the pastor was talking about love, I got the feeling that he only meant the kind that everyone could approve of, the kind that meant subservience to all of this greater good, all of these rules in fine print...

And that wasn't fair exactly. Hadn't Delilah always been good to me? Hadn't Mrs. O'Connell always been willing to help? And Paige and Kathy were not strangers to the church. They didn't all have something wrong with them, some gaping hole to fill, need for the degradation, or craving for someone to tell them what to do. They just parsed out the good and left the bad, like with anything. And those ladies from their committee might have been a little much for me, but it sounded like they did real good.

So I felt a bit guilty, as the pastor bid us good day and wrapped things up. But the place was all about forgiveness, I vowed to do better going forward, to judge the religious less, and I felt lighter as we sifted through more people, trying to escape. I had made my peace with it, but it didn't get to eat up half of my day off, and the morning was nearly gone.

Before I stepped over the threshold, I sent out a quick prayer to anyone who might be listening. I hoped that Inez Santiago would be alright. I hoped her brother would, too. That their mother would have them both back soon.

Getting out of the parking lot took fifteen minutes. Then as we cruised home, Mom and Dad spoke across me, with raised voices to hear over the wind rushing through the cab. "God, that was long!"

"Yup."

"If they pat themselves on the back anymore, they'll dislocate their shoulders."

Dad smiled and drove.

I felt just a bit embarrassed by what she said. It seemed childish. But like I was trying not to judge the religious, I decided not to judge her. Maybe in a few years, I would think of it all in some new way, and find myself aligned with my parents once again. Maybe I didn't know anything, maybe nobody did. It was freeing to realize it.

## Chapter Fourteen

Mom made a big, colorful salad with different veggies from the garden for lunch. Her homemade Italian dressing and some cubed pepperoni and sliced pepperoncini peppers gave it nice zip, along with shaved carrots, thin sliced radishes and purple cabbage. I snarfed two bowls at the counter while she then baked a chocolate cake for after dinner.

For a while, I hung out in my room. I caught up on homework and reading I had missed in school, getting it out of the way in an hour and a half. Then I listened to music, wasted time on social media, and just enjoyed being aimless, having nothing that needed to be done. It was the natural state of being for someone my age, and I was beginning to understand why.

Just a little over a month until graduation. Five weeks. I could do it that long. Once I was done with school, working forty or even fifty hours would seem so much easier.

When I emerged next, Dad was assembling the layers of a lasagna. Mom had brought out the bowl of salad and had layered and frosted the cake. I looked around for what needed to be done.

"Should I set the table?"

"Sure, and put the leaf in it. In the front closet."

There was still time before Paige and Kathy would arrive. All three of us sat on the couch and watched a few episodes of Friends.

I felt myself getting nervous as six o'clock rolled around. I wanted Paige and his wife to think that we were good people, decently sophisticated, I guess. I just wanted us all to get along. The Paiges brought red wine, were still wearing their Sunday best -as were we- and so we made a cute little party. I knew that I was biased, but it felt to me like the most exclusive dinner party in town, the best people to be around.

The night started with Kathy complimenting the house and the land, while the wine was uncorked and left to breathe, and I offered to take her outside to show her around, to the chickens and Mabel. She apparently loved horses, had one when she was young, and was ecstatic to go with me. Paige stayed behind with my parents.

Kathy was delighted by Mabel, of course, she was an exceptional horse with a lot of personality, she loved everyone that she met. A kind old soul. I was proud to watch Kathy feed her an apple, stroke her snout and her white mane.

"You know violin bows are sometimes made of horse hair? From the tails, though."

"Really? Do you play?"

"Not for years, now. I wish I had more reasons to play. It's hard, once you leave school. A lot of stuff gets harder; keeping up with hobbies, making friends, changing your ways… Pulling yourself out of ruts. We get set in our ways as we get older."

She was talking to me like I was a grown up, or at least like a person with thoughts and a mind of my own. I dug it, but I wasn't sure what to say in response. "Thanks for the warning."

"Not saying I'm stuck, I'm very happy! I just miss endless possibilities."

"That's kind of the part that scares me."

"You should try to enjoy it, while it lasts. Seems like you're doing a good job so far. You swung for the fences, going after the sheriff's job. Are you enjoying it at all?"

"I'm learning a lot." Like that I wasn't cut out and that I wanted to be a kid again. Back to infinite possibilities. But I couldn't chicken out now, couldn't fall on my face like that, publicly. I would have to think my next move through more carefully.

"That's good, there's a time for that."

"Let's head back in."

Kathy said goodbye to Mabel. "Goodbye old girl, it was very nice to meet you."

She made a good impression on both of us.

We headed back inside and Dad was pulling the lasagna out of the oven, steaming and bubbling, cheese browned in spots and looking mouth watering. Mom poured wine and shot a cheeky glance at Paige and I.

"Anyone going to arrest me if I let Evelyn have half a glass?"

"Not me," I said.

"Not my business."

Dad set the lasagna on a pot holder in the middle of the rarely used dining table. It barely fit in the small square of space designated for it, between the couch and the slider leading to the back. We all crowded in around it. Paige pulled out a chair for Kathy, and they sat together on one side. I sat across, noticing the sly look that passed between Mom and Dad over the gesture. Mercifully, they didn't make a joke about it. *Newlyweds*, I thought, something like that. Mom sat beside me, Dad sat at the end, the traditional place for the man of the house, but I didn't think he did it with some old-timey entitlement, it was just the last chair.

We passed the salad and garlic bread around, and cut thick squares of lasagna, scooping them from the pan with a spatula until the cheese pulled a foot long. The talk was small, how good the food was, Dad's recent jobs. Mom and Dad turned to plying Paige for answers about what we were working on.

"It seems Evelyn doesn't know what she's allowed to tell us and what she's not," Mom explained. "So?"

Paige considered. "You know that we had a body, a few days ago. Drug overdose. Designer drug. Trying to figure out where it came from. Can't go any deeper into it than that."

"You can count on our discretion," Mom said.

"I'm sure."

Dad asked Kathy what she did for work. He talked in order to be a good host, I knew.

"I cook the books for a few non profits in the area, do taxes at tax time."

"And?" Paige prompts.

"And I'm working on a novel, also."

"Oh! Really? We're all big readers."

I cut in, "Me, not so much anymore. What's it about, Kathy?"

"It's a young adult fantasy, first in a series that could go on indefinitely. It's about the folklore and mysteries in Appalachia -that's where I grew up- and also about growing up in general."

"Sounds good."

"Yeah."

"Very cool," Mom said. "I might like to write a book someday, although I don't know what I'd write about."

"What do you like to read about?"

Mom blushed, a rare sight. "Witches and fairies and love."

"You could try to think of something you'd like to see in those sorts of books, but haven't yet? I started my book because I wasn't finding anything about the mysteries of the mountains like I would have wanted as a kid."

"That's something to think about, definitely."

The lasagna gone, I cleared the plates while dad got out dessert plates and mom brought out the cake. When she took the cover off of it, everyone made appreciative noises. She cut slices for everyone.

Dad said, "Let's kill this bottle. Leo?"

He shook his head. "I'm driving."

"Kathy?"

"Oh, I suppose."

He drained the last of the bottle into her glass.

"Thank you... Great cake, too."

"Thank you."

Paige tried a bite and nodded, unsmiling as usual. "Very good... So I had a thought. Evelyn and I have a big load of clerical work to do, for this case. I have boxes in my trunk. It would probably take us a whole day to look through it on our own. If you three wanted to help, we could probably knock it out in an hour."

Mom was excited by the idea. "Oh wow. Police work? What if we make a mistake?"

"You won't. It's very simple work."

"Alright... Vince?"

"Happy to help."

We towed boxes in, five boxes, five people. Mom and Dad vacated to the kitchen serving bar, while Paige explained.

"We're looking for regular unleaded gasoline purchases. Check every receipt. Try to keep them in order. If you find one, let me know."

Dad put the radio on an oldies station and we all dug in, only the faint crooning of John Prine coming from the living room speakers and the sound of rustling paper for a few long minutes.

Mom erupted, "I found one! I got one!"

Paige crossed to her, held out a hand. "Good work. Here."

We kept leafing through receipts. Receipts for tolls, diesel, dues at the shooting range, equipment rental, more diesel, uniforms, night classes, more diesel, oil changes, wiper blades, air filters, detailing, diesel, a welding company -probably to repair a cage in one of the cruisers- and on and on, more of the same. Each of us found at least two slips for regular gasoline in our boxes, Dad found four in his box from January, Kathy found three in the box from February. I wondered if the new year was when the sheriff and his men got involved with the drugs. If they started moving the stuff in January, and the kids found a pound of Blue 82 and overdosed in January, things had gone off the rails immediately, they weren't very good at espionage.

With a stack of receipts, the last box tucked away, Paige and I sat at the table. I logged into our pay system and he showed me how to check the numbers of the expense reports associated with the receipts, how they were filed, who they registered back to. Of the thirteen slips, six of them had Paige's name on them in the system, but four of the payments went to an account he didn't recognize.

"Got something to tell me?" I joked.

He had made notes on his pad of each of the dates and times of the gas purchases. "I had a feeling it would turn out like this. Maybe one or two of these should have come back to me, not this many... So rough timeline: Raegan and co. get involved in the drug trade in January, they're dumb enough to submit their gas for reimbursement but smart enough not to do it in their own name, they use mine because I've always been a thorn in their side... End of January, the party at the marina happens, they start to cover their tracks better, just in case. They probably also start looking for someone with medical experience, just in case. They get their chance in March when Dennis Wright drives drunk and sideswipes that car." He was keeping his voice low, it was supposed to stay between us law enforcement officials.

"All circumstantial, though, right?"

"Yup."

"How do we prove it?"

"You tell me, Sheriff."

Mom and Dad and Kathy were pretending not to listen, sitting at the kitchen counter. Their chit chat suddenly died down, though, they wanted to hear how I would answer Paige's question.

I thought about our evidence. Most of it was circumstantial. The receipts were something, but I couldn't think of a way we could trace who had actually submitted them or gotten the payment. We had only one student willing to admit her involvement at the marina, and she couldn't confirm that the drugs had indeed just washed up... But the drug dog detecting trace particles in the boat, and finding the hidden compartment, that was something solid.

"You put the tracker on the boat. It's the only solid thing we have, and they'll take it out eventually to -I guess- pick up more drugs."

"If they do, the tracker isn't enough. We need to see them depart with no drugs and return with drugs, no plausible deniability. That could take weeks, or even months. They might never take it again, if they suspect we're onto them. But then... I suppose if they *could* drive where they're going, they would have from the start. They must need to go by boat. An island?"

"There are islands in the Tennessee?"

"Some. Small. We should look into that. And keep an eye on the marina, make sure that no new slips are rented by anyone we think is involved, no other boats are taken out, either, lent to them, I mean... And in the meantime?"

"Backoff of the witnesses, act casual... We could keep looking into other Blue 82 cases along the river, if we do it quietly. Lull them into a false sense of security, and hope they're stupid enough to make another drug run."

"How are me and you gonna cover the boat -all the boats in the marina- 24-7?"

That I didn't have any clue about. It put a sinking feeling in my gut. I was at my limit, already. "Who can we use?"

"Maybe Wilensky." She was the only female deputy. "We rode together a lot before you showed up. She's by the book, got no love lost for Raegan. She's on maternity leave, but I bet she'd love to get out of the house a night or two of the week, if it's just surveillance. That still leaves... roughly nineteen shifts to cover throughout the week."

"You really wouldn't trust anyone else in the department?"

"No, not with these stakes."

"I've got people..." I didn't let myself look and Mom and Dad. "I could deputize people, right? My classmates? Of course, we all have school, but get five, get them each to take a shift, after school until sundown, or curfew, whatever?"

Paige frowned at that. He didn't like it. "Technically, if they're eighteen, you can deputize them. But that's a slippery slope."

"It's just surveillance, like you said. So you cover most of the day shifts, while we're all in school... I guess that makes me the night shift."

"I don't like that," Mom declared, no longer pretending not to listen.

"It's just surveillance..."

"When will you sleep?"

"After school, I guess."

"So, three fifteen, you're out of school. You come home, take care of Mabel, eat, shower. Say you get to sleep at four -I'll be generous- and your teenage deputies are going to want to be home by what? Nine on school nights, probably. Ten, if you're lucky."

Paige said, "I don't think there's a better option. I'll take over at six, she can get a catnap before school."

"And school's out in five weeks," I said. "I can make it that long."

"You might not be sheriff that long," he said. "The next town hall is this Wednesday, they'll probably vote to put your recall on the ballot. It will take a few weeks to arrange a vote, maybe a month."

It was beginning to feel like my salvation, but I didn't want to show it. "Right. So, I can do it, Mom. I have to, while it's still my responsibility."

Kathy said, "I think that's admirable. You two seem to have done a great job instilling values into your daughter. And you can deputize me, too, Evelyn. I'll take the day shift on Sundays so Leo can have a day off."

He smiled gently, but he said, "You don't have to do that-."

"It's already done."

"Okay," I said. "Thank you. Dad? Can you pick me up at six and then run me to school?"

"If that's what you need. But won't you need a car?"

I considered. The parking lot was completely exposed at the marina. Anyone going to take the Sheriff Department's boat would have to park there, too, and would see someone surveilling the place, right away. The area around was mostly residential, big old beach houses, one restaurant with a gorgeous patio and fourteen dollar appetizers. Delilah's uncle had taken us there, one day last summer. He lived two houses down, in one of those old beach houses, although his had seen better days. I was sure that I could see the marina pretty clearly from his porch or back yard, if I had a pair of binoculars.

"I know someone who live on the shore. He'd let us use his driveway, maybe let me camp out in his sun room, even."

"Who's this?"

"Delilah's Uncle Bert."

"I don't know how I feel about that," Dad declared.

"He's sweet." I didn't want to say what I really meant.

"I really don't know how I feel about that."

"Dad, he's… he's gay." A flaming old queen who had always liked me. He couldn't be too fond of cops, so if I worked the corruption angle, he would probably play along. He wrote a few jingles we all knew, and he ran the community theatre program year in and year out.

"Oh, Bert, that's right. I know him, Hun…" Mom asked, "Are you starting tonight?"

I hadn't realized that my shift was about to start. It was past eight o'clock. It had been a slow day, but the week had caught up to me. I was ready for bed, sure that I would sleep straight through until my alarm in eleven and a half hours. I felt queasy at the thought. When my silence lasted a few seconds too long, Paige sighed.

"I'll take the first shift. And tomorrow's day shift. Kathy, that means we've gotta go. Thank you, Lassiters."

"Thank you so much, it was all delicious."

Mom and Dad said goodbye and waved, letting me walk the Paiges to the door. I said, "Thank you…"

"You earned a day off." But so had he, of course. "Just log in and approve my overtime. I'll expect some pimply kid to relive me at three-thirty. I'll park at the restaurant, tonight, but call that Bert guy, make sure he's okay with a black man camping out in his driveway, going forward."

"Will do, I'll text you the address."

He opened Kathy's door for her, then closed it. We stood in the cool night, in the light from my dingy, little red house's front porch. Moths fluttered around it. Paige had his arms crossed. "If anything happens while you're on the job, I'm your first call. I'll be there in under five minutes, so there's no reason for you to ever get closer or investigate on your own. Is that understood?"

I was his superior, but he was telling me how it was gonna go. I wasn't about to argue with the guy covering my shift so that I could get some much-needed sleep. "Yeah. Be careful."

"Will do, Boss."

"Thank you so much," I said again.

Chapter Fifteen

At lunch the next day, I wolfed my cheap chicken patty sandwich, side salad and grapes. I barely tasted it, washed it down with chocolate milk then caught my breath. I told Scott and Delilah to stay put, along with Debbie Brown and Michael Chessani from our usual group. Then I went to collect Abigail Springstead, who I knew had called the cops on the party that originally gotten Marcus, Joe and company all busted. She was the editor for the school's online newspaper, the captain of the varsity volleyball team, a theatre kid, the 'me' of the type-A's, and they all looked at me like I was an alien when I approached their table.

"Can I borrow you for a minute, Abby?"

"What is this about?"

"Extra curricular activity, it would look great on your college apps."

"I'm already accepted to Vanderbilt and MTSU," she said, pronouncing it phonetically.

"Just come on." Brat.

She did follow, and when I got back to my table, Veronica White and Sandy Sackett had joined. I shooed them away. "Give us some space, girls. Thank you."

"Yes, Sheriff." Sandy giggled as she went, she had a crush on me. I had too much on my plate to consider it.

"Alright -sit down, Abby-." Debbie was glaring at her. She had been at the party that Abby had snitched on. I sat, too, and leaned close; the cafeteria was loud and I couldn't have anyone overhearing us. Joe and Marcus had plenty of friends around. "Alright, I've gathered you all here because I need help. The town needs help. Harry Santiago, especially needs your help. I can't tell you too much about what's going on, but it's big shit. I need twenty-four seven surveillance, and only two of my deputies can help. Hopefully, that's where you come in."

"Hell yeah," Scott murmured, already excited.

"Thank you. If you could each take one shift a week, three-thirty to ten -if you can do it, if not, then nine- we can cover our bases. You would just watch, you'd call me if anything happened. No danger, and I can deputize you for your troubles. Plus, once I'm not sheriff anymore, I'm going to help Deputy Paige get the job, and he'll write you a letter of recommendation that will help you with college, scholarships, job applications, the works." A few of their faces were still doubtful. "And you'd be doing something really good, and it's just for a few weeks, until graduation, and I really need your help. Please."

Scott said, "You know I'll help."

"Me too," Delilah agreed.

"I guess," Debbie said. "It sounds kinda cool."

"Do I get to wear a badge?" Michael asked.

"You can have my plastic one."

"Okay then. I'm gonna get a plastic gun, too."

"Jesus, just be careful." I had a sudden image of Michael claiming to be a sheriff's deputy, spinning a silver toy pistol with an orange tip around his finger and getting shot by one of my deputies, or a uniformed cop… but he was white, and so -I thought with a hint of shame- he would probably be fine. Debbie had rolled her eyes as he said it; she was black and she would never say something so foolish.

Everyone looked at Abigail. She leaned back in her hair and crossed her arms. She wore a tight, pink cardigan, her orange hair was in a long braid draped over her shoulder. She stared at me, played with her braid. "Being deputized is good… the letter of recommendation is better, if you actually get Paige elected. But he got, what? Twelve votes last time?"

"Fourteen."

"Right. Sounds like a dark horse if ever I knew one. So, sweeten the deal."

"What do you want?"

"I want you to write me a letter of recommendation on official Sheriff's Department letter head, that I can keep in case the whole Paige thing never materializes. And if this case you're working breaks, I want an exclusive interview with you that I can shop to the local papers."

"Alright."

"Exclusive. That means you don't talk to anybody else in the press."

"Alright." I offered her my hand across the table.

She reached out to shake it, then opened a black binder that she always carried. Took out a pen and made a little chart as she spoke. "Let's figure out shifts. I can't do Mondays, Wednesdays, or Fridays..." she made x's under her name, next to each of the three days. "Anyone else have conflicts?"

"I can't do Mondays," Scott said. "Wrestling."

"I can't do Mondays or Tuesdays," Delilah said. She went to Scott's wrestling meets and tutored after school.

"No Fridays for me," Debbie said.

"Actually," Scott said, surely remembering his mother always needing a ride to and from the bar, "I'd better not do Fridays, either." I could read him like a book, and I knew that he was thinking that his mom didn't really *need* to be hitting the bar on Thursdays, too.

Abigail made her x's, luckily Michael had no extra curriculars or family stuff during the week. "So... Wait, Evelyn, aren't you taking a shift?"

"I'm the overnight," I said.

"Oh." I thought I saw a hint of respect on her face. "So, Debbie and Michael, who's taking tonight?"

Michael sighed. "Fuck, I'll do it."

"Okay, I'll take Tuesdays. Debbie, Wednesdays?"

"Okay."

"Scott, Thursdays? Delilah Fridays?"

"Yeah, that works." She spoke for both of them.

"Decided, then. What are we surveilling at the marina?"

I looked around, made sure that nobody was too close to our table. "This has to stay between us. Is that understood?"

"We understand."

"We're watching the Sheriff's Department's boat, slip three. Nobody should be onboard without my knowledge, so if you see anyone around it, you call me. Delilah's uncle Bert lives near the marina, and he's okay with us being on his property, just introduce yourself before your shift, he'll be expecting you. If you have a car, you can park in the driveway. If not, the backyard…"

"Knowing my uncle, he'll probably invite you all inside and feed you and serve you sweet tea."

"That's weird," Michael muttered.

"Bert Stokely," Abby said as she realized it, "He directs the community theatre, right?" She chuckled when Delilah nodded. "Oh that's great. Have fun, boys."

"He's harmless," Delilah insisted.

I agreed, "He is. He's sweet."

"Anything else?"

"Deputy Paige will be at Bert's place when you get there. You'll relieve him, I'll relieve you at ten. Ten is okay with everyone, right?"

A chorus of affirmative answers.

"And you're all eighteen, right?" They were, and the lunch room had started to clear. "Okay, real quick, everyone raise your right hands, repeat after me. I solemnly swear that I will perform with fidelity-."

"I solemnly swear that I will perform with fidelity…"

"-The duties of the office to which I am appointed."

"The duties of the office to which I am appointed…"

"-I swear to support the constitutions of Tennessee and the United States."

"I swear to support the constitutions of Tennessee and the United States…"

"-And the laws of Elviston County."

"And the laws of Elviston County."

"I pronounce you all deputized." I had pulled it out of my ass, as best I could remember it from when Paige swore me in. I didn't know if there was some official act which I was supposed to perform. It was going to have to be good enough. "Welcome to the force."

*

Since it was a Monday, and Scott couldn't drive me home, I walked. I moved briskly, the day was warm and I started to sweat, but I was losing valuable sleeping time. I felt a bit drowsy, still I didn't know if I could go to sleep. When I got home, I said hi to Mom, ate a granola bar as I walked out to Mabel's stable. I gave her a workout, brushed her, gave her a treat. My new shift meant that I would be able to take care of her every day, as I had promised to, and as she deserved.

"Wish me sweet dreams," I cooed at her, kissed her snout. As I walked back to the house, I wondered what the other deputies would think of me not being around, or only checking in occasionally... Would they think I had thrown in the towel? For the best, if so.

I laid down around four. There was too much light coming in my window, I was not really tired. I dozed off for a bit, but then I tossed and turned some more, feeling anxious. I wasn't sure why; it should be a cakewalk compared to actually patrolling and canvassing witnesses, trying to track down a lead in the Blue 82 distribution. I would just sit and watch the boat in the distance, in a cozy sun room, with a big iced coffee.

Mom came to wake me and I could smell the coffee she was brewing for me when she opened the door. "It's time."

"Okay." I put jeans back on, shoes, sidled out.

"Leftover lasagna." She took it from the microwave and slid the plate to me.

"Thank you." I didn't feel tired really, didn't feel anxious anymore. I just felt numb as I ate. "Wish me luck," I said when I was finished. "Hope I don't fall asleep and screw this all up."

"You won't."

Dad waited with his keys in hand, scrolling on his phone. It was nearly ten o'clock when we pulled into Bert's driveway, a long, dirt affair that must be a beast in the wintertime or wetter parts of spring. Dad surprised me by climbing out.

"I want to meet this guy."

Michael met me at the door, he had clearly been awaiting my arrival. "All yours, nothing to report."

"Thanks Michael."

He zipped his hoodie up and went hurrying down the street in the dark. He must live close by.

Dad raised his fist to knock, but Bert's silver hair and dangling cross earring appeared before he could. "Oh. Hi."

"Hello! Evelyn, so good to see you, and you must be Evelyn's father, handsome fellow, not that I'm surprised. I met your lovely wife a few times over the years that the girls have been friends."

"Vincent."

"Bertrand Stokely, pleased to make your acquaintance. Did you want to come in?"

Dad looked at me, I shook my head, pushed him back toward the car.

"No, that's not necessary. He just wanted to meet you. Bye, Dad. Thanks for the ride, I'll see you in the morning. Anyway, hi Bert, good to see you! Thanks so much for helping us out with this. So you met Paige and Michael today… Was everything alright?"

"Oh yes, two very polite young men." He ushered me inside, shut the door behind us.

His house was bright, lots of windows, one story and had seen better days. The appliances were old, the furniture antique, a brown leather sofa, dark wood curio cabinets full of little nicknacks that Bert was always happy to explain the interesting origins of. A hula girl lamp. A bust of some man from long ago. A miniature phone booth. And walls and walls of books, lots of plays and books on writing, directing, acting. A healthy record collection as well, mostly oldies and showtunes.

When I first came over with Delilah, I had commented that I was glad he hadn't been swept up in the minimalism craze, and he had been quite flattered and taken with me from that first moment.

He brought me through the kitchen and living room, and out onto the enclosed back porch, or the sun room, as he called it. Neat wicker patio furniture had already been moved to best view the marina around the neighbor's house and the restaurant in between. A pair of binoculars sat on the sill. I felt a twinge; I had forgotten to bring a pair.

"This is where you'll want to be, I think. Good view of the boats, you'll see."

I did see. Lights on poles lit up the marina. The docks were empty, the pavilion and parking lot, too.

"You're very nice to let us use your property, and sit in your house…"

"Oh, I'm happy to help. What can you tell me about all of this? The others were mums the word."

"Well…" I had to tell him something, this nice -and probably lonely- old guy who was being so helpful. "We need to keep things quiet. We don't know how much of the sheriff's department could be involved. There are definitely some of them… And the department's boat has been used for some unsavory things, so that's why we're keeping an eye on it. We don't know how long it might take."

"Corruption! How exciting. I was already so impressed with you, when Delilah told me about you winning that election. Now I'm just… -Wow!"

"Thanks."

"Could I help? I'll take a shift. I'm not cut out for overnight, but during the day? Any weekday would work."

"Sure, I bet Paige would appreciate that. He's the day shift. And it would give us time to do normal sheriff stuff, keep up appearances. I'll ask him."

"Okay, just let me know. It's about my bedtime, but did you eat?"

"I did."

"I could make you an Arnold Palmer?"

"I've got my giant iced coffee."

"Well if you want something after all, help yourself. You know where the bathroom is… I'll leave you to it."

"Good night. Thank you."

He disappeared back into the house, and I settled down into a wicker chair. Through the binoculars, I could make out the details of the sheriff's department's boat. But I didn't really need the binoculars to make out that there was nobody on the dock or in the marina at all. For a few minutes I kept a close vigil. About 10:15 I realized that I was in for a long night, a long week, a long month. I sipped coffee. I set my phone on the windowsill, but did not allow myself to open it.

Chapter Sixteen

By the morning, I was fighting to keep my eyes open. The sky lightened, the wide waters of the Tennessee turned from black to grey-brown, but I would not get to see the sun rise, not so early in the year, not before I crept through the dim and cluttered house on creaking floorboards, trying not to wake Bert. It was 6:02 when I slipped out into the yard. Paige was already parked in the driveway with a pair of binoculars visible on his dashboard. He rolled down his window.

"Nothing?"

"No."

"Get used to it. That's most of this job, hurry up and wait."

"Yeah... I have to go to school, now..." I wasn't tired, exactly, now that I was standing, breathing the cool air deep into my lungs, but my head was buzzing. I had the feeling the exhaustion was going to hit me hard and fast.

"Get good grades."

I turned to go, but he stopped me.

"Evelyn."

"What?"

"I checked my old notes, I've kept them all, since I started at the department. Two of the gas receipts that came back to me were actually mine. Of the other four, I was on the job for three of them. Two I was riding with Wilensky, she could back me up, she would remember at least one, back in January, we were interviewing this guy with Tourette Syndrome at the exact time the gas was being pumped. The last I was riding with Campbell, but nothing in particular that hour. I just thought that I'd let you know, in case you wanted to double check my alibis, be thorough."

I blinked. "I don't. You didn't have to do that. But that's good, that you kept those notes, in case it's ever in front of a jury."

My Dad pulled up in his truck and I sidled over, slid in. Dad waved to Paige, then drove us home. My Dad didn't talk much, so he didn't ask me how my first night of surveillance had gone. Just turned on Johnny Cash and drove.

I didn't want to nap, I knew that if I laid back down, I wouldn't want to get up again. So I went out to tend to Mabel, first thing. When I came back in, Mom was just heading out to collect eggs, and Dad was cooking some at the stove.

"Hungry?"

"Load 'em up." I started another coffee.

He set a full plate in front of me.

I stared at the fluffy eggs, suddenly feeling sick. Nibbled on a corner of buttery toast.

Mom came back in, and she filled the silence. "You don't look well, Evie... Do you really think you can do this?"

"If I make it through today, I'll adjust. Tomorrow will be kinder," I threw her own words back at her, picked up my fork and forced a few bites of eggs down. I would need the protein. I had to go to school, keep my eyes open, I could sleep afterward, for a few hours. I would adjust. I had to believe that.

School was a blur. Mrs. O'Connell asked if I was okay during English. I told her I had worked the night shift and she fawned over me, told me to make sure I got some sleep tonight and that I was taking care of myself. As if that's easy to do. At lunch I checked in with Abby, made sure that she still planned to take her shift after school. She did, and double checked that nothing had happened during my watch. I assured her she would know if anything had, which wasn't exactly a lie. Word spread fast in small towns, I was sure that she would, indeed, hear when anything happened. And I didn't lie to her, I would give her an interview. I wouldn't compromise the case, though.

Two more classes after lunch, I sat through trying to push information down into the soft, grey matter of my brain. But my brain seemed to have grown a shell, and the ideas my underpaid teachers were trying to impart just slid off the smooth surface. I was a zombie, my attendance was only for the sake of my mother and keeping up appearances, not to mention that it would look bad if the county's sheriff was a truant.

By two o'clock, I couldn't do it anymore. I walked out and headed home. Mom was home when I walked in, and I held up a hand. "Don't, please. I need sleep. I'll stay all day tomorrow, I promise."

"Okay." She went back to reading.

I didn't think it was very like her to let me off the hook, but I wasn't about to question it. I tended to Mabel -I could not let her slip through the cracks like I could with a stupid Physics class- then took two minutes to pee and make sure that my alarm was on, then collapsed into bed.

My sleep was dreamless and felt like it lasted only an hour or two, not six, but when I woke up, I felt more like myself. Dad brewed coffee for me and threw a pork chop back in the pan, while I wolfed a piece of blackberry pie and then a salad.

"You ready?" He asked, sliding me the pork chop.

I knew he meant for another night of surveillance. I nodded, picked the pork chop up with my hands and ripped a strip off with my teeth. It made him chuckle, but Mom was aghast.

"Evie."

I stuck the whole pork chop in my mouth before I turned to her, shaking it back and forth and growling like a dog, then asked around it, "*Rrrr* -What?"

She broke, trying to hide her smile with her hand. "Stop being crude."

"I thaw that," I stood and crossed to where she sat on the couch, taking the pork chop in my hand and smacking my lips. "Want a kiss?"

"From those greasy lips? No thank you."

"Suit yourself! Let's roll, Dad, I'll take this to go."

"Yes, your highness."

When we got to Bert's, he and Abby were waiting on the porch, someone I presumed was her older sister was waiting on the street in a beater Ford Escort station wagon that had to be older than me.

"Nothing happened," Abby reported, a bit disappointed. "Bye Bert, see you tomorrow."

"Bye Abby, can't wait."

They must know each other from theatre.

Bert ushered me in. "Mind if I stakeout with you for a bit? I made popcorn."

"Of course, it's your house."

We sat on the wicker furniture and munched through a big bowl, with Bert looking through his binoculars and reporting in, "Nothing yet... Abby's a smart cookie, are you two friends?"

"Not really. Different circles."

He excused himself to bed after an hour, and I waited out another long, boring night without an app to scroll through mindlessly or a book to read. I cracked one of the windows and pressed my face to it, breathing in the scent of the cool breeze coming off of the river, like decaying marine life and nature and some sweet, spicy river weeds growing on the bank.

The next day was better, but only a little. I dragged myself through the full day of school, Scott drove me home. I got a solid bit of sleep, but it was still hard to roll out of bed. Mom had coffee brewing for me and a sandwich, pickle and a piece of pie waiting for me, I guess nobody had felt like cooking.

"Dad had to go fix a burst pipe at a client's house. I'm taking you to work."

"Okay. Thanks."

"I'll probably pick you up, too, so he can sleep in."

"Is that the secret to a happy marriage?" I crunched into my pickle.

"Plenty of sleep? No, that's not it." And her sly smile told me what she thought the actual secret to a happy marriage was.

"Yuck."

The night dragged like the day had, but I was coming to appreciate the silence and the peace of my surveillance shift. The shifts driving around doing sheriff shit had gone by faster, but they hadn't left me much alone time, and suddenly I had it in spades. I shut the overhead light off and felt like I melted into the dark, but then I wanted to sleep too much and turned it back on.

At the marina, something finally happened. Two cars parked and a dozen young adults, probably college kids all spilled out. They carried coolers and tote bags and piled onto the biggest boat, taking off onto the river. That was after midnight, and I was still watching when they returned after three, stumbling, leaning on each other. Probably driving drunk, but I couldn't be sure.

I called in an anonymous tip to the local police and hoped for the best.

The rest of the night was uneventful. In the morning, I crept out of the house. Paige was two minutes late, which wasn't like him. He rolled down his window.

I reported, "Some college kids had a party on their boat. Nothing else."

"Thought I'd remind you that the town hall is today."

"Shit. What time?"

"Five o'clock."

"Shiiit." I bent over to catch my breath and try to calm the blood rushing around my head. I was tired, bone tired, still. I was limping through but not really adjusting, and the town hall would cut my sleep for the day down to probably three hours. "Do I have to?"

"It's on the agenda, they're going to vote to recall you."

"I'm gonna vote to recall me!" I wheeled away, embarrassed by the sudden tears in my eyes. I didn't understand it, I didn't even feel sad, just numb and staticky in my head.

Paige stayed level. "Remember why you started this. You wanted people in this town to change, or to at least get them talking. This is where they're gonna talk."

He was right, damn it. I nodded. "You'll be there?"

"Yup. Your parents will probably go, but if they don't, let me know and I'll pick you up. Wear your uniform."

*

I was overdue for bed and working on a headache when Mom and I walked into the community center, which was the old high school's gymnasium. The wooden panels marking a basketball court were still at our feet as we sat among folding chairs. The hoops were retracted, up against the rafters along with a soccer ball that Scott got perfectly balanced up there. It took him a week of sophomore year, hundreds of throws, but he did it.

A podium had been wheeled in, a long table at the front had a few of the busiest busybodies sitting at it. People milled around, sipping coffee in Styrofoam cups. I eyed it when we walked in, the big silver carafes dripping into their black trays, but Mom told me 'no'.

I had said, "I think no sleep might be better than only getting like two or three hours."

"That's your sleep-deprived teenage brain talking. No coffee."

I was legally an adult, a registered voter and the sheriff of the entire county, but she was still my mom and she drove me there. I sat down without coffee.

"Shouldn't you mingle?"

I looked around. Mrs. O'Connell and her husband were around, she smiled and waved at me, I smiled and waved back. I saw the ladies of the Friends of First Methodist, they were gathered around Raegan. Delilah and her parents, and Bert too. Kathy and Paige had come in, but they were talking to people at the door. I saw Dennis Wright. I saw clients that I recognized of my father's. My doctor. Marcus Campbell and his handsome father. I shook my head.

"They're gonna recall me, no matter what. I'll say my piece but I'm not gonna play nice."

My friends all drifted over as the head of the committee rang a bell -shouldn't they have a gavel?- and called the meeting to order. Everyone sat, the hall was half full. The agenda was read: First, funding drive ideas for the Fourth of July fireworks and festival. That was riveting. Everyone and their mom suggesting can drives, penny wars like we did in grade school, car washes, even selling tickets to a talent show like we were in a cheesy sitcom. I watched the clock in the back and saw half an hour of sleep slipping away. Second item on the agenda was a petition for new signage; a stop sign that a few women who liked to hear themselves talk went on and on about, saying their children played in the street, that people took the turn going too fast, blah, blah, blah. Another twenty minutes slipped away.

The man who led the meeting was bespectacled and boring looking, in his forties. Was he some kind of city manager? Did he get paid for chauffeuring us all through boring land?

"The third item on the agenda is the recall of Sheriff Evelyn Lassiter," the chauffeur read off his notes. "For those who don't know, Miss Lassiter was elected just two weeks ago. Although she technically meets the mandatory qualifications for sheriff, there are some who believe that the qualifications are outdated. We're going to open the floor to anyone who wishes to speak, although because we believe that this is going to be a hot button issue, we're limiting speaking time to three minutes per person. Who would like the floor?"

Mrs. O'Connell was the first to raise her hand and jump to her feet. Seeing her standing there, pretty, blonde, pregnant, I actually felt a surge of hope, of appreciation for my town.

"I'm Evelyn's English teacher at Elviston High. I know that Evelyn is a very intelligent and promising young woman. I think it's wonderful that she got so many other young people interested in voting, and making an effort to better their community!"

Scattered applause of agreement rumbled from the crowd.

She sat down, satisfied.

Raegan stood. "Pardon me for disagreeing with a school teacher -the old ruler scars on my knuckles itch just thinking about it-," polite chuckles, "-but some of us disagree. I'm Dax Raegan, I was sheriff of Elviston County for quite a few years. A few of the other deputies wanted me to come here and speak for them, because they fear reprisals…"

I rolled my eyes. Paige saw even though he was behind me, and gave me a subtle nudge, meaning to cut it out.

Raegan went on. "The deputies feel that Miss Lassiter has made a mockery of the department, and the town, and the whole county. They just don't think that any teenager could be competent in the role of sheriff, let alone one with a radical anti-police agenda."

Marcus said, "I saw a Tiktok video that Evelyn made with a boy, saying 'all cops are bastards'."

Raegan nodded, then sauntered toward the door. Apparently, he had said all that he had to say. On the way, he caught my eye, gave me a dainty wave with his fingers. He mouthed what I thought were the words, 'I'll see you later.' And he winked at me. It made the back of my neck prickle, put a pit in my stomach.

"Hold on!" Delilah had jumped up and spoke over the muttering. "I was there at the time, the underclassmen boy was the one who said that, not Evelyn. She was just standing near him, she couldn't have known what he was going to say. Mrs. O'Connell is right. What Evelyn did, getting almost a thousand young people to register and vote for her was incredible. She showed real leadership in getting elected, and she represents a need for change in our town. Under Sheriff Raegan, we were stagnant for years, or... you could even say we were going in the wrong direction. His Blue Lives Matter flag was an insult to the Black population in our town, with everything that is happening in our country. And we all voted for Evelyn because we felt like the law enforcement was ineffectual."

To my surprise, Abby stood and added her voice. "To recall the sheriff that we voted in without giving her a chance to do the job would be an insult to the majority that voted her in, and to the spirit of democracy!" I knew that she was trying to protect her exclusive story, but I appreciated her strong words anyway.

"Here, here!" Bert pumped his fist. "The kids are right. Give the lady a chance."

One of the ladies of the Friends of First Methodist stood up. "Hi there, Marge Hamilton. I hear what the young ladies are saying, Miss Lassiter was voted in by a wide margin. But I also know that a recall would take a few weeks to organize. A month would certainly be enough time to put it together and for the public to make their opinions heard with any campaigning. A month would be long enough, also, for Miss Lassiter to find her footing and prove herself as sheriff, or else for the town to get a feel for her not being a good fit. The young people voted her in -as I understand it, it was a secret campaign- they can vote again, and with the entire town being in on the vote, this time, democracy can decide the issue, fair and square, with everything out in the open."

That was a popular statement. A few people called out, "Agreed."

A man I didn't know stood. "Let's recall her, this whole thing was a joke. It was a good one! But it's over."

I couldn't help it, I chuckled. A few people turned to look at me. Paige gave me a nudge from where he sat behind me. Delilah and her uncle looked back, nodded encouragingly. I stood. I didn't really know what to say.

"Hello, everybody. I'm Sheriff Evelyn Lassiter... First, I'd like to say that this whole thing wasn't a joke to me. It was a little bit selfish, I know that now. I wanted to make the town a better place, but I wanted to help myself, too. Get a leg up, cause it's hard out there... I've done my best to be selfless since I took my oath, I've been doing the job, full time, and staying in school, too. It has been really hard... I'd be willing to step aside, if I thought that I had helped. If we could just fund some sensitivity training, and mandatory body cameras for all cops and deputies. Our law enforcement has a history of incompetence, racism, and abuse of power, not just in this county, but in this country... We need to work to undo the ingrained rot, and we need to be held accountable. If we could achieve that, I know that the people of this town would be happy to elect a qualified sheriff. Thank you." I wasn't sure if I should name Paige, being that I wasn't very popular at the moment. There were plenty of people really considering what I had said, but there were also some people shaking their heads, glaring at me. I had badmouthed America. Political suicide.

Kathy stood up behind me. "I agree with the sheriff. I support our police, but we need accountability from them. If they have nothing to hide, they have nothing to fear."

Mom took my hand as I sat back down. I nodded to Kathy.

The city manager said, "Funding for law enforcement is decided at the state level, it is not in the purview of this committee or the town, Miss Lassiter. We're discussing the recall, right now. Would anyone else like the floor?"

The crowd was all done, it seemed.

"All in favor of scheduling the recall vote for…" He consulted a calendar. "May 28$^{th}$? Oh wait, that's no good. That's the day after Memorial Day, let's give it another week. June 4$^{th}$?"

"Aye." Three of the four others sitting at the front table spoke up and raised their hands.

"And I make four." The city manager took a note. "Opposed?"

One woman raised her hand. "I'm opposed."

She looked at me and I nodded my appreciation, even though I wanted them to recall me. I was glad to have an end date for my suffering. The last week of May was the last week of school, for seniors, a little over a month away. Graduation was the Sunday after the recall, June 9th. I would have a free and clear and fun summer to look forward to.

"Motion passes, we will hold signups for poll workers after the meeting, thank you."

I stood again. "That's fine, but I'd like to put the matter of raising funds for my proposed changes on the agenda, please. If we can raise funds for fireworks, we can raise funds for improving our law enforcement."

"Our agendas are decided a month in advance and advertised so that the town has time to respond. I can put it on next month's agenda, for the meeting on May 22nd."

"Okay."

"Alright Miss Lassiter, please come up with a specific number as to the funds you are seeking and a breakdown as to what they'll go to before the meeting… And some fundraising ideas wouldn't hurt."

I nodded and he moved on to the next point in the agenda. Glancing at Mom, I nodded to the door. The Stokelys stayed behind, Paige and Kathy were already heading out. We made our escape.

Outside of the hall, with the warm sun baking the parking lot blacktop, Kathy slowed up. "Let me get your number, Evelyn. I'm going to whip up a design for some lawn signs, get a few friends involved to go door to door handing them out and spreading the news. They may just want to meet you…"

"Thanks Kathy."

Chapter Seventeen

"Who's staking out the boat, right now?" Mom asked as she drove us home.

"Wednesdays are Debbie's."

"Ask her if she can stay until eleven, or midnight. You need sleep."

"I shouldn't… I told them ten when they agreed to do this. They have school tomorrow."

"So do you."

"I can't." I was dead tired, I knew it would be worse after I slept a little, I would have to drag myself out of bed after an hour or two of sleep.

"You can ask me for help, you know."

"Good to know."

She turned down our long driveway, and at the end I saw a cluster of vehicles; a sheriff's department cruiser, a big red truck, and a big silver truck with a single-stalled, silver horse trailer hooked onto the back.

"Is that Paige?" Mom had tapped the brakes at the sight of all the vehicles.

"I don't think so." I didn't like the look of it, and when I saw someone leading Mabel around the side of the house, I popped the door open and ran.

"Evie, wait!"

My legs were pumping, lungs burning and head was rushing as I ran up the drive. I heard the engine rev behind me, Mom following and whipping sideways to block the driveway. I charged up to the man in some nondescript uniform leading my horse.

"What are you doing with her!?"

Kipling materialized from alongside the trailer, he swept a beefy arm out and intercepted me from getting close to the man. "Hold it, Missy."

"Don't touch me!" I shouted, and made a grab for the reins they had on Mabel. "What are you doing?"

There was another pencil-necked and polo-wearing man holding a clipboard standing alongside the trailer, and when he spoke, I whirled to face him, saw Raegan standing next to him, leaning on the trailer, arms crossed, lips pursed to keep from smiling too big.

Kipling answered my question, still blocking me from getting close to Mabel, while I was trying to block the man leading her. "We got a tip that you had a horse here without the proper acreage. County code states you have to have more than one acre to own a horse."

"That's ridiculous!" Mom had caught up to us, she swept me back behind her and squared off against Kipling, who was a few inches taller than her. "Our lot is 1.2 acres, we've had surveys done, you can check them!"

The pencil-neck answered, "I'm from the county survey offices, I just measured the property, it's coming in at .95 acres."

"You're wrong!" I shouted. "You're lying!"

He pushed his glasses up his nose, unamused by my accusation. "Well there is a degree of error in using the handheld tools, only, but we're backed up several weeks out for a full team to come out."

"So you're taking our horse over five-tenths of an acre?" Mom was blustering, her voice furious and frightening. "Measured with tools that you know are inaccurate, and with every past survey done on our property telling you that you're wrong! Whose pocket are you in? Raegan's? I want to talk to your superior, right now!"

Kipling said, "You ladies can run it up the flagpole on your own time, right now these men have a job to do. Step aside and let them do it, or I'll arrest you." He stepped back and away from me, arms raised, inviting me to try to interfere again, hoping that I would.

I had prickling eyes, fury welling up in my throat like a balloon about to burst, and I stepped toward him, but Mom reached out and caught my arms. "-No. It's okay, we're gonna figure this out."

"This isn't right," I squeaked out, my fury popped and turned into pain, I no longer wanted to scratch his eyes out, just lay down and cry. Tears spilled over, so Mom pulled my face into her shoulder.

"Sh. I know. It's gonna be okay. Raegan, you've got no right to be here, you get off my property!"

I peeked over Mom's shoulder. Raegan held his hands up, shuffled over to his red truck and left, having to drive up onto the grass to get around mom's car. At the end of the drive, Paige's car was pulling in. He stopped behind Mom's and climbed out, dressed in street clothes, he hurried over.

"What the Hell are you doing, Warner?"

"Just doing my job," pencil-neck answered.

"You pushed things around for this to jump the line? I know you didn't do it for nothing. The state licensing board is gonna hear about it." I had never heard him with that bitter edge in his voice.

I put a hand out as Mabel passed me, she craned her head so I could touch her snout. "It's okay. I'll see you soon, I promise." I was still crying, and I felt indignant anger bubble up again; Paige should not be seeing me like this, neither should Kipling, they were both my subordinates. I bent over, I felt like I was going to be sick. "Fuck. We're just gonna let them take her!? We can't do anything!? I'm the goddamn sheriff!"

Paige said, "I'm sorry. For now, you have to let her go."

I felt like they were ripping my heart out, seeing my old girl nervously trot up the metal ramp into the trailer, having to be coaxed and dragged the whole way. She was so old, my mind was spinning with thoughts of her tripping and breaking her leg in the back if they hit a pothole, or her thinking I had given her away and dying, not knowing where I had gone. People could die of broken hearts, I bet that animals could, too. "Where are you taking her?"

"Glue factory," Kipling quipped, and it blindsided me so much that I buried a squeak in my hand.

"That's not where she's going," Paige rushed. "Where is she going?"

The man who had loaded her in swung the back gate closed on the trailer, cutting off my view of her. The back of his shirt was embroidered with 'Elviston County Animal Control'. "Reed City Shelter has room for her, she's going there."

"And they won't stop Evelyn from seeing her horse, isn't that right?"

"I expect so."

I broke away from Mom and hurried after him as he headed for the cab of his truck. "Be careful with her! She's old! And she gets special feed for her hooves, she's prone to abscesses so you have to keep an eye on her, especially her right front leg! And a hardener if it snows. You have to tell them."

"She'll be taken care of," the man said, and I heard sympathy in his voice. "Take your hand off the truck, please. Step back."

I forced myself to move back, sinking my teeth into my lip. The truck started, started to pull slowly onto the grass. Mom came and stood by me again, and Paige, too.

I wiped my face, I had pushed my emotions down just enough that I could speak without my voice shaking. "Can I fire him?"

Kipling had climbed into his cruiser, waited to exit the property behind the slow moving truck and trailer.

Paige said, "Those would be the reprisals they spoke of earlier. They're frowned upon."

"What can I do to him?" The pit in my stomach was cold. I felt capable of anything in that moment.

"You can move him to the night shift for a week straight, then alternate him back to the morning shift, so he can't adjust. You can send him for a psych eval, he'll hate that. Just use the words 'erratic' and 'confrontational' on the form, I'll send you the one I mean."

"Thanks."

"You need me to cover your shift tonight?"

I shook my head, but his kind offer had poked a hole in my resolve, tears threatened again. It took me thirty seconds to breathe through it before I could answer. "No. I'll keep doing this as long as it takes. When they recall me, you can deputize me, and I'll sit and watch that boat all summer, while everyone else goes off to college, if that's what it takes to catch these bastards in the act."

"You had better get some sleep, then."

"How'd you know to come down here?" I asked.

"Campbell told me. I guess he didn't approve."

"And Dennis Wright must have told Raegan and Kipling about Mabel," I realized. "He told them how to hurt me."

"We'll get them all in the end. It only takes one of them to flip, one solid piece of evidence."

I nodded, I was beginning to feel numb. "Thanks for coming."

"I'm filing a complaint about Warner as soon as I get home. He can't be in someone's pocket and work for the county. There might be something we can do to get your survey redone, sooner rather than later. I'll look into it. Payday Friday. I'll see you."

"Yup."

I went inside and crawled into bed. My alarm was set for nine-thirty. I had less than three hours, and what I really needed was twelve and a long bubble bath, and some nuzzles from Mabel. But nothing was going to give if I didn't keep at it.

I slipped under, had anxious dreams about my teeth falling out and zombies closing in. When I woke, I realized something wasn't right. It was dark, the way it should be, but there wasn't coffee brewing, my alarm wasn't going off on my phone. I checked the time, and the display said that it was after four-thirty in the morning. I jolted upright. I was instantly pissed, thinking I had slept through it, Mom and Dad had not woken me -even though I knew it wasn't their responsibility- and that Debbie surely would have left when I didn't show up by 10:05, last night.

And in those unmonitored hours, Raegan and his goons could have slipped onto the boat, taken it up or down the river and picked up ten pounds of Blue 82, enough to supply local dealers for months, and I could have lost my chance to get justice for Harry Santiago and the dead and braindead kids and for Mabel. To make it so that Inez didn't have to pursue her justice any longer, and to bring her home safely.

I hurried into the kitchen, unlocking my phone as I went and tapping the button to wake up the Keurig. But the first message on my phone was from Mom.

*Took your shift. Get some sleep. Love you.*

I exhaled, shuddering all over, tension releasing. I bent over the counter, breathed deeply, in and out. I felt like I had been pierced with something; appreciation, I guess. I could go back to sleep, but I didn't feel the need to. Instead I enjoyed a slow cup of coffee, scrolling on my phone for the ease it gave me, transporting me away. Then I showered, swept the kitchen floor, unloaded the dishwasher and started making pancakes so that I would have some ready when Mom got home, just after six.

The cakes sizzled in the pan, smelling like apples and cinnamon, I stood and stared out the window over the sink, into the back yard. The grass brown around the chicken coop, Mabel's stable, empty… The back yard was where she belonged, and to have her not out there felt wrong, the space looked empty.

Mom dragged herself in slowly, and laid her purse on the counter. "Hey."

"Thanks. I cleaned a little, and made pancakes."

"Yum, I'm starving. I scheduled the survey, paying extra for them to come from Grace County, apparently their findings would be valid in our county, as well, and they had less of a wait. It's three Tuesdays from now, one o'clock. Not so bad, see? We'll have Mabel back in no time."

"Yeah… Thanks. I'll pay you back tomorrow when I get my first paycheck."

"Okay."

I sat next to her at the counter, flipped through my notes as I chewed pancakes. Saturday would mean another card game between Rodney Bean and his associates. We could follow Daniel Reiter, since he was out best bet. After that? We needed to hunt down some new lead, and I couldn't do that while watching the boat overnight and going to school during the day. Saturday night when Wilensky was on duty and Sunday during the day when Kathy took a shift were our best and only chances to make it happen.

Dad got up early. When he came out, the first thing that he did was to wordlessly pull me into a hug. We all had breakfast together. They were exchanging glances as I served them pancakes. I picked up on some weirdness.

"What's this? What's that look?"

Mom the mind reader said, "Dad was just suggesting with his eyes that we tell you about your graduation present to cheer you up. I think it's a great idea. You show her, it was your idea."

Dad whipped out his phone, flicked around in it for a minute, then slid it across the counter to me.

I couldn't help it, I smiled as I leaned over and looked at it. "What's this? The lease on a brand new hotrod? No, it's a ticket to..." I zoomed in. "The Walkmen? Oh wow, I didn't know they were back together!"

"We're going to Atlanta, all three of us, just like last time. End of May. Con-graduation!"

"It's great, you guys, thank you." I went around the counter and threw my arms around both of them. They patted my back. I would have preferred a car, of course, but my parents were never going to have that much money, and they had taken me to see the Walkmen ten years ago, when I was eight. It was my first concert, a special day and night.

We had headed to Nashville early, eaten great barbeque, stood in line chatting to other fans, my parents bragging about me, people calling me an awesome little fan. The show was cool, but seeing my parents singing along and dancing together had been cooler. I'd felt so grown up, I'd told all my friends about it at school the next day. Back then I couldn't have named you two Walkmen songs, but I had developed an affinity as the years went on for their sometimes harsh but always thoughtful sound. Mostly they sounded like Mom and Dad to me, though.

Mom excused herself to get some sleep, and I schlepped to school. I was early, I met Delilah and Scott by her locker and told them what had happened.

She was aghast. "They took Mabel? I'm so sorry, I can't believe that."

Scott pounded a fist into the locker. "Sons of bitches!" He had met Mabel only recently, and only a few times, but he was decent like that.

I nodded. "I knew when we started this, that it would make some people mad. I never imagined this… How have you been? I feel like we hardly see each other, when we do, I'm so tired and out of it, and we're always talking about me and my problems."

They smiled, exchanged a glance with each other. I could see that they had been feeling the same way lately, apparently talking about it with each other, but they would never say such a thing, not when I was going through so much.

Delilah said, "I'm good. I got a job for the summer at the Swirl."

"Oh really? That's great!" The Swirl was the busiest ice cream shop in town, down by the water, right on the lake. It was where the big money was for kids like us, if you didn't want to be sheriff, that is.

"Yeah, and my comic got like four hundred more followers since you got elected, I think being your friend has something to do with it."

"That's great. And you?"

Scott shrugged. "Same old, same old. I'm planning on a lazy fun summer before starting college. Might be our last chance, you know?"

"Fair enough, it does sound nice… I'm glad things are going well…" The bell rang, a warning that first period began in five minutes. "Whose shift today?" I couldn't remember the schedule.

"Mine," Scott said.

"Right… We're gonna get them. They're not going to bully their way out of facing justice."

"No, they won't."

"We won't let 'em. I won't fall asleep on the job, I promise, E."

## Chapter Eighteen

May meant that Tennessee got warm. It was extra hard to focus in classes at the end of spring, especially when it was also the last spring of our youth; flowers were blooming, the clouds formed like some oppressive force up above bringing static in the air that could raise the hair on the back of your neck, make you twitchy, and then the rains came and there was a release, a moment to breathe, but they never lasted long.

Teachers sensed it all in us. 'Senioritis' they called it. Like we weren't right to be panicking that we were losing childhood forever and were unable to cling to it. Anyway, they took it easier on us at the end. Maybe they remembered the end of their own senior year; how the best parts of adulthood were dangled out in front of us but still out of reach while the best parts of childhood had been shucked off long ago. We had to get jobs but couldn't get good ones. We could fall in love but it wouldn't last. We were chomping at the bit to get going but there was less potential than ever before, and it was frightening.

The break in school-work had come in the nick of time. A small mercy, along with my teenage deputies not missing any of their shifts. My brain wasn't cut out for hard work anymore. It was mostly just watching the boat in the dark and sitting through classes, absentmindedly taking notes to play catch up with on Sundays.

Paige had talked me out of following Daniel Reiter all the way home after last Saturday's card game. Pulling Rodney Bean over the week before when he was all over the road had been one thing, but to pull over another member of their group would probably give away that we were still digging into the Blue 82 network, not just looking into the shooting of Frank Gillespie. Maybe. If more of them were actually involved in the drug trade. He wanted me to wait another week, another week of surveillance on the boat, see if anything happened, but nothing did. And I lost a lot of sleep that week, had to give up valuable hours to transport a detainee to the county jail and take a speeder with a warrant in, to maintain appearances in case Raegan and co. were watching me.

I got my first paycheck the Friday after Mabel was taken. I stared at it, in my office, wondering if it was worth it. It wasn't. There would be a time when I would be happy to see a chunk of change like that, but for the moment, I really wanted to go to a drive-in movie or to the beach with my friends, to a throwback concert with my cheesy parents. I wanted to be lazy when I wanted to be lazy, to read some popular book that would never live up to the hype, and spend time with Mabel in her golden years. Another two weeks sloughed off uneventfully meant another paycheck. My savings account was padded. I could buy a decent set of wheels, or pay for my first semester of community college, probably. It didn't really matter, though.

Paige and I sat on yet another Saturday and went over the other cases of Blue 82 in surrounding counties while parked behind a low billboard on a state road, in the afternoon. Cars zoomed by and we focused on the notes we had been sent from other law enforcement agencies. Paige knew someone everywhere, he didn't say that he trusted them, exactly, but it was better than trusting a complete stranger. Looking at other officer's notes and reports didn't give us much. There were names of plenty of small-time dealers who had been apprehended, but would they give us anything? No. They hadn't turned on their sources when arrested to save themselves some time, why would they now, when we had nothing to offer?

Paige did a little clicking around on the cruiser's laptop. "This guy, Bruce McCafferty -a dealer recently caught holding Blue 82 in Chattanooga- was in the same prison at the same time as Daniel Reiter. Same cell block, too."

"That's something. We could ask prison guards if they were associates. It sounds like we should really be following Daniel Reiter…"

"Can't do that and stake out the boat. And we're in pretty deep, there, already."

"Yeah, we can't let up. Can we track Reiter's locations through his phone?"

"Not without a warrant. And we have no probable cause for one."

"So we're thinking that Reiter is the middle man, who goes between the local dealers and the cops."

"Maybe one of many. We don't know how big this pyramid scheme is."

"So where does this happen? Where could it happen? I don't think that Dennis Wright would go in that deep. So: Raegan, Kipling, Campbell."

"I think Campbell just got dragged in because of his nephew. Probably temporarily."

"Maybe, if we believe that they really found that pound of dope washed up on the riverbank. But he could have found it in his uncle's possession, somehow."

"I really don't think so, I've worked with Campbell for years."

"Okay…" I was inclined to trust Paige's instincts. "Raegan. You know him better than I do. Would he do the dirty work himself, or would he delegate it to an unstable lackey like Kipling?"

Paige chewed on that question for a full minute.

The survey was in a few days, I could have Mabel home by the weekend, I hoped. Unless Raegan had bribed or threatened the surveyors of Hope County, too. Unless we actually were on slightly less than one acre. Unless Mabel died before then. Mom or Dad took me out to see her almost every day, at the expense of more sleep. She always trotted over, happy to see me, still looking decently spry; her hair was not falling out, she had not stopped eating because she missed me so much.

I didn't feel betrayed. I wanted her to be okay more than I wanted to be her whole world. I guess that was love.

Paige was done thinking. "I don't see Raegan trusting someone else with something so important. Maybe they would go together, but I think he would definitely be there."

"So maybe we should be sticking to Raegan like glue."

"Except he's not sheriff anymore, he lost a lot of his ability to cover up after himself. I'm betting he suspended operations, or even called it off entirely."

"You think that's why nothing has happened with the boat for weeks?"

"Probably."

I sighed. While I thought that our vigilance was getting us closer to the end game, I could bear it. But he was telling me that it had all been for nothing. I could tell from looking at him that it didn't bother him in the slightest, or just that he was used to that sort of thing. "Can we push them to act, somehow?"

"Got a pound of Blue 82 we could dangle in front of them?"

My temper flickered. I flung my notebook onto the dashboard. "So just keep waiting for them to screw up? I hate this!"

He hardly glanced over, his subtle face which I was becoming quite good at reading showed distaste at my outburst. "That's the job." He folded his arms, looked out at the passing cars on the road.

I simmered, watching him sit there like he was better than me, I felt my Mother's attitude engage in me. I felt a smile forming, forced a chuckle. "Oh ho ho! This guy thinks he's Raylan Givens!" His face twitched with irritation, just a momentary lapse, and combined with my exhaustion it made my chuckles turn into full on belly laughs. I bowed over in the seat gasping for air.

Paige tapped his fingers on the steering wheel, licked his lips, took a breath trying to calm himself down. But he couldn't stop himself from saying, with a cold voice, "I'm not Raylan Givens, and you're not Nancy Drew."

I was still laughing, it was turning into a shrill cackle. "Clearly!"

Paige sighed, then he was chuckling, too, shutting his eyes and putting his face in his hands, hiding his smile but laughing with me until my hysteria faded enough that I could stop, wipe my tears, catch my breath. When he spoke next, he was serious.

"You walk around being sarcastic, acting like nothing affects you. I know why you do it. I don't blame you. I don't see the world getting any better... But I don't think never investing in anything is the way to deal with it. That just hurts you, in the end. Robs you."

I dabbed my eyes, sniffed, looked away. I felt uncomfortable with him speaking so candidly, like I might as well be sitting there naked. I wanted to crawl out of my skin. "What do you suggest then, Sigmund?"

"Don't try to take the world on. It's not your burden. Carve some space out for yourself, let yourself care about what you can control. 'Water your own garden' is what Kathy would say."

"Kathy's a smart lady."

\*

It was dark when Paige drove me home. Wilensky was on shift for the night at Bert's, but I would stay up most of the night, anyway. I had finally adjusted. I liked my quiet Saturday nights in my room, snacking, scrolling, reading. I had settled in with a bag of Doritos and was finally about to listen to Maggie Rogers' new record when my phone rang. It was Paige. I felt myself deflate.

"What's up?"

"Got a situation. We got a tip about a party, apparently there's a lot of underage drinking happening."

"Where's it at?"

"Here in town. Lethe Street."

A nice subdivision. My friend Debbie lived on Lethe Street. "Do I have to come back in?"

"If I bring anyone else, I'll have no choice but to book everyone. If you go, you have some discretion…"

I didn't want to go. "I mean, they're breaking the law, right?" But I had been to a couple of parties in my day. It was pure luck I hadn't been at the one where Marcus, Joe, and Monica all got busted. Some of the people at the party would almost definitely be eighteen, they wouldn't get a slap on the wrist that could be expunged with some community service.

"You want these people to vote not to recall you, don't you?"

I couldn't say 'yes'. Even if I planned to continue to stakeout the boat all summer -and I wasn't sure that I still did, if there was no point- I wanted it to not be my responsibility anymore. I wanted it to not be my fault that I couldn't find Inez or help Harry.

Paige deduced as much. "You don't want a recall attached to your name. You want to show the town that you did the job, that your classmates still support you and what you stood for, and then resign on your own terms."

"Okay. Pick me up?"

"I'm pulling in right now."

I threw my uniform shirt back on, attached my badge and fake sidearm.

When we pulled up to the bland two-story house on the sprawling yard, there were four cars crammed into the driveway, another parked along the curb. Paige flicked the lights on, and we jumped out of the cruiser. Music was thumping through the walls, there were strobe lights on the lower level, visible through the windows. The music cut out first, then the lights.

A window was flung open on the side of the house, a boy tumbled out head over feet, hit the ground, took off running. I twitched, starting to give chase, but Paige stuck out an arm.

"He's gone."

Paige pounded on the door but didn't wait for someone to answer, flinging it open. "Elviston County Sheriff's Department, let me see hands." He was shining his flashlight into the eyes of a cluster of terrified teens, who had all come together, safety in numbers. His hand was on his gun, he scanned the open-concept first floor. "Keep them here, I'm going upstairs."

I had my light out, too. I checked faces, registering most as familiar. A few from my grade, a few from the Juniors. A dark face made me do a double-take.

"Damn it, Debbie."

She looked down, ashamed. "I know. You don't have to say it."

"Is this your house?" I couldn't remember.

"No, it's Corey's."

Corey Chalmers raised his hand. "Hey Evelyn. Sorry we didn't invite you, but, you know…"

"Who was that who just bolted out the window?"

Everyone clammed up.

"He didn't drive here, did he?"

"No."

"Alright." I looked up as Paige marched a couple down from presumably one of the bedrooms. I recognized them. They were our age; whatever they were doing up there -besides the drinking- was legal. There were eleven people left in the house, total. All things considered, it was not a big deal.

Paige said, "I want keys to all five of those vehicles, right now." He held out his hand.

"They're all in a bowl in the kitchen," Corey said. "Not like a key party! Just making sure nobody drove home."

I leaned around the corner of the single wall on the first floor, where most of the appliances were placed. On the nice marble kitchen island were bottles of Absolut, Jack Daniels, and Malibu. And in the center, a bowl of keys. I nodded to him.

"You were all spending the night, that was the plan?"

Debbie piped up, "The girls were spending the night at my house, across the street."

Paige paced back and forth, staring the teens down. "Well, Sheriff, what do you think? I think we should throw the book at all of these teenage delinquents." He was good, didn't raise his voice, didn't oversell it.

One of the juniors I didn't know pleaded, "Please, Sheriff…"

I bit my lip, pretending to consider. "We're not going to arrest you. But you're calling your parents, you're detained until they come get you."

It was a long two hours, with sets of parents showing up to claim their children. Most were embarrassed and apologetic, grateful to us for not charging their wayward youths. A few were outraged with us, questioning the legality of holding the kids, the cars, questioning them without parents present, blah, blah, blah. Paige would make quick work of telling them that they should be grateful that the sheriff had elected not to arrest their child, and them too, for negligence, while we were at it.

When Debbie left, I asked if she were still going to take her shift at Bert's. She said, "Of course."

We were left with two boys. Corey's parents were out of town. He got in touch with his aunt, who had to come from Chattanooga. And that left us with a sixteen-year-old boy who couldn't reach his mother. He sheepishly told us that she was probably already passed out for the night. We drove him home, pounded on the door.

When a woman appeared, she was haggard looking, bleary eyed. I explained the situation to her. "Your son was at a party where there was a lot of underage drinking going on. He's not being charged, this time."

She rolled her eyes, snatched his arm and dragged him inside. "Get in here. Sorry." She shut the door in our faces.

It was nearly 3am when Paige dropped me off once again. I was mostly adjusted to staying up nights, but I still had lost sleep from the week to catch up on. I looked at the new Maggie Rogers record open on my laptop; I also needed to come up with fundraising ideas for the money to put the whole department through sensitivity training, and equip them with body cams. So far, all I had was 'cop dunk tank'. I shut the laptop. I would be in a better headspace for it all, after some sleep.

Chapter Nineteen

I got a few stink eyes in the hallway on Monday. Somebody -presumably from the party- even hung a massive 'Recall Sheriff Lassiter' banner across a row of lockers near mine. I was walking with Scott when we turned the corner and saw it. He stalked over, snatched it down and balled it up.

"Sorry…"

"It's alright." Really, it was. Nothing could touch me; I was seeing The Walkmen that night, Mom and Dad were picking me up after school and we were going straight to Atlanta; Michael had agreed to stay until I got back, even if it was one in the morning, which it very well might be. I'd had to offer him a hundred bucks.

"Are you telling people about the recall? Getting them to tell their siblings, the other schools?"

"I haven't been worried about it. If they recall me, they recall me. Delilah did mention setting up a new Facebook page…"

We were very near the end of the school year, seniors got out a week before everyone else. And the end of the year meant finals, study guides and whole classes devoted to practice tests. Monday was easy for me, I had slept something like fourteen hours between Saturday night and Sunday morning and Sunday afternoon. I was looking forward to seeing the Walkmen. It wasn't even about the band, so much... they were good, live music was cool, but what I was really craving was being carefree, being a teenager for the night, hanging out with my family. Mom and Dad were like giddy kids at the breakfast table that morning.

When I saw Michael coming toward me in the hallway after the last bell rang, something heavy settled in my guts. His face pinched with shame. I held up a hand when he was still a stone's throw away.

"Don't come any closer."

"Evelyn..." He shook his head.

"Don't do this to me, Michael, it's the fucking Walkmen concert tonight!"

"I don't know who that is, but I'm really sorry, I can't do my shift watching the boat today."

"At all?" My voice squeaked out, betraying my helplessness.

"I'm so sorry, my parents are making me go to this wake for an aunt I only met like two times, but she was family..."

I forced myself to nod, couldn't speak for a moment. "...Okay. Could you take another day this week, if I can get someone to switch?"

"Yes! I could! Any weekday is fine."

"Okay, I'll let you know."

I sent out a mass text to the other teenage deputies. Debbie was my only real hope, but maybe it would be no big deal for her to switch, to stay late. I crossed my fingers as the dots appeared, showing that she was typing.

*GROUNDED. SORRY :'(*

Her crying emoji hit too close to home, I felt tears start to well up, tried to tell myself it could still happen. But Bert had said he was no good on an overnight. I could not ask Wilensky, who was already giving up two nights with her baby, and whose husband worked during the week. I pulled up my past messages with Paige and started to type the message. Then I stopped, and did the mental math for how many hours he had worked the past week, how many he would work, this week. I couldn't do it. He had done too much. I couldn't go.

I opened my locker back up, stuck my face in and gulped a few big breaths, feeling them rattle around in my lungs, smelling the metal, hurting every second. My nose prickled and ran, the tears spilled over. I forced it down. Mom and Dad were probably outside, already, her in a nice dress, him in an old band shirt. I couldn't make them late. I swallowed my feelings and slammed the locker, hurried outside.

It was a spectacularly long and lonely evening, imagining my parents holding each other and swaying in the front row to *Line By Line,* bouncing and singing to *The Rat.*

Tuesday was a bit groggier; I could think of nothing but the survey happening when I was in school, and of Mabel coming home. When Scott drove me home, I saw

Mom standing in the door as we came up the drive. She waved a paper in her hand, and I knew that the survey had come back the way that we wanted it to; we could go and get Mabel. It hit me all at once. I clutched my chest, heart about to beat through my ribs, and shut my eyes.

Scott awkwardly patted my shoulder. "I can drive you out to get Mabel, if you have a trailer, or rent one."

"That's okay, Dad has a client who's going to lend him one, probably as soon as he gets home."

We did just that, and I hugged her around the neck when she was finally tucked back in her stall, where she belonged. She huffed and whinnied, seemed very happy to be back. I had no hope of sleeping at all, did my homework out there with her, by the light of my phone.

Wednesday was a blur, and I was still foggy when I woke up from my afternoon nap and Dad drove me to Bert's to relieve Debbie.

She was sheepish and had been quiet around the lunch table since the party. "Hey, nothing to report. Thanks again for last weekend…"

"Yeah. Thanks for not abandoning your shift."

"We're almost done, right?"

It made me cringe to hear it. I had told them we would be done when school was done. But I had to keep it up. For Mabel, for the Santiagos, for justice. If they all tapped out -and I couldn't blame them- I would have to park myself at Bert's half of any given day and most nights, too. And it all might be for nothing.

"Almost…"

She got picked up. Bert was sitting at his kitchen table and waved for me to come in.

"Hello, Evelyn. Another day in paradise, huh?"

"Yeah."

"You know the way."

I moved through the house and settled into the comfortable wicker furniture in the sunroom. Bert still took a day shift on Saturdays, but didn't bother to sit with me, anymore. Like the rest of us, he wasn't expecting anything to come of the surveillance anymore. He went to bed early, and I shut the light off on the porch, watching the marina in the dark, with crickets chirping outside, a few birds calling up above, their claws clicking on the metal roof.

A car pulled into the lot at the marina when I had been sitting for only an hour and a half. It was not so unusual; about once a week, some college kids had a boat party, or a few middle aged dads snuck out for a cruise with their buddies. I played those situations by ear, called local cops if I thought it was really necessary.

Still it was something. I whipped the binoculars up, focused them, found the figure walking across the parking lot, adjusted the focus. My heart skipped a beat.

Kipling.

"Oh shit." I jumped to my feet, blood rushing to my legs, fight or flight, but neither of those was an option. I bounced in place as I found Paige in my contacts and dialed. "Pick up, pick up, pick up- hey! Hey, Kipling's at the marina!" I lifted the binoculars again, found him walking down the dock, toward the Sheriff's Department's boat.

"Are you sure?" He had just been asleep.

"Yes I'm sure!"

"I'll be there in five minutes, don't do anything, just watch."

"He's getting on the boat."

"Let him. What's he driving?"

"His big red truck. Chevy."

"Good. I'll set up on the road, pull him over when he leaves. I'll call you back when I'm in position."

"Okay I'll be-." He had already hung up.

The lights on the upper deck of the boat came on, shining out in a big ring on the water, illuminating the way. Kipling had cast off the line tied to one of the deck's large support posts. I couldn't hear the engine engage from Bert's deck, but I could see the black waters start to churn at the back, the wake kicking up as the boat surged forward into the wide river, then in a big arc started to cruise upstream. I watched it for a minute, then two, with it getting smaller in the distance, finally disappearing around a bend.

I felt chilly, suddenly. Something was finally happening, and I was stuck watching. In less than five minutes, Paige called me.

"Yeah?"

"I'm in position. Just let me know when Kipling gets back, if he's alone, if he's carrying anything. Did he have anything on the way in?"

"No, nothing."

"He was alone?"

"Yes." My voice came out weak, I couldn't catch my breath.

"Alright. I'm going to hang up, now. Call me when he gets back. And Evelyn?"

He wanted me to say, "Yeah?"

"Stay exactly where you are. Keep your eyes and ears open, but don't do anything. Understand?"

"Yeah."

"You've done good work. Let me take it from here."

He hung up before I could say 'thanks'.

For over an hour, I waited, standing by the window, peering at the dark river with my anxious sweat cooling under my arms. I was wide awake, felt wired. I checked my phone every other minute, checked the time, looked for any message from Paige. There was nothing, no relief, just time stretching cruelly on. Eventually, I realized that I wanted to be closer, I was desperate to be.

Slipping out the back door in the sunroom, creeping around the deck, I had to take my eyes off the river and the Department's slip of the marina for a few seconds. I ran through the night, past two dark and still houses on the road, then up to the closed restaurant, the last building before the marina. I crept around it, keeping low, out onto the back patio that faced the river. I slunk between upturned tables on chairs, each with their own closed up umbrella.

The night was cool, with an infrequent breeze. I parked myself at the corner of the patio, shielded by the glass of the industrial railing. It was dark enough that nobody would possibly see me; I could see the slip clearly without binoculars, now, still empty. I could also head back along the deck, hop the railing, slide down the embankment and be in the marina's southern parking lot in only a few seconds, if I had to.

It was a few more minutes with my heart in my throat and my lungs burning, panting, legs shaking where I crouched. Then the lights appeared on the river, coming around the bend. I shielded my phone as I woke it up, not wanting to give away my position. Dialed Paige.

"What's happening?"

"The boat's coming back from the... northeast? From up river. It'll be docked in a minute or two."

"Stay on the line."

We both fell silent.

Even though he did not speak, I could feel his presence on the line, in the white noise of the connection. I felt easier for it. My body melted into a kind of nervous thrumming, as taught as a bow string ready to loose an arrow, while my mind was thick with the thought of: *This is it. This is it. This is it.*

The boat's engine rev was audible from where I was perched and watching. It pitched down in frequency. The wake grew smaller, the movements oddly graceful as Kipling cut the wheel and reversed the boat neatly into its slip. I was struck with the knowledge that he was actually good at something; that he had done this before, how many times? How many clandestine trips, meetings at midnight, how many pounds of dope had they smuggled into our county to help our hopeless generation poison itself? I felt a surge of hatred for him, watched him like a hawk as he tethered the boat and stepped onto the deck.

He was still alone, looked much the same as he had before his trip. He sauntered easily down the dock, up onto the grassy stretch between it and the parking lot. He spared only a casual glance around and did not spot me. He held nothing but his truck keys. He wore a jacket but it looked snug on his broad frame, I didn't think he could be hiding anything under it, but I could tell from his gate that he wore his sidearm.

When I was sure that he was out of range, I broke the silence to fill Paige in. "He's getting in his truck, now. He's alone. He doesn't seem to be carrying anything, but he's definitely armed." And saying it made my voice tremble with fear; Paige was alone, out there. I could see the night going horribly wrong, suddenly. What would a man like Kipling do to save his life as he knew it, his livelihood and reputation all at once?

"It's alright," Paige said, hearing my worry.

"I can get to you in a minute." I didn't know it for sure, but he was probably on the next corner.

"No. Stay where you are. We need to have eyes on that boat every second, in case he left the drugs onboard."

"But you're alone..." I was thinking about Kathy, about having to deliver the news if her husband was shot, killed, while I was kept safe and still technically his superior. It made me feel sick. Suddenly the drugs seemed superfluous to what I had started this all to do. I didn't want it that badly, if it meant my partner could be killed.

The red truck was pulling out of the lot.

"I'll be fine."

"Stay on the line," I ordered, with as much authority as I could muster.

"I will, and you stay where you are, no matter what happens. Watch the boat."

I heard his car start on the other end of the line, I could hear his breathing, I thought that maybe he had stuck the phone in his breast pocket. I forced myself to watch the boat, as he had told me to. He was right; we had to help Harry Santiago, and I felt -perhaps foolishly- that bringing an end to the corruption would somehow bring Inez home safely, too. In the distance, from the corner of my eye, I could see red and blue lights start to flash through the trees, in between the last row of houses before the marina. I automatically squinted for a glimpse of Paige's car, or the truck, but I couldn't see them.

My breath coming faster, I looked back to the boat, rocking gently in the waves. On the other end of the line, I could hear the siren, the short burst of acceleration. I prayed to whoever might be listening: *Please be okay. Please let this be the end of it.*

"He stopped." Paige was filling me in, then he spoke to dispatch. "Dispatch, Deputy Paige here, pulling over a red Chevy Silverado, plate number ESM370, registered to Eric Kipling. Suspicious activity."

I couldn't help but to look that way again. I could still see nothing. My body was sure that I was about to hear a gunshot, I knew that I would take off running in an instant if I heard Paige in distress on the line. I looked at the boat again, did a double take.

Someone was on the dock, dressed in a dark hoodie, face mostly obscured, walking fast toward the slip.

"Oh no," I murmured. I had heard a door open on the other end of the line, Paige getting out of his car, I could hear rustling that was surely him approaching Kipling's Chevy; it was a jacked up truck, Kipling would have high ground, his movements would be shielded.

"Let me see some hands."

I couldn't ask Paige what to do in that moment; I would distract him from Kipling -that second could be fatal- and I would clue Kipling in to the fact that we had the boat under surveillance. He might suspect, but he couldn't know. The second that he did know, he might become desperate, dangerous. The scrawny, hooded man was almost to the slip; I could hear his footsteps on the wood of the dock, he was looking around, paranoid, better at this than Kipling, more used to it? A hardened criminal?

My heart was in my throat. My legs carried me before I had even decided the move, keeping low, moving along the back of the restaurant's deck. As soon as the hooded man's back was to me, I launched myself over the railing. One of my feet caught on it, and I ate shit, hitting the ground hard, face first, then rolling, rolling, down the hard embankment. It was damp at the bottom, I was close to the river. I found my feet and looked around, making sure the hooded man hadn't seen me fall and bolted.

No, I could see him still, on the main deck of the boat, disappearing inside the cabin, heading down. He was picking up the drugs, I knew. The second he left that boat, all of Kipling's culpability would be gone; he had just been going for a late night joy ride, and whatever some unknown person had planted or had on him when he left the boat was none of the Department's concern. Not proof of collusion beyond a reasonable doubt.

Paige was saying, on the other end of the line, "Open the door with your right hand, keep them where I can see them. Step down."

Hearing it, I thought that he was out of the woods.

I knew what he had told me to do, but I couldn't let the hooded man leave the boat. He would take our case with him, all those weeks of lost sleep and tedious surveillance, all paying dividends to this moment. I ran up the embankment on the other side of the ditch, it was shallower, it took two seconds, and in my hands, suddenly, was my air pistol. I made the wood of the deck and tried to step softly. Took one big step over the back of the boat, followed with the other foot and then I was on the main deck, steadying myself as it rocked beneath me. I was looking into the dark, open mouth of the doorway leading down to the galley, and I was trembling all over.

When the dark head and torso appeared, it sent a spike of fear through me; my body wanted to turn and run but I couldn't move. I said, "Freeze. Sheriff's Department," and it sounded more like a suggestion than an order.

I heard three things, seemingly all in the same instant. On the other end of the line, Paige said my name. In the dark stairwell leading down to the galley, I heard a thud, then another, then another, something with a bit of weight tumbling backward down the steps. And then I heard, along with a flash of movement that made me fling myself backward, turning to run, a click of a hammer being pulled back on a gun.

I heard the gunshot and the sound of it was such a blow to my senses that I was sure that I was hit, then I heard myself scream, and I was falling. I had launched myself back into and then tumbled right over the boat's back railing and was enveloped by cold water the next second. When I surfaced, I was sputtering and choking on muddy water, my legs were kicking frantically to keep me afloat while my hands were feeling my torso, searching for the bullet hole that I was sure was there, I wasn't registering pain, just cold, shock. There seemed to be nothing wrong with me, my extremities were all moving.

Pounding footsteps raced away on the dock above me. I floundered in the water, looking for a way out. I spun, headed for the bank past the end of the dock, having to swim hard to get there. I trudged up it with water falling off of me, grasped for my phone in my pocket; my air pistol had fallen somewhere.

My phone's screen was dark but I put it to my ear anyway, looking around the dimly lit parking lot for any sign of the hooded man. "Paige? Hello? Shit!" My phone was a goner, the hooded man was nowhere in sight.

Standing on the grassy slope next to the end of the dock, dripping, I had to take a knee. It sank in that I had just been shot at, and it sank in heavily. Mom and Dad would hear about it. I was crouched over there, in the dark, with the river moving placidly to one side of me when the red and blue lights fell on my face. I realized the siren was blaring, although I hadn't really noticed its approach.

I forced myself to my feet, waved a hand.

Paige vaulted out of the car and came running. "Evelyn! Are you okay?"

"Yeah. He shot at me."

"What happened?" He whirled, hand going to his gun, checking our surroundings, his hand swept me back toward the car, sticking me behind it, shielding me.

"A guy was going on the boat, to get the drugs, probably. I had to stop him, or our case would be blown."

"I told you to stay put."

"I know. Is Kipling-?"

"-In the back. Stay here."

I bent down to look. Kipling was in the backseat, scowling through the metal mesh. Paige went to look on the boat, holding his gun in one hand, his flashlight in the other. When he returned, he held out my air pistol.

"Dropped this on the boat. The guy who shot at you dropped the drugs, I guess you really scared him. I'm gonna call in State Police to secure the crime scene, and it's time to turn over what we've got to them."

His voice had a strange quality to it. I took a guess. "I screwed up. I let him get away, and now Kipling has plausible deniability." I didn't get a look at the guy's face, we had no way to track him down.

Paige glanced over. "You screwed up by not following orders, and putting your life in danger while armed with a bb gun."

Oh. That. I was still focused on our case. "We've got evidence of collusion, right? Between how they failed to investigate in the Santiago case, the missing drugs from the evidence vault, Kipling taking the boat, then this guy showing up a few minutes later?"

"And the coordinates of the boat, where Kipling went. We'll get someone out there, right away, that should nail them to the wall. Or him, at least."

"But not Raegan."

"We'll see. Criminals turn on each other all the time."

## Chapter Twenty

It was a long night, first waiting at the scene for the state cops to show up -and with the adrenaline worn off, my body was twice as heavy to lug around as it ought to be- and then taking Kipling back to the station. He didn't say a word on the way. Just simmered in the backseat.

Paige had put a call in to the Internal Affairs Bureau, in addition to the State Police. IAB was sending a detective in the morning to take our report, around 9am. It was only just after four in the morning that we finally sat down, across from Kipling, in an interrogation room. I got the feeling that we each wanted something else to report, when IAB showed up.

We had Styrofoam cups of coffee, all three of us.

"Anything happens to my truck, you're both gonna be sorry." It was the first thing Kipling had said for hours.

"Your truck will be fine," Paige said. "Now's the time to tell us everything, if you want us to mention your cooperation, when we pass it along to IAB."

Kipling sat back, arms crossed, stared at Paige. Snorted, like he thought it was hilarious. "Everything about what? You got me taking the boat for a spin, so what? You want to write me up, *Sheriff-*," he hissed the word. "-Go right ahead."

Paige said, "We're leaning more toward suspending you, right Sheriff?"

"That's right." He hadn't suggested it before hand, but there was no need. I was just following his lead.

Kipling chuckled angrily. "You two can make your plans, do whatever you want. I think I'll let my union rep and my lawyer handle things from here."

"That's how it is?" Paige asked.

"Yeah, that's how it is."

"Alright." He stood. "If you want to act like a criminal, we're gonna treat you like one. We'll hold you for the full forty-eight hours."

"Oh that's horse-shit!"

Paige was heading for the door, I followed. He held it for me. When it closed, leaving Kipling behind inside, we stood and faced each other.

"Forty-eight hours?"

He checked his watch. "Four and a half, really."

He meant before IAB showed up. I was due for a nap and then I was due for school, but I would miss part or all of the day if I had to. "What are you thinking?"

"Campbell. We keep it vague, tell him we're handing evidence over to IAB at nine, it's his last chance. He'll take it."

"We going to him?"

"Yeah. Right now."

We drove out to his apartment, a unit on top of a strip mall in town, a bachelor pad. We woke him just after five. He was rubbing his eyes when he answered the door, but when he saw us, his face sobered immediately. He shook his head, shook the sleep off.

"What's this about?"

Paige said, "Raegan, Kipling, the Santiagos, Blue 82."

"What makes you think I know anything about all of that?" His voice was soft, his eyes were searching.

"We've been working this for a month, now. We have State Police on the scene at the marina, and we're bringing IAB into the fold at 9am. So this is your last chance to come clean to us."

"Alright. Come inside."

There was only a small sofa inside, so he sat on it, and we stood. He lit a cigarette and took a long drag before beginning to talk. His face was handsome once, but lined from years of hard sun and sleepless nights, and the smoking couldn't have helped.

"I wasn't on shift, that night. Marcus called me, panicking. He told me about the drugs at the marina, the kid he left seizing, said that he didn't know what had happened after that, or what was going to happen, but could I help him? I changed his diapers, taught him to throw a ball. His dad wasn't going to do it, he was a pansy. I thought that keeping him out of trouble was the right thing to do, at the time. I've realized since then that I was wrong, should have let him take responsibility for his actions…

"But anyway, I went down there. Raegan and Kipling were on the scene. I didn't ask them for anything specific, I just asked them to keep it confined. There was a kid already dead, that night. Another one in serious condition. Why the Hell they decided to pin it on the brown kid... I mean, he was an easy target, for this community. He was older, he was selling pot, he was there, and he shouldn't have been. It's no excuse. Raegan, he was happy to help me out. All he wanted in return was for me to fill out the form, like I had logged the brick of Blue 82 into evidence."

A recorder was set on the coffee table in front of him. He stared at it for a minute, leaned forward, flicked the ash from his cigarette into an ashtray. When he spoke next, he was trying to sound more upbeat. "I'd understand if I lost my job over this, but you'll put in a good word, right, Leo? I don't want to lose my pension. You know I did the job for fifteen years, I did it to the best of my abilities, upheld the law. I don't think one mistake should erase all of that."

Paige said, "Your involvement was minimal, you're cooperating, now... Hopefully nothing has been done that can't be undone."

Campbell nodded. It seemed he had more to tell. "I regretted what I'd done pretty quickly. Raegan started asking me to bend the truth for him, in little ways. I booked a guy named Daniel Reiter, I was told to cut him loose. Raegan was the sheriff, I was the sheriff's deputy, so I did as I was told. You understand. -Well, maybe you don't, Leo. You've always been a stickler. I always respected that, about you. How strident you can be. You know I voted for you, two years ago?"

"Thank you." No hint of a smile on his face, but maybe in his voice.

"And you-." Campbell pointed at me, sinking back into the couch cushions. "I voted for you, too, Sister. Marcus told me about your campaign, he was worried you would mess things up for him, but I thought it was time for a change in leadership."

I couldn't help it, I blushed. "Thanks."

Paige asked, "Is that everything you have to tell us?"

Campbell inhaled, sighed. "Not quite. I didn't like Raegan having leverage over me. I also didn't feel right about what they -what we- did to Harry Santiago. So I went by the Santiagos' place, one day. I wanted to see if there was anything that I could do to help them out. The mother was asleep when I got there, so I just talked to Inez. Smart girl, shrewd. She called me out, although her voice shook when she did, she was trying her hardest to get me to give her something that she could use. Started out with 'Haven't you people done enough', worked her way around to 'If you were any kind of man, you'd stand up to your sheriff'... The sheriff, at the time, being Raegan, of course.

"I tell you, she smelled blood in the water. I guess it makes sense, why else would I have been there, except if I was guilty? I didn't give her the details, but I told her that I was sorry for how it went down. She wanted to know why it happened. I was flustered, to have that teenage girl working me over like that, and I guess I wasn't used to holding onto guilt. I smashed a few mailboxes when I was young, but nothing like this. I know that I shouldn't have, but I told her to leave it alone, that the people who were supposed to be there to help, they weren't, this time.

"Well, she took that and ran with it, I guess. Disappeared the next day. I feel responsible. She called me once, she had my card. That was the night of the eleventh of May. She gave me an address, said that there were underage kids doing the stuff. She didn't say her name, then, but I knew it was her. I guess she felt like she could trust me, that far, to break up a party. They got wind that I was coming, somehow, anyway, and had cleared out by the time that Stanton and I got there."

"Where was that?"

"Abandoned building in Reed City, the old feed mill."

One of the locations that Harry Santiago had given us. Inez knew about it, too. She had taken it upon herself to investigate, and that had put her in with bad people, doing bad things. I shuddered to think about it. How was she living? Was she safe? Was she trading favors for a bed, a couch, a floor to sleep on? Was she snorting that shit to blend in, to get deeper into the mess in hopes of finding something that she could tie to Raegan? All because she couldn't trust the sheriff's department to do the searching. All because she loved her brother so much.

I said, "Do you have any idea where she might be? Where else she might have gone? Any leads on who might have been at that party, that night, so we know where to start looking?"

"I don't have any idea, I'm sorry. That's everything that I know. Is it enough?"

"Hard to say," Paige answered. "But I think it might be."

"Not going to arrest me, are you?"

"Not as long as you're not going anywhere."

"I'm not running."

\*

It was still very early in the morning, the sky had lightened to a pale blue overhead, and in the east, to gold and orange. Paige and I climbed back in the cruiser, in the lot of the strip mall, so we were looking out at Main Street, at a few cars rolling past with their headlights on. Heading in to work the morning shift, or home after a very late night of clubbing, or back home after a hookup with some Tinder date who's going to ghost them, heading to the hospital, or to grab an Egg McMuffin.

"Can we swing through a McDonald's?" I asked, but then remembered, "-Oh, wait. We're supposed to be boycotting them. Palestine. How about a gas station? I'm starving."

He obliged, buying a pair of peeled hard-boiled eggs for himself out of the cooler and his usual sugar free sports drink. I got a piece of breakfast pizza, a sleeve of powdered mini donuts and a giant coffee that was half hot chocolate. I wiped powdered sugar off my work shirt after we had munched and thought for a minute.

"We should bring Raegan in."

"We don't have enough to hold him."

"We don't need to hold him for long. We bring him in, hope that scares him or Kipling into turning on each other. Even if they don't, it might be enough to make Inez see that we're on her side, get her to give up her crusade, get her home safe…"

"I don't like the optics. State Police might see it as a revenge thing, bad blood between us and the old guard. The girl probably wouldn't even know."

"She probably had a rough night, wherever she is… Trying to clean up the mess Raegan made. We need to end this."

"We did what we could, and we got some good evidence to hand over. You should be proud. I should take you home…"

"No. Let's hit up Daniel Reiter, we know he's involved, let's get him to flip."

"If only it were that simple."

But he did search the address and start the car. Nobody answered the door at his last known address, it looked empty inside the run down little house, no car was in the drive. Paige called in an APB.

"Is Rodney Bean out on bail? And the woman who runs the sex shop, let's hassle both of them."

Pounding on doors at the crack of dawn was not a good way to make friends. The woman who ran the sex shop where Reiter and Bean played cards on Saturdays answered the door of her cute white house in a leopard print robe. She had last night's red lipstick smeared across her cheek, ligature marks on her wrists.

"What do you want?"

Paige said, "We're looking for an associate of yours, Daniel Reiter. Is he here?"

"Here? No. Why would he be here?"

I stated, "So he's not handcuffed to bedframe?"

"No…" She dragged the word out. I took it to mean that Reiter wasn't cuffed to her bed with fuzzy pink handcuffs, but somebody sure was.

"Do you know where Reiter might be?"

"What's this about?"

"He's going to want to hear what we have to say. He is going to be brought in for questioning in connection with the illegal substances flooding the county the past few months; either by us, this morning, or by the State Police, this afternoon. And by then, it might be too late for him to help himself out. And for you, too, if you're involved."

Her smudged eyes widened. "I can pass along your message, but that's got nothing to do with me."

"Alright, thank you for your time."

At the trailer of Sybil Wright and Rodney Bean, I noticed a 'Recall Sheriff Lassiter' sign at the end of the drive. Seeing it gave me a sense of pride. If shit stains on society's underwear like Rodney Bean wanted me recalled, then I was doing something right. Our knock garnered yelling.

"What the FUCK!?" The greasy, wild-haired man stomped over and flung the door open.

Paige had shoved me behind him in the second that the footsteps had approached, his hand was on his weapon, still holstered. "Sheriff's Department, show me your hands."

Rodney's hands went up. The livid anger turned to a knowing scowl on his face. "Oh, what the Hell do you want now? I haven't skipped bail."

"We're looking for Daniel Reiter. Any idea where he might be?"

He groaned. "That's what you're waking me up for? I've gotta work in a couple hours, that shit's unconstitutional."

"Daniel Reiter," Paige said again. "Where is he? Where's he going to be?"

"What do you want with Daniel?"

"We have some questions for him, he's going to want to answer them."

"I don't think you know Daniel," Rodney skeptically muttered. He crossed his arms. "If you've got something to offer Daniel, maybe you've got something to offer me."

"I'll offer you not following you around and tossing your house and your car whenever we feel like it. You holding right now?"

"His eyes are bloodshot," I chimed in, "I think he's high."

"You just woke me up, of course my eyes are bloodshot!"

"He's agitated," Paige said.

"Hysterical, paranoid." I had learned by now that a degree of obfuscating the truth was necessary in law enforcement, when dealing with the lowest hanging fruit, the dumbest of criminals.

Rodney groaned, a groan that was childish. "Daniel has a girlfriend, her name is Kelly Korman, with a K. Maybe he's there. I don't know. Leave me alone."

"Thank you for your cooperation."

We turned to go, with Paige keeping one eye on Rodney as we descended to the cruiser.

He muttered, "Pigs," as he shut the door.

Paige veered the cruiser off of the dirt driveway and ran over the flimsy 'Recall Sheriff Lassiter' sign on the way out.

Kelly Korman lived in another small house that had seen better days, outside of Reed City. Two cars were parked in the lot, one registered to Daniel Reiter. The sun was hanging low in the sky but getting higher above the tree line. It was quarter past six when Paige knocked on the door.

Daniel Reiter answered, rubbing sleep from his eyes. A bleach-blonde woman peered over his shoulder.

"Mr. Reiter, we're going to need you to come with us."

## Chapter Twenty-One

We had Reiter in an interrogation room as seven o'clock rolled around. Paige had gotten him a cup of coffee. Reiter was more put together than the likes of Frank Gillespie, Rodney Bean. He looked sober, even with a day's stubble, his reddish blonde hair askew, and bags under his eyes.

Paige explained. "We have Deputy Kipling in interrogation room one. We have State Police at the marina, where last night, a drug deal went down on the Department's boat, and someone took a shot at Evelyn. State Police are also on sight at an island upriver from Chattanooga where the drugs were acquired. This network is crumbling, IAB is due at nine, this is your last chance to do yourself a favor."

Reiter looked indignant at the suggestion, he crossed his arms. "What does this have to do with me?"

"You have connections to Frank Gillespie, who overdosed on Blue 82 after being shot. To Rodney Bean, who was caught carrying it after your weekly card game. We have a CI that puts you at the center of this. Are you going to wait for the walls to close in, trust your associates to leave your name out of it, while they're doing hard time?"

Reiter kept his voice low. "I don't think you've got anything."

We were standing. Paige leaned closer over the metal table. "Are we going to find gunshot residue on your hands?"

"Do you have a warrant?"

We didn't, but I thought from his answer that he was the one who had shot at me, at the marina. It sent a chill down my spine. Reiter wouldn't meet my eye. Paige and I stepped out, stood outside of the locked door once again.

"Someone has to give," I said.

"You sure hope so," he replied, "But it's not always the case."

"We know he's involved!"

"Not beyond a reasonable doubt, and not enough for a warrant."

"Campbell implicates him…"

"He says that Raegan instructed him not to charge Reiter, that isn't enough."

"We can work on his girlfriend, the others from the card games. What about Jason Geraci? He's the competition, maybe he can point us in the right direction. We can bring Dennis Wright in."

Paige nodded, his face had gone unreadable. "I'll do what I can, and I'll handle giving IAB the rundown when they get here. We did what we could, we shut this down for now, and maybe it's enough to get Harry

Santiago's charges dropped. But for now, Raegan is still untouchable, and Kipling and Reiter will probably be out of here, today. Grab your stuff, I'm taking you to school."

I did a double-take, looked between him and the clock. "No. I need to be here."

"You don't. Let it go, focus on your future."

I felt morose as he drove me to school. I was early, had time to eat a sullen second breakfast before Delilah showed up.

She took one look at me and asked, "What's wrong?"

"We don't have to watch the boat anymore."

She helped herself to a few of my grapes. "Why's that?"

I took her through the night's events. When I mentioned the perpetrator taking a shot at me, her mouth fell open. She looked around.

"Oh my God. Evelyn…"

"All for nothing. All of it. All those nights."

"Not for nothing. It sounds like the State is going to shut down whatever cook shack is out on that island. And Kipling is going down, right?"

"Maybe. But Raegan isn't unless someone else flips, and they can tell we don't have enough, they can sense it, somehow. Or else, they've all been around cops too long, they know not to trust when we say we've got them pinned to the wall. Paige seems to think there's nothing else we can do."

"Look on the bright side."

"What's that?"

"You get your nights back, just in time for summer. You did get a crooked deputy off of the force."

"There might be enough to drop the charges against Harry Santiago. His sister might be able to go home."

"That's great, isn't it?"

I knew that she was right. I was just too proud, too hungry for justice or revenge to enjoy the small victory. I wanted Raegan behind bars. Daniel Reiter and Rodney Bean, too. But mostly Raegan. I took the last few green grapes in my cup and pushed them across the table to her.

"How have you been?"

She shrugged, sheepish. "All signed up to go to CSCC."

"What?" I was flabbergasted. "You? Community college? You're the smartest person I know."

"Well, it's not all about how smart you are. Even with a few scholarships, it just doesn't make sense not to get our basic credits out of the way, you know?"

I nodded, forcing a smile. "You'll do great, no matter where you go."

It stayed on my mind for a while. I would have thought that Delilah's parents were well-off, financially. I guess appearances can be deceiving. Delilah wanted to study marketing and graphic and web design, anything to get her comic off the ground, so that she could draw and create for a living. I had heard her talk about the design programs at multiple colleges, never Chattanooga State Community College… I hoped she wasn't too disappointed. I hoped that her talent and her brains would get her where she needed to be, regardless of her alma mater.

The school day was long, I struggled through. Something about the long night, the adrenaline that had pumped but long since left my system made me more tired than I had ever been before. I dreaded going home, since it would mean explaining everything to my parents. I considered omitting the shooting, but I could not lie to them after all the help that they had given me.

Paige called me after school, as Scott was driving me home.

"What's happening?" I answered.

"State Police went out to the island where Kipling went last night. They arrested one man, James Earl, and found equipment and supplies to cook large amounts of Blue 82. He hasn't said a word since his arrest, not even with his lawyer present and advising him to cooperate. Kipling and Reiter are stonewalling, too. If it was Reiter on the boat, last night, he was wearing gloves. And so was Kipling, must have been, or else the pound of Blue 82 on the boat was wiped clean of prints. I tried the girlfriend, I tried Jason Geraci, I went to Dennis and Sybil Wright. No one is talking."

"How can this be? Since when are criminals so loyal?"

"They're probably serving their own interests. They'll turn on a fellow low-life quick enough, but a former Sheriff? Raegan has connections, it wouldn't go well for them after the fact."

"So where are we?" I asked.

"IAB thinks we can't charge Kipling with theft, just write him up for misconduct. He has past write-ups, so it would be within your rights to let him go. Or play the long game, suspend him but let him get back to duty, hope that he screws up again."

"How can that be all that we can do? We knew the boat was smuggling drugs. It was empty, and then he took it out to that island, and then there were drugs on it."

"He has reasonable doubt because we know that someone was on that boat, handling the drugs, after he was."

"I should never have let Reiter onboard," I said, with a heaviness in my stomach.

"There was nothing else you could have done."

"Not with a toy gun. But if I'd carried my real one…"

"It would have made no difference. You wouldn't have stopped him from going onboard. If you had gotten into a shootout, you would be dead."

"So what now?"

"Get some sleep tonight. I'll see you after school, tomorrow?"

"Alright."

We hung up. Scott was driving, but he kept glancing over at me, could read my mood easily enough.

"Hit a road block?"

"Big one."

"You'll figure it out." He shrugged. "You're smart."

"I don't feel smart, right now." All of that time, wasted, thinking that catching someone in action on the boat would be enough. I realized that a part of me wanted to weep for that wasted time, but the tears weren't coming.

"You probably just need some sleep."

I nodded. We were turning down my driveway. When Scott put the truck in park, I unbuckled, turned and threw an arm around his shoulders for a quick hug. "Thanks."

"Anytime." He rubbed my back, was blushing when I pulled away.

I climbed out and ran inside; it had started to rain.

Mom and Dad were both home, as luck would have it. Apparently Dad had been scheduled to do a roof, and the incoming rain had pushed the project back. They had texted me when they woke up, I had sent them only a perfunctory reply to let them know that I was alright and that I would see them after school.

I sat them down on the couch and walked them through the night's events. Dad crossed his arms and glowered as I discussed confronting the man on the boat, him shooting at me. Mom pinched her mouth an instant after I saw her lip tremble, her face froze as she looked away. They were Mad.

"Where was Paige?" Mom was the one to ask.

"Arresting Kipling. It's not his fault, he told me to stay put, no matter what. In fact," I said it as I realized it, "If I had stayed put, we could have maybe followed the guy who came to get the drugs. And maybe we'd be somewhere in our investigation."

"What do you mean?" Her tone was still icy.

"Basically nothing came of it all. We got Kipling for misconduct, but not enough to charge him for the drugs, because the guy on the boat got away. And even though our tracker puts him offshore of the island where the drugs were being made, it's not enough. Nobody is flipping on each other, in this network. We have nothing on Raegan besides Deputy Campbell's word that he was ordered to let Daniel Reiter off the hook, and the apparent failure of Raegan and Kipling to investigate the Santiago case. It just looks like good ol' boys being bros and letting their friend's nephew off of the hook."

"Burying the Lede, here, Eves," Dad muttered.

"You were almost killed," Mom agreed. "Our only daughter. We didn't spend all this time raising you just to end up burying you. I think this has gone far enough, you should resign before they can recall you, anyway-."

"-No, I can't do that. I'm sorry that this scared you so much, it scared me too. I'm not going to be doing anything like that, again. For now I'm going to get some sleep, but then I'm going to get up and start thinking about how to get these sons of bitches."

"Language," Mom said, a reflex.

My parents were crestfallen, they looked to each other and said nothing for a long minute, communicating with their eyes. I stood awkwardly, third-wheeling, for as long as I could take it. Then I headed for the sliding door to head out back.

"Okay, good talk. Chores, eating, sleeping, plotting to do…"

\*

In the morning, I was up at five, my sleep schedule was a mess. I sat with a coffee and some peanut butter toast on the little back porch, pushing the swing back and forth with one toe, rocking gently in the twilight. I had no messages from Paige, nothing new seemed to have developed.

Dad got up at six, and by then, I had tended to Mabel and was ready for second breakfast. I had heard him stirring, going to the bathroom, so I had started him a coffee.

"Good morning," I said. "Coffee's on. Can you make eggs?"

"Didn't I hear the toaster already?"

I threw on a Hobbit accent. "I've had one, yes, but what about second breakfast?"

"Hm," he chuckled. "You're in better spirits."

"Been thinking about some things we can look into today. There has to be some little detail we can trace to Raegan. Like, something that Delilah said yesterday… It's all about money, so where's the money going?"

Dad turned the oven on, put butter into the pan. He cracked eggs into a glass bowl. He started whisking them. It was a long, silent minute before he spoke. "I'm worried about you, Eves. You could have been shot-." His voice cracked with emotion, his shoulders slumped, he set the bowl down on the counter with a clatter. I could hear him taking a few deep breaths, trying not to cry. It was a thorn in my side.

"I know."

"Do you?" His voice came out sharp, skeptical.

"I'm sorry. It was dumb not to listen to Paige, I know that, now. I'm not looking to get into any shootouts, I promise."

He heaved out a big sigh. "Okay. I hear you. How many eggs do you want?"

"Two and a half, please."

He cracked one more egg, whisked, seasoned. When he poured them in the pan, they sizzled and a puff of steam rose up. He added some fresh cracked black pepper, stirred them with a wooden spatula.

Mom got up, she had big bags under her eyes and looked her age, for once. She looked at me, then poured herself a glass of water, straight from the tap, and chugged it. I felt guilty, wished she would put me out of my misery, start in, pop the balloon of tension growing bigger in between us.

Instead she pulled on her boots and went outside with the egg basket.

Dad set a plate down in front of me, spooned eggs onto it. "Brr…"

"At least it's pizza day at school."

## Chapter Twenty-Two

We couldn't get bank records without a warrant, but we could get cell phone records. We perused them in my office after school, highlighting recurring numbers, long conversations. It was tedious work. It was the second to last week of May; I had one week of school left, only four days, because Monday was Memorial Day. There was to be a parade, basically the entire department was to be on duty that day, between patrolling and actually monitoring the day's events. Still, Paige was on board with me firing Kipling when he showed up for his night shift at eight. We set our papers aside, and waved him into the office.

He was dressed for duty, he was armed. He squared his shoulders and held his head high as he walked in; he had to suspect that he was at least being suspended.

When Paige shut the door behind him, moving around to the side of my desk, I stood, too. Kipling folded his arms. Said nothing.

"You're relieved of duty. Permanently."

"As long as you're sheriff, you mean." He had a snakelike smile.

"Turn over your badge and sidearm."

He inhaled, exhaled, getting red in the face and steaming like a tea kettle, but still smiling, still looking down at me. I realized that I was more scared of him than someone like Raegan; Raegan had a mean streak, too, but his was more controlled. This guy was a pipe bomb ready to blow. He unhooked his badge, set it down on the edge of my desk. His movements were slow. He unhooked his gun, it took a second longer. Paige had his hand on his own gun, standing back against the wall, watching closely, ready to pull in an instant. Kipling laid the gun down, as slowly as a person could, not breaking eye contact.

"It's alright," he said. "I've got others."

Then he turned and walked out.

"You should start carrying your own gun," Paige said, he was simmering.

"Not gonna happen. Let's get back to work."

We were both prepared to stay late, that night, had our sandwiches and ate them as we searched up public records of the names and businesses that Raegan called most often.

"Family he's supporting?"

"I don't think that there's anyone. Ex wife, she remarried years ago so no alimony. No kids. His mother lives in Florida, her husband was a vet and had a pension as an electrical worker, so she's living well."

"His sister owns a restaurant in Chattanooga. Could it have been struggling, you know, Covid?"

"I don't think so, not still. According to social media, it's pretty hard to get a table there. And Laura Raegan looks like she's living well."

"Can't always tell," I said, thinking of Delilah and her parents. "Okay, what about just blowing the money on himself?"

"I don't think so… he eats out a lot, but last I knew, he had a loan on the truck and a mortgage."

"We should check into that. There's the evidence of collusion, between the Santiago case and Campbell's word, that should be enough, right?"

"Maybe. If we ask the right judge."

I went back to scanning the records. "What's this, Trillium Springs?"

"Trillium Springs… assisted living facility. Not only old people, but handicapped adults as well."

"Could he have a grandparent there?" I couldn't imagine he would have a grandparent still alive, but stranger things had happened.

"Could be. Won't know until we take a drive over there."

"Now?"

"Now."

It was not visiting hours, but of course having a badge opened up certain avenues not available to the public. The sliding glass doors were locked, the front entrance was dark. We went around the back, where a light was on over a white metal door, a keypad on the side.

Paige knocked, dialing the number for the facility at the same time. It rang and rang, finally going to a mailbox. He knocked again, pounding louder, this time. The lot behind us had a few cars in it, one spot reserved for the employee of the month. Nothing was moving but the leaves on the trees overhead, the blades of grass on the lawn across, where a neat little path led to a gazebo and small pond.

Someone opened the door. A man in scrubs in his twenties stood there, blinking in confusion. "You're not my pizza. What's up?"

We showed our badges. "Can we speak to you?"

"I guess so." He wavered between inviting us in, then stepped out into the night with us. "What's up?"

"Dax Raegan, former sheriff. You know him?" He was looking at me, afraid to look Paige in the eye, I thought, so I took the lead.

"The sheriff, yeah. He comes around sometimes."

"What for?"

"Visiting…" He was uncomfortable; I thought he might be high.

"Who?"

"I don't know if that's okay to say…"

"Have you sworn an oath?" Paige demanded.

"…No?"

"Is that a question?"

"No."

I redirected, being the 'good cop'. "No oath, no responsibility. Who does Raegan know here?"

"He's a resident, his name is Hank Cottonwood."

Some recognition registered for Paige, he got his phone out and seemed to do a search, while I pushed for more details.

"Is Raegan paying for Hank to live here?"

"I wouldn't know that."

"How much would that run somebody?"

"Um… it's the nicest one in town. Maybe three or four grand a month?"

"Hm…" I leaned over and glanced at Paige's phone as he tilted it toward me. The article he had pulled up was old. Hank Cottonwood had been a high school football star in Elviston, more than thirty years ago, then he was in a pretty horrific car crash that left his girlfriend dead. His own injuries were not specified. "You work with Hank?"

"Help take care of him, you mean? Yeah."

"What kind of care does he need?"

"Uh…" He hesitated again.

"Be our confidential informant, we don't even know your name, we're just gathering some facts."

"Okay… Hank is brain damaged. He couldn't take care of himself, change his clothes. He's pretty much on auto pilot, if you take him to the bathroom, he'll go, but if you forget, he'll mess himself. He'll eat whatever you put in front of him. He seems to like being outside, especially at the koi pond."

"Thank you. Anything else?"

Paige shook his head.

"Goodnight. Enjoy your pizza."

\*

We called it a night, no hope of getting a warrant for Raegan's financials so late. We planned to work a double the next day, Saturday, so that I could still, hopefully have my Sunday off. I got a good night's sleep, ate a hearty breakfast, packed a lunch and plenty of snacks. Dad dropped me off.

When I walked in, I got the sense that something was up. A few pairs of eyes turned to me as I walked in; not only the deputies on duty but also those of a few familiar men. Jason Geraci and Roy Brighton, the dope dealer and the diner manager from Reed City, both suspected by Harry Santiago to be people Inez might have gone to for help.

I hurried up the hall the rest of the way, went through the door. "What's going on?"

Paige met me. "Inez is here. She'll only talk to you."

Jason and Roy were both putting on a tough front, on edge. I added, "What's with them?" as we passed by.

"I think she was scared to come alone. They want to protect her."

My heart skipped a beat. I hurried into the interrogation room, setting my backpack down. Inez sat across a metal table from me. She looked unhealthy; big bags under her eyes, bloodshot, having seen too much for her young age. Two Latina women in their forties stood flanking her, I thought that they were sisters. Her aunts?

"Inez… Are you okay?"

"I'm alright… You're the new sheriff, huh?"

"Yeah." I shrugged.

I felt self-conscious, talking to the girl, younger than me and braver, too. While I had been working within the bounds of the law as diligently as I could with my seventy-five to eighty-five hour weeks, she had been diving into a world no girl should ever have to. I could only hope that she hadn't suffered anything irreparable, and that she had gotten something that was worth her trouble. But I couldn't just ask her. We had all failed her.

She wasn't volunteering anything. She stared at me, then turned her gaze to her cup of coffee, sweet and creamy, with four packs of sugar empty on the metal table. She picked one up and ripped the top strip the rest of the way off, rolled it into a tight coil between two fingers. "You said you were going to clean up the town, when you were trying to get elected... is that what you've been doing?"

My guts twisted. "I've been trying. Paige and I have been trying." I nodded to Paige, standing beside me. She glanced up, but then focused back on me. The adults were a non-factor, it was basically just the two of us in the room. "We've been trying to help your brother, too, and we might have done it, cast enough doubt on the case against him, the validity of the investigation... We're just waiting on the legal process to catch up."

That made her face change, she blinked a few times, showed very cautious optimism.

"Do you have something that could help us?"

She nodded. "You talked to my mom and my brother, you probably know by now that I ran away to try to help him, somehow. Catch Raegan in the act. It wasn't easy."

She stopped again, set the rolled up strip on its side, tore another one, a straight line, from off of the empty sugar packet. Started rolling it up. I got the feeling that she was either still high or coming down from something.

I prompted her, "Tell us about it, please."

She nodded, took a deep breath. "I knew a few people in the drug scene. I never did drugs, before, but that doesn't stop a person from knowing a little about them. A lot of it is hiding in plain sight, these days... I just started asking around, meeting new people, with new stuff to sell. Acting like I wanted to get my hands on some, even start selling it, myself, crashing on people's couches. I wound up at parties on the weekends. People my age and younger, all the way up to their thirties, forties, hosting these things, living their best lives, feeling young again. Using people..."

Another torn off strip, rolled up. She set it down, picked up her Styrofoam coffee cup and chugged.

"Would you like some more?" Paige asked.

She shook her head. "You can't just ask people who their supplier is, but I kept a close eye on the dealers I knew to see who they were getting their stuff from, then went to the next rung up, and then asked if someone could get me a large quantity of Blue 82. I got ahold of a few cell phones, hid in a few closets, stayed after everyone else went home, not always hiding, sometimes just making myself look too wasted to leave, or making myself useful..." A hint of shame and a lot of anger crept into her voice. Her nose crinkled with distaste.

I wanted to get up and hug her, or reach across the table and take her hand, but it would be totally inappropriate. As it was, one of the women with her put a hand on her shoulder, the other rubbed her back, smoothed down her hair.

"I spied on people, basically. So another rung up from the people I could get in with easily, to their bosses, to their supplier, I met Daniel Reiter. I gave a fake name, I was going as Anna Salazar. I said that I wanted an ounce of Blue 82. I showed him money. I borrowed it from Roy and Jason, I didn't tell them what it was for, they just wanted to help me... He put me off for a week, saying he could get it, but he needed to hit up his guy. I went to get it, he tried to stall some more. I said I couldn't wait anymore, I had clients lined up, whatever. It had to be tonight. This was last Saturday...

"He said that he would get it. I was supposed to wait at his house, he had made some calls and was going to pick it up. I had two cell phones, one was just a cheap burner. I hid my iPhone in his seat cushion, used the tracker app to follow him. Jason drove me, we stayed a ways behind him, when he went out of town, into the woods, out toward where all the factories are... When he parked, I went on foot. Jason didn't want to go, the whole thing was outside of his comfort zone, the... the people in his line of work, they don't do that sort of thing to each other, it's frowned upon, to say the least.

"He parked down the hill, and I went creeping through the trees, on foot. I saw Daniel Reiter parked by this shack that the Elviston parks department uses for equipment, for maintaining the trails. I guess Reiter has a copy of the key. It was raining, he waited inside. I waited until the truck pulled up, that was about a half an hour after I got there. It was Raegan. When he got out,

Daniel came out, too, and started making excuses... Here, I got it all on my phone..."

As she got it out, I glanced at Paige, he nodded.

On the video, the sound of hundreds or thousands of falling raindrops created a kind of white noise. Then we heard breathing, rustling, the crinkling of leaves as footsteps landed; Inez, moving through the woods. A faint sound of inorganic material as she leaned against the side of the Parks Department's outbuilding. Then a voice that had to be Daniel Reiter's.

"Raegan, whoa, whoa, what are you doing here?"

Raegan's retort was hot, I mean *hot*. "What am I doing here? What the FUCK do you think I'm doing here? I told you, you deal with me and only me. I told you I know everything that happens in my town, and I told you we were shutting it down for a while, then I get wind of you trying to cut me out and bring in whatever filthy shit you can get your hands on!" He was seething, and a peek of video of the two of them standing there came into view around the slate grey corner of the building. He was jabbing a finger into Daniel Reiter's chest, Reiter was glowering, but not fighting back like you would expect him to.

Reiter's voice was tight, he was hardly holding back. "We had a deal, but if you're done, you're done."

"You're operating under the false assumption that just because I'm not the sheriff anymore, that means I'm no longer in charge. Well I've still got deputies that will turn your life upside down, and I've still got a thirty ought six in the truck with your name on it." His voice had dropped down, deadly serious.

"Can't stop the flow of commerce."

"Like Hell I can't. This is my town. What I say goes."

Reiter held his hands up, pleading innocence. "People are going to need their fix, they're going to get it. You wouldn't know what it's like, to need it and not have it. If you don't want to be a part of it anymore, just let me use your connection, we'll keep it clean like you like, we'll renegotiate our split to keep your palms greased."

"I said it's too dangerous right now. You try to go behind my back again, any more kids get their hands on that unclean shit -cut with whatever laxatives or drain cleaner or cheap Mexican Fentanyl is lying around- and I'll hold you responsible. I'll kill you, Reiter, do you hear me?"

"I hear you."

The video ended there. I sat back, heart racing. Just like that, Raegan was on tape, complicit. If it was admissible, that was. And I thought that it would be. I tried to remember laws about consent around recording people without their permission; if it was in public, it was fair game. And was the land that they were on public land, if it was the Parks Department's? What about Hearsay? Even if the video wasn't admissible, Inez had heard it all, she could testify to it.

"You did a great job, Inez," I said, although it felt shameful to say it. "But why did you wait a week to come forward?"

"I was worried about a lot of things. Raegan or Reiter putting the pieces together, if me being found made the news… they could realize that I was the one. And I was worried that you two might be clueless, since you didn't seem to be making any headway for the longest time, if you were looking into Raegan or Blue 82 at all. I was laying low, trying to figure out what to do, maybe send everything to the State Police or news stations. Maybe I'd be protected, as a whistle blower. I just didn't know what to do. When we saw that you had brought Kipling in, and Reiter, the family decided I could come to you, as long as we were smart about it."

"I'm sorry that it took us so long," I murmured. And then, etiquette be damned, I reached across the table and took hold of one of her hands. "I'm sorry that you had to do it."

Paige pulled up a photo of Dennis Wright on his phone. "Do you know this man?"

She studied his face for a moment. "I think so. He has big teeth, right? Someone did too much of that stuff at a party that I was at once. He showed up, looked like he had just rolled out of bed. It was the middle of the night, maybe 2am. He took care of her, I saw an IV set up, when I peeked in…" She redirected, "If you thought you could get my brother out, already, this should definitely do it, right?"

I looked to Paige to answer that one.

"Yes," he said. "We'll make copies of this, and turn it over to IAB, along with taking another run at a few of the people we know to be involved. They'll be tripping over themselves to turn on each other, now. We'll want to get your statement on paper, if you'll just sit tight. Evelyn?"

I rose to step out with him.

Inez said, "That's a toy gun you're wearing, isn't it?"

I reached for it automatically, stopped my hand. "Yeah. I can't shoot anyone, guns scare me. But I still had a job to do…"

She was looking at me with judgment, and I couldn't blame her. Paige and I stepped out. I exhaled and bent forward, low enough to touch my toes, hands on my hips, trying to focus on breathing.

Paige gave me a pat on the back. "It's alright. This is good."

"I know. It just sucks that she had to do it. Is she going to be safe, if we send her home?"

"I think so. Especially once we arrest them all, and it hits the news. I'm going to make some calls, you get her to write down her statement, how she came to be in a position to record that footage."

"Okay. You're not going anywhere?"

"Not without you, no. This is a delicate situation, him being the former sheriff, and there being bad blood between you, you just fired Kipling. And warrants can take a day, even in normal cases. I don't think we'll be going to arrest Raegan anytime today."

## Chapter Twenty-Three

We drove Inez home ourselves, both her aunts going with her. I was sure to thank Roy Brighton and Jason Geraci on our way out, assured them that she would be okay. They had deceived us, it was true, helped a teenage truant and runaway, but seeing the girl's determination firsthand, I was sure that there had been no other way, that it was better than they had helped her, provided her some small safety net. The girl's aunts rode with us out to Reed City, to the trailer where her mother had lived alone, those past weeks. Paige and I stayed in the car while they all got out.

We watched the reunion at the front door; could see inside from our position on the driveway. Inez had to stoop to hug her mother, her mother's face scrunched up into a sob before her daughter's body blocked our view of her. I felt lachrymose.

Paige did not want to bring Reiter in, to give him a chance to flip. He wanted Kipling, so that we could hit Reiter with everything the law allowed, for taking the shot at me. The problem was that neither of us thought

Kipling was likely to talk to us, or to turn on Raegan. We had nothing new on him from the last time we spoke, after all, and he had as good as threatened me after I fired him.

But Reiter was not our only option; there was the man who had been cooking up the Blue 82, out on the tiny island in the Tennessee. His name was James Earl, he was being held in Chattanooga. After submitting our new evidence to IAB and filing charges with the District Attorney, we took a drive over there.

Memorial Day weekend meant a good bit of traffic, and we sat idling on the bridge for a few minutes.

I said, "I can't believe this is finally happening." I had been excited, at first, my heart had raced and my foot had been tapping frantically the whole while I sat with Inez and her aunts as she wrote out her statement, as we copied the video. I was ready to go, but then once I was in the car, my nervous energy faded and I felt sluggish; more than a month's worth of exhaustion catching up.

"Could be looking at Racketeering charges..."

We drifted forward. The cause of the gridlock turned out to be a small fender bender up ahead. Local PD were already on the scene, but Paige stopped to check that they had it under control and got waved off.

"This is good for your recall campaign," Paige said, after a minute. "You delivered on all your promises. To help Harry Santiago, hold Raegan accountable, clean up the town."

"Thanks. Good publicity for you, too. I don't want to be recalled, but assuming I'm not, I'm resigning the second I get the results. And then I'll spend a week rallying the kids again to get you elected, then I'll rest."

"You've earned it."

At the State Police Department precinct in Chattanooga, we were greeted at the front desk by a uniformed officer. He was unimpressed by us.

"You *must* be Lassiter and Paige." He eyed me. "Wait here." He picked up his phone and hit two buttons. "Got your yokels here."

Paige crossed his arms and stared the man down. For over a minute we waited, and the man at the desk seemed uncomfortable under Paige's unflinching expression, didn't look back up and pinched his mouth into a straight line.

When a man in a suit without a jacket came through the open doorway where we could see a bullpen, he was friendlier. "Sheriff?" He assumed Paige to be the sheriff, offered his hand.

Paige did shake it, but then said, "Deputy Paige." He pointed to me. "Sheriff Lassiter."

"My mistake." He shook my hand as well. "How about that? You two can come with me. We've got Jimmy in interrogation, he lawyered up and hasn't said much, he's a real 'fuck the government' type, we know him pretty well. Comes into town to do his shopping like once a month, prior drug charges, did about four years. We'll let you talk to him, you're being recorded and I'll observe. I'm Detective Rodgers, by the way."

I thanked him as he opened the door to a little room not unlike our own back in Elviston. The metal table with a loop welded on for handcuffs to feed through.

Jimmy Earl was wearing a pair, and they clinked as he moved around, trying to get comfortable, the chain was not long enough to rest them in his lap. He was scruffy, with a gold tooth and hooded eyes.

"Who's this, now?"

"Sheriff Evelyn Lassiter, Deputy Leo Paige," I introduced us.

His lawyer was a woman in her forties with dyed hair, firetruck red, and blue eyeshadow. She wore a jacket and skirt, no panty hose. Probably a public defender. "Judith Greer. Have you come to offer my client a deal?" Straight to it; it was a Saturday, after all, and her pay was probably shitty.

Paige said, "We came to offer a chance to cooperate. If Mr. Earl wants to be the first to do that, it would probably go a long way with the DA."

"That's not good enough-," she started to say, but Earl interrupted.

"It doesn't matter, I've got nothing to say to them."

"Well hold on," I said. "You might change your tune when you hear that we filed charges against Dax Raegan this morning. We're waiting on a warrant to arrest, but it's just a matter of time. We know he was controlling the sale of Blue 82 throughout the county, working with Daniel Reiter, Frank Gillespie -who's dead- and deputy Eric Kipling. We know that you were providing that Blue 82. If you're scared of him, you don't need to be. You should make a deal for yourself."

"Hold on," Greer said. "It sounds to me like the former sheriff was using his authority and a healthy dose of fear to run an illegal organization, and that my client was coerced into making illicit substances."

Paige said, "Your client has priors, this isn't just going away."

"If you want him to help you make your case, you need to get with the DA and get something on paper."

We stepped out of the room.

Detective Rodgers was ready. "We already have a call in, we're waiting on the finalized offer. You want some coffee? There's some donuts, too."

"I'd go for a donut."

It was over an hour for the call and email from the DA's office. Detective Rodgers spoke with them, and passed along the message to us that the offer on the table was to be the only one, that more than likely Earl wasn't going to like it, that it was up to us to sell it.

We went back into the little room, took our seats across the table.

"Can we take these damn things off?" He jingled his cuffs.

"Not our house, not our call," I shrugged.

"Alright, Jimmy," Paige took over. "For the amount of a controlled substance you were caught with, and obvious intent to distribute, you're charged with a Class A Felony. You could be looking at sixty years. If Raegan confesses before you, and multiple deaths from Elviston are attributed to your product -one of them was a kid, you know, a few other kids overdosed and had permanent brain damage- you'd never be a free man again in your life." He waited.

Jimmy Earl had been staring intently at his own hands. He forced himself to look up, nod that he understood. "What's the offer?"

"Fifteen years. Out in nine with good behavior. This is the only offer that the DA is willing to make. If you don't take it, and tell us everything, you'll die in prison."

He looked at his lawyer, who just whispered something in his ear that took all of half a second to say. Probably 'take it'.

A copy of the agreement on paper went to his lawyer, signed and witnessed.

Then Jimmy Earl filled in the cracks for us, at his own vainglorious pace. "I was always good at chemistry in school, so this career path made sense to me. Some people think it's easy, it's not easy! You have to keep your ear to the ground for new developments in the business, just like anything. Keep an eye on the market, keep up with demand. And I could make a lot more if I were one for the marketing side, but I'm not. Everyone you meet wants a cut, usually more than they deserve, so by the end you've got enough to get by, but it's not what it should be, for how hard that shit is to make. It takes days of careful cooking, constant observation. They say God made the world in six days, rested on the seventh. I cooked for five days straight, and rested on the sixth.

"This whole involvement with Raegan started back in January. Somebody had robbed me, end of the month. I shot at them -I had a right, they were on my property! But they got away with some stuff. I think they must have dropped a brick while they were turning tail, how else would those dumbass kids have found it? The ones that overdosed at the marina. I didn't sell that shit, so I don't see how I'm responsible..." He waited, looking between us and his lawyer.

I nodded. "Go on."

"I don't know how Raegan traced it back to me, he said he had a lot of connections, 'friends in high places, friends in low places', he said... Maybe it was just process of elimination. But find me, he did. He had it over me, you know, he pretty much set the terms, they weren't exceptionally unfair and one of his conditions was that I only dealt with him, that made things easier on my end, I didn't get much sleep, you understand, it cut down my anxiety to have one contact, less risk of getting caught. He was the sheriff, you know. Some protection came from that.

"His other condition was that I refine the process, no cheap add-ins that would make the stuff easier to overdose on. I think he saw himself as a hero, for that, or else it just helped him justify it. I cooked for and sold to only him for a couple of months, it went smoothly. Then he lost the election. I guess he lost to you, huh?" He studied me again, apparently had just put it together.

"Yup."

"He said we had to stop, temporarily. He thought that he would be sheriff again in no time, a month, maybe. It was more than a month after that, I guess Kipling got impatient. I knew Kipling, he had been there for about half of Raegan's collections, so when he came to make another pick up, I went with it."

"When was this?" Paige was taking notes as always.

"A few nights ago. Wednesday night, Thursday morning, technically. I got the call from Raegan that morning, ass crack of dawn. That I was in deep shit, I'd better watch my back. Said he'd kill me if I so much as said his name. Y'all were busting down my door not fifteen minutes later."

"Tell us about Daniel Reiter," I prompted.

"He was a connection from before the Raegan days. He called me a little over a week ago asking for product. I acted like I was going to give it to him, but I wasn't going to cross Raegan, I told him about it, right away."

That tracked with what we knew to be true. There were i's to dot and t's to cross, we spent another hour between having him write his statement, filling in Detective Rodgers with what else we knew in the case, and talking next steps. We had Reiter with a reasonable degree of certainty on drug charges, what with multiple people putting him in Raegan's organization, but we didn't have him on trying to shoot me, and Paige wanted it to be so.

The only person who could pin that on him was Kipling. And with the writing on the wall for Raegan, it was time to bring Kipling in again, either way. His warrant had come through by the time we crossed the bridge and were back in Elviston. With it came a message that Paige was to call the DA's office.

I felt anxious when he told me that. Could Raegan have so much pull, that he could make the whole thing go away? I didn't think so, not with so much evidence, so many people to swear to witnessing his crimes.

Paige called as soon as we parked outside the department. There were more cars in the lot than I had ever seen; a pair of State Police cruisers, a few extra I recognized of our coworker's. I had called them in to patrol and man the department while we went with the State cops to arrest Kipling. We thought we needed the extra force, just to be safe.

"This is Deputy Paige, Sheriff's Department…" He waited, probably being patched through. "Hello? Yes… Yes, I understand. Thank you." He hung up, turned to me. "The District Attorney took the charges to a judge, who is granting the warrant for Raegan's arrest. The judge, however, has known Raegan for years, of course. He specified that we are not to arrest Raegan before the Memorial Day parade, and we're to let him surrender himself quietly."

"The parade?" I was dumbfounded for a minute, sleep deprived. "Oh. He's a veteran."

"He's in the parade every year. Usually carries a rifle in the American Legion's color guard."

"Those aren't loaded, are they?"

"Blanks. You're staying here, you know."

"What? No." He meant to go and bring in Kipling.

"It could be dangerous, he's the more unstable personality of the two of them. Your parents would kill me if I let you go, and we don't need you."

"We'll wear vests, I'll sit in the car, but I'm going!"

"No."

"I'm your boss," I snapped, folding my arms.

"No. You can be there when we bring Raegan in, I'm not worried about him as much. You'll get your moment. But Kipling has threatened you, and he's an irrational fool, so get out."

I scowled at him, but he stared right back, unflinching, and in the end, my respect for him won out over my stubbornness. I popped the door and got out. "Call me as soon as you have him." I would be worried all the while, I knew.

I watched out the window of my office as the men and women in the parking lot strapped on bulletproof vests. They had a blueprint of Kipling's house spread on the roof of one of the State cruisers. It looked like Paige was following the lead of a man with a big hat and badge; a lieutenant? It made sense; the force was largely theirs. The Elviston County Sheriff's Department had been short-staffed when I had started, and we had lost Raegan of course, Wilensky to maternity leave, Kipling to his misconduct, Campbell was on unpaid leave pending the results of his own IAB investigation.

The line of cars rolled out of the parking lot.

I looked at the work schedule; the one for the following week was already done, the one after would be the week of my recall. I made two potential schedules, one for if I lost my recall -it spread the schedule for patrols quite thin- and one for if I won the recall, deciding that I would finish the week or maybe two while cajoling the local busybodies to throw together another election.

I kept checking my phone. More than an hour passed, and I became sure that something was wrong. But I couldn't call Paige. If I called him in the wrong moment, and his phone was on? Was he alright?

I was so anxious that when it finally rang, I jumped halfway out of my skin and dropped it. It was Paige calling. "Hello?"

He went right into it. "Kipling wasn't at home, his cell phone isn't pinging anywhere, and his mother seems to think that he was going away for a while. I put an APB out, but it looks like he's in the wind."

## Chapter Twenty-Four

I found it hard to focus as Paige and I patrolled for a few more hours that Saturday. It was equally hard to sleep, that night. I didn't like the thought of Kipling out there, somewhere, knowing that we were trying to find him, feeling persecuted, feeling the walls closing in. He had to know that his associates were in custody, and that they had turned on him. I wondered if he had gone to Raegan.

Sunday was my day off. Kathy had wanted me to go to church with her and Paige again, since the recall vote was on Tuesday. I didn't want to go, but she thought it could be crucial. I dressed up, did my makeup, talked to the ladies and sat through a dull service. Afterward Todd Brooks -of wing tips and hair gel- cornered me by the free coffee.

"Hey there, Sheriff… Tough luck about the recall."

I shrugged. "I'm not worried. Are you registered?"

"Of course, I'm a progressive young man of a certain age… Don't want to tell you how I'm voting though, if I do, it might not come true." He winked, was smiling slickly.

"Uh-huh. Nice talking to you, again." I veered off, moving for the door. I had searched him in the database, after our last meeting. I knew that he wasn't criminal, just a bit odd.

Abigail Springstead caught me in the doorway. "Hold on, Sheriff. It's time for our interview."

"Do you even go to this church?"

"Do you?"

"Touche. Right here?"

"No. Let's sit down by the trees."

I told Kathy and Paige to go without me, asked Mom and Dad if one of them could come and pick me up. "You've got maybe fifteen minutes," I told Abby.

"That's plenty." She had her phone out, started recording with an app. "Take me through everything."

"You won't share this before tomorrow, will you?" I wasn't necessarily worried about Raegan, he had to know by now that the net was closing in. It just seemed like the thing to say; the DA had specified that Raegan was to be allowed to surrender, after the parade, with dignity.

"If that's what you need."

"How do I know I can trust you?"

"Don't insult my journalistic integrity, Evelyn…"

Safe in the holy cloisters of my humble home once again, I spent some time on social media. I posted on my 'Reelect Evelyn Lassiter' Facebook page, started by Delilah, reminding everyone that the vote was coming up, to overnight their mail-in ballots if they hadn't sent them in already, or find their polling places. I also outlined what I had achieved so far, and what I still hoped to.

I had no homework, I was heading into my last week of school. Mom and Dad had planned for us to make our own pizzas. We played rummy while they were in the oven.

"You're working during the parade, tomorrow?"

"Yes."

"We'll look for you."

They would be there, of course. Parades were a big deal, in a small town. And my Grandpa led the parade every year. He was the Commander of the Elviston American Legion, the head of the color guard. A Vietnam vet, short and stout, gray haired and a smoker for more than fifty years, so his laugh was like sandpaper, but still infectious. It would be a full day for him, I knew. A lot of the Legion vets couldn't drive or really get around anymore. He would pick them up anywhere in the county, even if they just needed to get to the doctor, and especially for a parade, so that they could get dressed in their old uniforms and relive their glory days. He thought there was no greater duty than to serve those who had served their country. He drove a big truck with a king cab to pile them in, hauling wheelchairs and scooters in the back.

He was decent and proud, like that. He would probably think that me getting myself elected sheriff and running up a Black Lives Matter flag next to the stars and stripes was a shameful display. I wouldn't know; we hadn't spoken in months. He was hard to talk to, these days, with the contention dripping off. Of course he would still give anyone in the family the shirt off his back, but he couldn't carry on a conversation without railing against the liberals.

I missed the man he used to be before Fox News and Donald Trump got ahold of him.

I looked over the plans for the Memorial Day parade in my room that evening. I had the order of marchers, including a few 'floats' which were mostly just trucks with banners strung along them to cart veterans too old or disabled to walk. I had last year's plan as well which stationed a deputy every few blocks along Main Street, with cruisers parked and road blocks erected at tributary streets, plus one driving around the parallel streets keeping an eye on things. I saw no reason to change it.

A little after eight o'clock, I got a message from Deputy Stanton, who was on duty, saying that Kipling's truck had been found at a truck stop on the highway just outside of Reed City. Either he had abandoned it and hitched a ride out of town, knowing he wouldn't get out of the state himself, or he wanted us to think that he had, or, more probably -because he was a dumbass- he had been taking a leak in the bushes when he saw the cruiser pull up, and had taken off running through the woods, on foot, but in country he knew well. I could picture it vividly, him red in the face, swearing and sweating as he ran, a few drops of piss on his pants.

I didn't see him running. He had lived in Elviston County all his life. He had unfinished business; he still wanted revenge on me. I bet that truck was the last thing he had, besides his guns. He thought I had taken everything from him.

I checked the locks on the doors and every window in the house, all were secure. But as I laid down, thoughts of the glass being broken on the far side where I wouldn't hear it, and Kipling coming creeping through the house kept me awake. I got up a little after ten, made a coffee as quietly as I could, got my Dad's rifle out of its cabinet; I knew where he kept the key. Holding that rifle in my lap, -sitting in one of the hard wooden kitchen chairs so that I wouldn't get comfortable and fall asleep- with it loaded but with the safety on, I didn't feel anxious like I had shooting recreationally at the gun range. I actually felt calmer. I didn't entertain thoughts of shooting Kipling, or anyone. I didn't want to. I didn't know if I could. But whatever came next, I would be ready.

The front door was on my right, the curtains pulled over the wide windows. The slider through the kitchen was on my left, it was mostly exposed but it led to the backyard, the chicken coop. There was a simple wire fence out there that would trip a person up, or at least slow them down, make their approach awkward.

It was a long and dull night, but I had come to appreciate the act of spending time for the sake of vigilance, for my peace of mind. I respected myself, I realized. That was something that a year or even a few months ago, I would not have been able to tell you was missing from my life. I thought having the best friends, good grades, a great sense of style were the last word in accomplishments for a girl. But I must have been seeking it, subconsciously, way back when I ran my campaign and got elected.

At five to six, I unloaded the rifle. I opened the gun cabinet and was tucking it back inside as quietly as a mouse when my parents' bedroom door opened, and Dad slipped out. The house was a rectangle, the hall leading to the bedrooms was a straight shot to the gun cabinet on the other end, the living room's far wall.

He froze, looking at me.

I shut the cabinet, locked it, suddenly anxious. I hung the key back up on the hook on the bottom of the upper kitchen cabinets, among the coffee mugs dangling by their handles. Hit the power button on the Keurig.

Dad came to stand next to me. "What were you doing, Eves?" He didn't call me my full name, that was a good sign.

I started filling the reusable pod with pungent coffee grounds. "They found Kipling's truck but not Kipling. I just couldn't sleep, he blames me for his problems."

"Why didn't you tell me?" He sounded wounded, probably feeling emasculated.

"I didn't want you to worry. And I wasn't really worried, anyway. Just better safe than sorry."

He wasn't mad, he pulled me into a hug, squeezing me tight. "Stop growing up so fast."

"Can't help it."

Mom got up and Dad didn't mention the rifle or the Kipling situation to her. We ate omelets, I got dressed. When I came back out in my uniform, with my hair up and my makeup tastefully done, Dad blinked.

"Need a ride?"

"Paige is picking me up, he'll be here any minute. We have to set up road blocks and check for bombs and stuff before the parade."

Mom said, "Okay, we'll see you there. Be safe."

Dad walked me out, putting a hand on my shoulder as we stood on the porch and saying, "Hold on, Eves."

Paige was pulling up in a cruiser.

Dad went down to meet him, I stood back and gave them their privacy, although I was beginning to feel anxious again, even through my sluggishness. He wouldn't try to make me stay home, would he? I didn't want the morning to turn into one big fight, but I had a job to do, and I was going to do it. Mom taught me not to let angry men get the better of me, that applied to threats big and small, in my mind. If I stopped living my life because of Kipling, he had won.

Dad and Paige talked for all of thirty seconds, then Dad came back up to me. He put both hands on my shoulders, looked down at me. "I wish you wouldn't go, today, if there's an angry redneck on the loose. But I won't try to stop you. Just promise me that if anything happens, you won't be a hero."

"I promise."

"I want your phone on, I'm going to text you as soon as Mom and I get there. Tell me where you're stationed so that I can stay close. Until then, I want you with Paige at all times. Agreed?"

"Yeah. I'll see you soon."

"I love you."

"Love you too." I kept it casual, went down the steps, climbed into the cruiser. As soon as the door was shut, I asked, "What did he say to you?"

"Just to keep an eye on you, which I was already planning on."

"Did you get any sleep?"

"A little. I've got a good security system."

He backed down the drive, looking over his shoulder. When he stepped on the brakes suddenly, I lurched in my seat. My hand went to my hip even though my gun was essentially a toy, I whirled and searched the horizon through the back window.

"What is it?"

"A chicken."

I groaned, got out. As I hurried to scoop the errant chicken up, I was looking into the trees on either side of me, looking for any signs of movement. I saw nothing but branches bending low in a sudden gust of wind, the dew sparkling in the morning light. I ran the chicken back around to the coop, passed it through the fence. Ran back to the cruiser. When I got settled inside again, sanitized my hands from the bottle Paige always kept in one of the cup holders, I realized my heart was hammering. My hands shook, adrenaline had spiked and was receding.

It was going to be a long day.

## Chapter Twenty-Five

The roadblocks erected, the wide street emptied of cars along the old-fashioned looking buildings for a few blocks of downtown, the parade had plenty of space to creep through. It was three lanes wide; an eastbound, a westbound, and a turn lane, plus the wide sidewalk gave way for two-hour parking for a few cars on each side, in between fire hydrants on each corner.

There was a sound system, with speakers hung on streetlamps along with American flags. It played old patriotic classics, and some food carts had been erected, some played their own tunes, too, along with a cacophony of chatter, sizzling onions and peppers and hot dogs and brats on a grill.

An hour before the parade was to begin, people had begun to stake out the best spots in the front, with lawn chairs and blankets spread out, old folks, families with young children. In the half hour before, the rest of the sidewalk had filled. Most of the town had to be there, and plenty from Reed City, too. They were shoulder to shoulder, not troubled at all by the crowd. Kids bobbed and weaved between the legs of adults, holding snow cones and popsicles and ice cream. Some were hurling those little popping things at people's feet; an old man snapped at them but forgot his anger a moment later when he saw a friend, waved a hand over the crowd and shouted.

"Bill! Bill, over here!"

A lot of people were dressed in red white and blue, a lot of them wore shirts advertising branches of the armed forces, boasting that they were a proud Army Mom, a girl I recognized as being a year older than me wore one that said, 'I love my Marine', there was a whole flock of beleaguered looking Navy Wives.

Everywhere I saw faces I knew.

Lots of schoolmates. Marcus Campbell and a group of other senior boys wore crop tops. I didn't let his hip bones distract me for more than a second. Delilah was in the marching band, they were in their red and black uniforms, epaulettes and big hats with chin straps. She played the oboe. Scott was milling around; his mom was parked in the Ex Wife with a good view of the street, I guess the holiday meant that five o'clock came early.

Mrs. O'Connell, her husband and their litter of small children, all dressed up and faces painted. Her belly had grown massive, she was dressed as Lady Liberty with a green spiked crown, her youngest toddler had his hair styled like a torch and was hoisted up on her hip.

She saw me and called out, "Hi Evelyn!" Then, gesturing to herself, she added, "Getting a little more use out of my Halloween costume."

I gave her two thumbs up.

I saw Rodney Bean and Sybil Wright, they were with a toothy man who had to be one of her brothers, and his family. Dennis had been charged with Obstruction, and that was all, so far, but he was awaiting arraignment at the county jail. Operating without a medical license might stick, although the DUI was too long gone, and I didn't really want to see him in jail for long, anyway. I hoped and thought he had learned his lesson.

Daniel Reiter's girlfriend gave me the stink eye.

There was Melissa Arlington and her family, the picture of perfection.

Bert and Delilah's parents were in the front, ready to see her march, they all said polite hellos to me as Paige and I patrolled our block. Kathy and my parents stood together near the corner where we finally parked ourselves as the parade began. Grandpa led the parade, looking regal in his dress blues, holding a rife in the color guard. He didn't notice us, kept his gaze forward and his movements precise. There was Raegan, dressed the same, in formation behind him, with a dozen others ranging from early-fifties to geezer.

I bet that Raegan would turn himself in right after it was over, with local news crews around, with the town the most primed to 'boo' those of us arresting him as they would ever be. He probably wanted the dog and pony show, he was probably betting on a sweetheart deal considering his years of service and standing in the community or else he would go for jury nullification.

The crowd applauded and cheered as they passed, beaming, some crying tears of sorrow or tears of pride. I felt pity for the ones who had obviously lost a relative and were reliving that pain, slapping a Band-Aid of Nationalism on their bullet hole of senseless loss.

I also felt pity for the ones who led such small lives that the chance to celebrate their country -most of which they had never seen and never would- and mingle with friends and eat a hot dog was one of the highlights of their year. But at the same time, they all looked happier than I felt, so maybe I was the one who was wrong. Maybe neither of us was, we were just different, and I was just being self-righteous, like the church service all over again.

And at the same time as I was turning it all over, I knew that I was lucky to be an American. I was grateful to be, too. I wouldn't say 'proud'. America had been embarrassing me a little too much, lately. I wanted to be proud of her, but she wouldn't let me. So I could feel my patriotism and my conscience wrestling inside me, like a couple of babes in star-spangled bikinis Jell-o wrestling on a hot, summer day.

Most of the buildings on Main Street had second stories, apartments over their shops. A dozen or more windows on the block where I stood alone, with the bright sun overhead gleaming off of them, making me squint when I tried to look inside them. A dozen or more opportunities for Kipling to perch with a rifle. He wouldn't need some fully automatic death machine, although he could surely get one if he wanted.

I was on edge as the parade languidly passed by. The marching band was playing Stars and Stripes Forever, and I had to keep reminding myself that I was not JFK.

When my parents had showed up, Paige had taken up his own station across the street. At moments when I felt anxious, I looked over and saw him there, scanning the crowd around me with intense focus, hand resting on his gun. There were shots of blank rounds coming from the rifles at the front of the parade, mostly in synch with each other, and on the odd beat of the drums, where they were supposed to be, and I tuned them out after the first few.

A truck strung with streamers rolled by. Grizzled veterans rode in the cab and in the bed, waving. The single traditional float built on a trailer and towed by one such truck was advertising the America Legion post, and marked the end of the short parade. A few of the spry members tossed out red, white and blue beads, handfuls of candy. Parents let their children flood the street to scoop up what was mostly Tootsie Rolls and cheap Dum Dum suckers. A girl barely toddling tumbled headfirst when she tried to grab a piece of that cheap, chalky blue and yellow bubblegum, started bawling. Her mother scooped her up and rocked her, shushing.

When I heard the gunshot, I didn't register it as being wrong for a full second. Nobody else did, either, although it came from beyond the back of the parade. Faces turned that way, smiles froze, chatter stopped midsentence but the band kept playing their tinny rendition of America the Beautiful. I blame the grogginess for not putting it together until the first woman screamed, and the whole crowd of women and children echoed her half a second later, radiating toward us at the front.

Paige drew his weapon and ran into the street. On the next corner, Stanton and Wilensky did the same, I started to follow them instinctively but my father materialized at my side and caught my arm. Kathy was beside us, eyes wide, terrified, watching her husband hurry toward danger, alone in the street.

"Get back," I told her, giving her a push in the direction that the crowd was going; she hesitated for an instant, but then went.

"Where are you, Sheriff!?" A shout came from up the road.

The street and sidewalks emptied, the crowd surging back into the tributary roads, between the relative safety of the buildings, but plenty lingered there, peering out to get a look at what was happening.

With the crowd thinning, I found myself waving them by, catching a girl a few years younger than me and shoving her on, saying, "Go, go!" I couldn't run with them, as much as I wanted to, they were my responsibility. I could see Kipling in the middle of the road. He had a gun in his hand, had just fired up into the air, but lowered his arm so that the barrel pointed at the ground. He found my father and me, his eyes narrowed, teeth bared, face red and sweating. There were still people fleeing around us, terrified parents scooping their kids up, half the marching band had run for the buildings on our side, half the other. Dad tried to move me but Kipling barked out an order that froze us in place.

"Don't you move, Missy!" Kipling's gun hand had twitched, but his arm did not raise; he was still aiming at the ground but that could change in an instant.

Dad looked at the last few stragglers moving around us like a rock in a river; I knew what he was thinking, because I was thinking the same thing. That Kipling didn't want the civilians in the way, didn't care about them, but he might start shooting if we made a break for the jewelry store, the last building on our corner. A lot of people would be in the crossfire. Dad planted himself, reaching back, holding my arm in a tight grip to keep me behind him. My heart was in my throat and my body was telling me to run, but I couldn't move a muscle. I peered around Dad's shoulder to keep an eye on Kipling, I couldn't help it.

Three of my deputies were standing in the street. Wilensky and Stanton were two points in the triangle, closer to Kipling. Paige was dead center, a few steps back. Two more deputies came from the next block up, from behind Kipling. All had their guns raised, and several shouted orders.

"Drop it!"

"Put your hands up!"

Kipling hollered, "Nobody move!" And his voice shot up into a higher pitch, a frantic cry.

He was twitching in place, not looking behind him, not looking at any of the deputies, just at my father and me. Nobody was going to shoot him yet; his gun was still pointed at the ground. He looked unsure, suddenly, like he hadn't thought it through, didn't know what came next. That probably made him more dangerous.

"What's the plan, Eric?" Paige kept his tone calm, his gun was steady in both of his hands.

My legs were shaking, I could collapse at any second.

Kipling answered, still glaring at me, "I'm not going to jail."

"That's not up to you," was Paige's cool reply. "I'll shoot you in the leg. You'll be in jail and in pain, if you don't drop that gun."

Kipling took a step, he was unsteady and about to fly off the handle. "That little BITCH has it out for me!" He jabbed the air with a finger, the hand that didn't hold the gun. The one that did trembled, but stayed down, like the thing was weighted down. Hating someone was one thing, actually shooting them was something else. But he took another step, sneered at me. "Are you scared?"

I nodded, found my voice. "Yes." I was scared, and I was scared for my father, still silently and resolutely standing in front of me.

"In over your head?" Kipling asked, next.

"Yes." I would say whatever he wanted me to. They would shoot him if he tried to shoot me, that was for sure, but I couldn't know that he wouldn't get a shot off, hit my Dad. My nerves jangled but my common sense told me to keep him talking. Self-preservation was a powerful thing. He had to have it, too. It could still win out.

"Put it down, Eric!" One of the deputies inched closer behind him. They were spread out wide on the sidewalk, so that they were not in the cross hairs of the ones closer to me, vice versa.

"You don't want to do this," the other said. His tone was softer; were they friends? Had they worked together for years? Would they be able to pull the trigger, to stop him from shooting me? Most of them didn't like me…

Kipling heard them, he looked less sure. Beads of sweat dripped down from his hairline, into his eyes. He wiped them with his free hand. When he spoke again, his tone was more level. He still addressed me. "So you're the sheriff, you can get yourself elected, play with the big boys, but at the end of the day, you still need a man to protect you."

I nodded. "You're right."

He liked that, smiled for a second. "You kids don't know about right and wrong, these days. You don't know about consequences!" His voice spiked again, he was getting himself worked up.

"Eric, what the Hell are you doing?" A new voice came from behind me. I stole a glance and couldn't believe it. It was Raegan, dressed up, unarmed, walking up the street like he wasn't afraid at all. He had an incredulous look on his face, hands on his hips as he planted himself in the center of the street.

Paige glanced over his shoulder, just a fraction of a second. He apparently weighed the new development, stook three big steps to the left, toward my side of the street. Wilensky followed his lead, they spread out more to make room for Raegan and Kipling to face each other.

Kipling looked from me to Raegan and back. "She ruined everything!"

"You ruined everything," Raegan shot back, as casual as could be. He crossed his arms over his chest. "I told you we had to stop."

Kipling couldn't believe what he was hearing from his friend and mentor. "You know I've got bills! New truck is forty grand! That ain't fair!"

"Life ain't fair. Can't blame the girl for that. You're acting like a little no-account *pussy*." He spat on the ground.

"Don't say that." Kipling's tone was less uneven but turned venomous. "You started all of this! You lost that election."

"You're right. I can't blame anybody but myself for how it went down, really… They say you can judge a man by the company he keeps… And I kept company with a bunch of stupid sons of bitches-."

Kipling's face pinched into a furious scowl and he brought his gun up, but the three shots that fired in the same instant hit him and knocked him off his balance. He never fired his gun, just hit the ground. The two deputies on his sides charged in, kicked his gun away, knelt and applied pressure to his wounds.

The boom of the gunshots hit me like a slap, Dad jolted. I was sure for an instant that Dad and I had both been hit. But then Mom was beside us, waking us from our stupor, and I looked down at myself, I registered no pain, Dad had no wounds, either. We held each other, all three of us, awkwardly. I saw Kathy run to Paige over Mom's shoulder.

"Leo!"

"It's alright, stay back." He let her hug him for an instant, but then broke away.

People had already crept back into the street, Wilensky was herding them back on our side, Stanton on the other.

"Stay out of the street!"

"Clear the street! This is a crime scene, give the man some room."

An ambulance had been stationed only one block back, and the medics were on the scene not one full minute after the shooting.

Over Dad's shoulder, I saw Raegan walking up the street. "Eric, don't you die on me, you pansy! I swear to God!" What he swore to, I didn't know, but I could hear his desperation where a minute ago he had been untouchable.

I heard one of the deputies demand, "Really, Sheriff?" And he was talking to Raegan, not me, of course.

Raegan answered, "Can't blame a dog for biting you if you didn't train it well… Lassiter!"

I pried my mother's arms off of me, she was crying. "It's okay."

I took a deep breath, still feeling shaky and surreal as I went to join them up the street. I could smell the alcohol and sweat coming off of Kipling from a stone's throw away. I said nothing. I didn't say 'thank you', I didn't think Raegan would want to hear it, and I hated him too much, even if I did owe him something, even if I knew that he didn't do it for me. He did have some kind of principals, I had figured that out, by now.

Raegan said, "Parade's over. You and Paige can take me in, now."

Of course. He looked plenty heroic, he looked good in his dress blues, half the town was still watching and so were the local news cameras. A tiny part of me wanted to think that they had planned the whole thing, but that was just the bitter hatred for them both talking, my self-pity. I shook it off. I could let him have his moment, not just for him, but for what he meant to the town.

"Alright." I waved Paige back when he went for his cuffs, took out my own. I couldn't let him be the one to do it, a bunch of them would see me as the bad guy, arresting the hero, the veteran, on Memorial Day, no less. Maybe the DA would be pissed, too, but I thought it was the right thing to do. Let them all say what they want, take it to the polls on Tuesday. "Dax Raegan, you're under arrest for the distribution of controlled substances, you have the right to remain silent, anything you say can and will be used against you-."

Alanna Malone pushed toward us with a camera, "Sheriffs, does either of you have a comment?"

"Get back," Paige got between us.

The boos had started, rose higher.

I raised my voice and kept Mirandizing. "You have the right to an attorney…"

The crowd thinned a block back, and we loaded Raegan into the back of the cruiser. He bowed his head, moved willingly, said nothing, just sighed. I watched his face as I closed the door, locking him in. His jaw gave a small clench.

"You alright?" Paige asked, standing at the side of the car.

I didn't want to seem weak, but I considered, answered honestly. "I can't believe that just happened."

"It's a crazy world." It seemed he had no words of wisdom for me.

"Do you think Kipling will live?"

"No great loss, if he doesn't."

"I couldn't shoot someone... are *you* okay?"

"I'm okay. And you think you couldn't shoot someone... Right now, that's probably true, and it's a good thing. In a couple years? If someone was threatening one of your friends?" He opened the door, slid into the driver's seat.

I hurried around to my side, climbed in after him. "Wait... Are you saying that we're friends?" I couldn't help but to smile.

"Seatbelt."

I pulled it on. "Okay Buddy. Thanks for caring."

He sighed, turned the blinker on and steered us out onto the road.

After a moment, I started to hum the theme from Golden Girls. "Hm hm hm *Being a friend...*"

In the backseat, Raegan started humming along, and that made Paige's façade crack; he smiled. Raegan added, "You're too young to know that show."

I glanced back. "Hank Cottonwood... He was your friend?"

"He *is* my friend. Going on forty years, now. Should see the place he was in, between when his father died and I took responsibility for him."

We passed from the part of town thick with businesses to a more residential area. It was a lovely day, sunny, not too warm, a soft, pleasant breeze even as we sat at a red light.

I said, "I understand that. But why did you have to hang Harry Santiago out to dry like that?"

He didn't answer for a minute. "I bet you've got a taste for it, now. In a few years, you'll do the training, come back the right way, be sitting where you are, now. Then you'll understand. Couple of kids overdose with a local dealer, he's older, you make the arrest. Even if you don't think he brought the stuff, this time. Next time, he will. And those kids' parents wanted justice, real or not. Seemed like the right thing at the time."

"He was poor, an immigrant, and he made a few mistakes. He was an easy scapegoat."

"Believe what you want about me, if it makes it easer for you. That's what we all do, to get through the day."

## Chapter Twenty-Six

Kathy had wanted to have a party at the diner on the day of the recall vote, but I had said 'no thanks'. With Raegan behind bars, and Harry Santiago's release imminent, I felt like I had accomplished all that I needed to. I didn't need to put on a brave face, I didn't need consolation, and I would rather be alone with my family, if I was, indeed, recalled.

We were watching the evening news, Tuesday, and Alanna Malone was on sight at City Hall.

"I'm here in Elviston, Tennessee, with the results of the vote to recall Teen Sheriff, Evelyn Lassiter, whose exploits have captivated the county, the state, and the nation. Sheriff Lassiter, of course, is the eighteen-year-old high school student set to graduate this weekend. In a world of academic competition and political division, she set herself apart and set out to bring the youth into the conversation of what some say is a racist institution of law enforcement in America. Along the way, she and Deputy Leo Paige -who once ran for sheriff himself, and lost- found themselves investigating former nine-term

Sheriff Dax Raegan, who was found to be embroiled in an operation to distribute the deadly designer drug, Blue 82. Two other deputies were caught up in the scandal, with one on administrative leave pending the outcome of an IAB investigation and another under arrest at Elviston Mercy General Hospital after a shooting at the town's Memorial Day parade."

A lot of it was bloated for the sake of intrigue, of course. If there had been national news coverage, it had been skimpy. Blue 82 was deadly, I supposed, but of course she would not be privy to how Raegan had been trying to keep the stuff that entered the county as clean as could be, that the overdoses had happened on the stuff that came in, before him. Kipling had been the one to take the brick of the old stuff cut with bad shit out of evidence, swimming in debt the way that he had been, reckless as he was. That was the stuff that Hiram Walsh, Ian McMahon and Frank Gillespie had all overdosed on.

When Raegan knew that we had him, he was proud to admit that he had been the one who shot Frank Gillespie. He was selling that tainted shit, against orders. Then he had started using it to numb the pain of the flesh wound, and irony signed his death certificate.

Alanna Malone introduced a man in his fifties, paunchy and balding. "Here's City Manager Ted Whitlock, with the tallied results."

"Thank you, Ms. Malone. I can tell you that this has been a historic vote for Elviston County, the highest turnout we've ever seen by a wide margin-."

She retracted her microphone to prompt, "And what were the results?"

"With a majority of fifty-four point eight percent to forty-three point two percent, the motion to recall Sheriff Lassiter has failed-."

My father whooped and my mother gasped, shaking me where I sat, managing a smile. I was distantly proud, but it was a small thing, compared to all that I had done already. I raised my glass of water in a toast, they joined me with a bottle of beer and a glass of red wine. "Here's to democracy, and I hereby announce my resignation-."

They whooped and cheered louder, making a two-person crowd.

"-Effective two weeks from today, or next week, Tuesday, if we can get Paige elected by then. The sooner the better. Whatever."

I had no doubt that the poll workers were on call to hold another election if I had been recalled, and so I wondered if I announced my resignation right away if they wouldn't cobble it together in just a week's time. Nobody would need time to campaign, after all. It was a small pay raise with hellish hours to be the top dog of a tiny county nobody had ever heard of before I came along. I felt reasonably sure that we could get Paige elected. My phone was buzzing like crazy with congratulatory texts.

I picked out the one from him, sent him back a quick reply: *YOU'RE NEXT* with a knife emoji, why not?

Finishing her wine, Mom said, "We had some news we were saving to congratulate you with if you won-."

"-Or comfort you with if you lost," Dad said.

"What?"

"The Walkmen announced more dates, they're playing Nashville!"

I clutched my chest, more for their sake than my own. I had seen the new dates announced and thought my parents would do exactly what they were doing. "Really? And we're going?"

"It's in October, think you'll be free then?"

"I'll make sure of it, thank you guys!" I hugged her first.

"We felt awful going without you, last time."

"I felt awful, too…" I hugged Dad. "You guys won't be bored, seeing the same show again?"

"No way."

"That's dedication… Thank you guys for everything, this past few months… I've decided I'm going to go to Chattanooga State Community College, at least for a year or two. Delilah's going there, and we can get our general education credits out of the way while we figure out what we're going to do. Plus I can stay here with you guys and Mabel a little longer, if that's alright."

"Of course," Mom said. "But… wasn't half the reason that you did this -became sheriff, I mean- that you wanted the leg up in getting accepted to schools, and scholarships?"

"Yeah… That was part of it. I could probably get a full ride, or close to it, somewhere bigger than CSCC… but there's not much point if I don't know what I'm doing, which I don't, or if I'd have to live on campus and be totally alone, which I'd hate. And if I left, and Mabel died, I'd never forgive myself for losing that time with her. Same if something happened to one of you…"

I felt my cheeks heat up. The shooting had put some things clearly into perspective, scary as it had been. I was not supposed to be a sheriff, not now. I was supposed to be a daughter, and a friend. I was working up to something sappy, and part of me hated it, but I pushed myself to keep going.

"I don't know what I want to be, but I know who I am. I have responsibilities here, so this is where I belong for now."

Dad said, "Happy to have you, Eves."

*

A few weeks later Scott, Delilah, and I laid on towels at the beach. Us girls were soaking up sun, while Scott was propped up one elbow, eating an orange creamsicle from the Swirl, which was just a short walk up the beach.

A kid ran by screaming, being chased by his older sister. He climbed up onto the three foot retaining wall that separated the sandy beach and lakefront from the grassy playground up above. Further down, a group of what had to be college students spotted him. One whipped a beer bottle so that it shattered against the wood right in front of him.

He screamed in shock. "Hey!" He turned and ran the other way.

I was on my feet in a flash, stalking over. "What the Hell do you think you're doing!?"

"Oh no." Scott hurried after, then Delilah did, too.

The burnout college boy who had thrown the bottle blinked down at me. "What's your problem?"

"You could have hit that kid. And people walk barefoot here, it's a beach! Pick up those shards, or I'll have you arrested. The sheriff's a personal friend of mine, and I've got him on speed dial."

"Arrested for what? Having a good time?"

"Littering, $500 fine. Public intoxication, up to thirty days in jail. Are you gonna pick it up, or am I gonna make that call?"

"Alright. Fine. Bitch."

I supervised the clean up while his friends laughed at him and gave him shit. Then we went back to our spot, laying down again. My heart was pounding, I had missed the feeling.

Delilah was still sitting, she raised her hand to shield her eyes and squinted at the line wrapped around the Swirl's little white building. "Glad it's my day off."

I said, "Glad I only have days off."

Scott made a fart noise with his palm pressed to his mouth. Then asked, "How many days until the Walkmen show?"

"A hundred and two days," I rattled off.

"Almost down to double digits."

Delilah rolled onto her stomach. "And how many days until classes start?"

I copied her, stretching out luxuriously in the warm sand. "Who cares?"

The End.

If you enjoyed #TeenSheriff Evelyn Lassiter,
Please leave a review wherever you buy books. It's harder than ever before to make a living as an author, and your review matters.

Turn the page for a look inside 'Witch Wife' which is an adult Fantasy novel coming November 21, 2024.

Chapter One

The metal of the box I'm in shakes and groans as the carriage jolts down the bumpy road. It's pitch black inside and my mind is just as cold and dark. I'm collapsed in a heap where they threw me. I reek of sweat and filth and urine; we've been traveling for a long time, maybe days, and I haven't moved a muscle. I couldn't if I wanted to. My body is spent. I've been running on fumes for weeks -almost no food left to be found- dragging myself around the country on horseback and aching feet and duty. On and off battlefields, swinging a sword and a dagger, opening flesh of my countrymen and in the same motion rending the muscles of my arms, still coated up to the elbows with sticky dried blood. I used to cringe at the sight. I used to worry about being clean.

Now I'm used to wearing the blood of strangers, friends, and my countrymen. It feels like it belongs on me. The last time I was truly clean -before the massacre at Youngstown, where the war was lost and I was taken-

I could still feel it. The skin around my eyes is tight with dried tears. I don't have anymore left in me.

My thoughts play on a loop the lives I took, the lives I lost, when I saw him for the last time as he was sliced across the chest, and collapsed into the crush of redcoats. I screamed my throat raw, tried to surge through the bodies to get to him, but hands were clawing me, arms encircling my neck, pinching my windpipe, cutting off my sobs and snatching me off of my feet. They were swarming on the fallen, putting down the wounded with savage slices of their rapiers, taking no prisoners except for me.

My exhausted and frantic mind hadn't understood it in the moment. But in the hours since, I have begrudgingly begun to consider what is happening. I can't help it. After I realized there was nothing inside of the carriage which I could use to swiftly kill myself, my mind turned strategic.

I have had encounters with British nobility before, although I never thought I left much of an impression. I had sat in on war councils for the last several months, at the request of the New World's prince, but I was far from one of the most important players in the war. I had earned no significant rank, only a Second Lieutenant. So they had not been collecting officers to make spectacles of, for trials in their courts, then to be publicly drawn and quartered, ripping their hearts out still beating while their guts barbecued on a nearby pit, smoking with foul black haze that burned the eyes… If I could opt into it, now, I would. I'd walk past the firepit and offer my hands up to be tied at the post. Anything to put an end to this cold, black Hell.

No, they were not collecting officers. What happened to Felix? He was a Captain. Merrick was a senior Lieutenant, and they cut him down without hesitation.

My hand twitches, and clenches into a fist. Sticky, smelly, sore. He mocked the way I pronounced it when we were promoted in tandem. 'Left-tenant'. My Englishness, the thing he hated about me when we first met, had become something to joke about over the years. His last thoughts will have been of me; his eyes found me in the moment the sword slashed his chest open, and his blood made a sickening crest in the air. I remember the sadness in his eyes, the regret at not being able to protect me anymore. I could almost hear him say, "Sorry, Kid." I press my face into the metal, which smells like pocket change and is cool on my cheek. I focus all of my energy and try to die. Heart failure, spontaneous combustion, undetected blood infection shutting down my organs one by one, quick and painless or slow and painful, I don't care. If anyone could just go out like a light, then in that moment, I would. But it can't be done. I have heard of widows dying of broken hearts, but it's a slower process. Probably I will have to wait. Not long though.

Wherever they are taking me, there will be something I can use. Something sharp. One quick slice, cut, impale my heart. Worst case scenario, I can starve myself. A slower and more ignoble end is probably what I deserve. Then there will be nothing, which is more peace than I deserve. Or maybe I'm a cynic, maybe Merrick was right and maybe he's waiting for me somewhere. Heaven or Hell, if we're together, it won't matter.

I'm about to slip into blissful unconsciousness when I feel the rocking of the carriage stop. It has happened a few times. Switching horses or drivers, I figure. But then the thing starts to roll again and a sound of grinding metal on metal echoes around my enclosure, I'm flopped over in the next second and roll to the back corner, banging against the wall as the carriage takes a steep incline. Then stops.

The door of my cage opens. Light floods the space that has been my private Hell. I shrink from it, it almost fries my eyes out of my head. There is a series of thuds.

A coarse English voice declares, "Food for the witch."

Before the door closes again, I see outlines of a few pieces of fruit and a few pieces of bread. A metal canteen. Darkness closes in on me again.

A witch, am I?

Am I? I thought I knew myself, once, but that was before all of the death. Now I am nobody. Practically formless in the dark. My body seems to have broken up and now floats around in the square iron box. The pieces might reconfigure in any possible combination, change me at the cellular level. I could be anything, and it wouldn't surprise me. A witch, a worm, a healer like Fiona...

I can't think of Fiona, now. I hope she is alive, unharmed, as much as possible, that maybe we lost Felix on the battlefield because he left it to go to her... Came to his senses... I put her from my mind. If I don't, I may lose my nerve at the last moment. She knew me longer than anyone, since I was born, and somehow, I feel that even she would not recognize me, now.

They don't draw and quarter witches. They sink them in lakes, or burn them. I have enough of my old self left to wish not to burn. But that will probably be the way it goes. If I burn or if I get my hands on something sharp, it will be much quicker than starving. I have been starving for weeks, and I am sick of it. I stretch an arm out that shakes and aches like it might snap off, grab a piece of fruit -an apple, it turns out- and sink my teeth into the bruised flesh. Sour juice floods my mouth, makes me choke with the sudden flood of saliva and how long it has been since I had food. Just like that, the haze is lifted. My body becomes solid in the dark again. I remember Snow White. I wish the apple were poisoned. But it's only sour.

*

Hours more, surely days. I ate my fill of bread and fruit when first it was tossed to me, ran out and grew very hungry again before finally someone opened the door and tossed in some more. The carriage I remain trapped in starts to sway gently, I know that I have been taken on a ship. We are crossing the sea.

They are taking me to England. It's an awfully long way to transport someone, just for a witch trial. The soldiers did not hear gossip about the English sisters aligned with the New World troops, one a healer and one a fighter, come to their own conclusions and take it upon themselves to burn me only to then send me across an ocean. Someone commanded the soldiers, they were looking for me.

Who could command soldiers? Royalty, certainly. I don't believe I was ever in the same room as anyone royal. Someone of significant rank in the British military might have commanded my abduction, but I never knew any of them, either. I try to think of other possibilities, but my mind gets stuck in a loop of playing the moment that Merrick fell over and over again, I can't help it. The numbness has faded some, I curl in on myself and waste what little water has returned to my system on a few tears. Existing hurts. I want it to end. I think crazy thoughts; I could take off a sock -filthy and sweaty as they must be- stuff it down my throat and try to suffocate myself. I hardly have any pride anymore, that's not what stops me. It's just that I know what a body will do of its own volition in certain circumstances. A body is a separate entity, sometimes, and desperate to survive. A mind is like a parasite, to the body's host. I didn't want to kill any of those people, but once I was on the battlefield, on the business end of their weaponry, my body took over.

Once more on our sea voyage someone tosses me food, throws in a full flask rather than retrieve the canteen and fill it. Probably it is dead to them, now. Bewitched. I had grown as used to starving as a person could in the past year, but I had never been without water for so long, and the thirst was impossible to get used to, or forget, even for a second. It started to drive me a little bit mad, or more mad, since I could hardly be considered in my right mind anymore. It ran out once again, though I tried to ration it, then so did the food.

I sit up in the dark, feeling more solid. I piss in one of the corners and am acutely aware of the reek all around me, on me. And also the heat, it's sweltering, and I am in a constant state of damp. A year ago I would have been mortified to be perceived as filthy, but my pride was dying a slow death over the last few months, then left me all at once when Merrick fell.

I consider banging on the walls and asking for water. I haven't quite decided to yet when the carriage moves again, more metal on metal, a steep decline as we depart the ship, then another bumpy road. I tense as we come to a final stop, a few hours later. The door opens. I blink and shield my eyes as they adjust.

Six redcoats stand outside the carriage, three on either side before a massive entryway of a castle of white stone, intricately carved and ornate. One reaches in and gestures for me to come closer.

I stay where I am, at the back.

"Come out, or I'll come in and drag you out."

And hands groping at me are always horrifying, and I'd just as soon get it over with, so I inch to the edge and lower my feet. When I stand, I wobble. My legs don't hurt as much as they did after the final battle, but they are still weak, and the muscles have not been used. The redcoat who spoke reaches out and takes my arm, which I shrink from, but he holds firm and starts to walk. I stumble but don't fall, another soldier from the other side latches onto my other arm. We trudge into a grand hall of marble floors, a carpet of red and gold embroidery stretching from the entrance to the elevated pair of empty thrones at the back. Royalty. I shudder.

I am taken up a narrow staircase, noticing ornate weapons hung up on the walls but sure that I won't be able to grab one and use it before I am apprehended again. I am shoved into a room and the door locked from the outside behind me. I am not alone.

There is a summer breeze drifting in past white gossamer curtains which I could probably use to hang myself. A woman stands there, a maid from the look of her. She has brown skin, a round face with a big plume of brown hair under her headscarf. She is well fed and has shrewd eyes even as her hands wring nervously on her apron.

"Bonjour Miss, hello…" A slight accent, she sounds educated, which is strange. "My name is Anita. I'm to be your handmaid while you reside here, with us. I have orders to help you bathe, and dress, for an audience with the King. There is food, also…"

A steaming tub in one corner of the room. I have as little hope of being capable of drowning myself as I do of choking myself to death. Some of the food is steaming, as well. A half a chicken in a white sauce, potatoes, carrots. A basket of rolls, butter and honey. A three-tiered silver tray of pastries and bite-sized cakes. A glass of white wine. I stare at it for a long moment, remembering how I used to dream of a spread just like it, while I was trying to sleep on the hard ground, shivering under a threadbare blanket, stomach gnawing at itself but at least I was in my husband's arms, with his soft, snoring breaths making my hair tickle my neck. I'd trade all of this for that in a heartbeat. But it can't be done. I can envision it so vividly that I feel like I should be able to climb into that version of my life, but I never can again.

I sit at the table. The only silverware they've given me is a wooden spoon. I could scoop an eye out with it but probably not kill myself. Picking up the chicken leg with filthy fingers, I tear into it.

"Your name is Irene, they tell me." Anita stands nearby.

"Irene Shannon." My married name tastes bitter. "Eat, if you want."

She shakes her head. "I'm alright, thank you."

I eat until my belly is full, then use the bathroom, then move to the bath where Anita waits.

"We had better wipe you down before you get in the tub. May I?" Her hands pause at the tie on the front of my white blouse. I nod. She pulls the strings, then I bend forward and she tugs the shirt over my head. I hear her intake of breath, meet her eyes as I shuck off my disgusting pants, then I'm standing before her naked. She is a fine looking girl -a few years younger than me, maybe twenty- and it might be erotic if I felt or looked remotely like a person. She takes in the sight of me with sympathetic eyes. My ribs and hip bones stick out, I'm dirty and bloody and hairy.

Anita has a cloth and a pail of warm water, and starts at my shoulders, scrubbing my skin. I stand perfectly still, feel warm rivulets run down the front and back of me.

"Where's your color going?" Anita asks, smiling a little and looking at me from the corner of her eye. "We could have been sisters when you came in. Half-sisters, maybe... Now you're white as a sheet."

"Do you know what they're going to do to me?"

Her smile fades. "No, Miss. I've known the king for years now, he has always been a fair man."

The water in her pail is murky and full of silt by the time she reaches my feet. I climb into the metal tub and ease down into the warm water. Merrick and I would bathe in icy streams after a battle, or whenever we were too ripe. I haven't had a hot bath in months. For some reason, along with all of my muscles relaxing, something gives inside of me, too, and I'm crying again before I know it.

Anita takes a clean towel and sits beside me, dabs at the tears and shushes me. "Sh. Things are scary right now, but you're young. They say that time is all we need to heal, and you have plenty."

But I am not young, I shake my head furiously. I have killed probably a hundred people, and lost everything and everyone. "I've had enough. I've had enough, I'm ready for it to be over."

"Sh." She lathers up the clean cloth with a bar of soap and starts to scrub me down again. She does not shave me, and so bizarre thoughts of being made a sex slave disappear from my mind. With all of the dirt left to be scrubbed from my hair and scalp, the tub is dingy and cold when I finally climb out, dry off. Anita combs my hair, which I am grateful for. I hardly think I can lift my arms repeatedly, have trouble keeping my head up. She lets my brown hair hang loose, helps me into a dress. I haven't worn a dress in so long. It's a heavy thing of expensive fabric, feels as out of place as they always do on me. The sleeves are too tight on my arms, which still hold some of their muscle, were once so strong, cleaving through flesh and bone and sometimes rough hide armor.

They have a pair of shoes with dainty little heels meant to go with the dress. They are much too large for my feet, so I leave them off. The dress drags on the ground, so my feet are hidden, anyway -they thought that I would be larger, taller, because I am a warrior- but I am only five foot, six inches. Felix was nearly a foot taller than me… Merrick a few inches taller.

With me finally clean and dry and fed and dressed, Anita knocks on the door and the heavy lock is opened from outside. The two redcoats wait there, and this time, they do not take hold of me. Maybe they are uncomfortable man-handling a girl in a dress, already putting from their minds the bloody, dirty, piss-covered murderer they escorted an hour before. I know that at my best, I am not bad. It's all the better if they let down their guard. If they let me get ahold of one of their swords, it will be over so quickly. I'll ruin the pretty dress the color of lilacs, stain it red. Show them who I am, or was.

The guards, however, seem alert. They take me back downstairs, through the main hall and into a bright sunroom. Sunlight streams through intricate stained-glass windows which depict saints, the Virgin Mother draped in blue. Different colored squares of light land on a massive rug, white and embroidered with gold, stretching almost the entire area of the room. Its worth could probably buy every building I have ever called home, and there have been many.

A small table is set for tea in the center of the room, and a man in a white blouse and golden trousers sits there, eating an afternoon snack of cake and fruits. Munching as he looks up at me upon my entrance, he holds up a finger, meaning 'one moment', sips tea and swallows.

He smacks his lips noisily and catches his breath. "Ah. Finally. Please, join me." It has the cadence of an order. He is a man probably in his fifties, balding but not quite there yet, unfit and pale. Several gold rings, several prominent features like his large ears and thick brow, and the way that he clearly views himself tells me that he is the king. The two redcoats move to stand, armed and at attention, on the nearest wall.

I take the seat offered. None of the three men present bother to pull the chair out or scootch it in behind me, as they normally would in polite society. It seems the pleasantries have gone out the window. I do not speak, wait for the king to finish chewing a purple grape. I can hear its skin pop when he first crunches it beneath his tobacco browned teeth.

"Tea?" He starts to reach for the pot.

I shake my head. "Don't like it. Never have." My voice is low. It's not timid, just tired.

"And you call yourself a Brit?"

"Not for some time, now. You know I fought with the New World."

"And you lost," the king declares, his tone as cheerful as the little rose frosted onto the piece of cake he grabs. "So a Brit, you remain. As such, I have a... well, let's not call it a charge to put to you... I have delightful news to share, and most heartfelt congratulations to offer you. You see, my nephew the Earl of Snowdon is in want of a wife. With our recent victory across the sea, it has been decided that the woman should be someone from the New World, to rebuild some good will between our nations. You are, of course, only tangentially related to nobility, but a more suitable bloodline can be arranged, along with annulling your previous marriage as far as the church is concerned-."

I scoff.

He blinks. "Something funny? Your king is welcoming you into the royal family, thereby allowing you to live the rest of your days in luxury rather than having you put to death for your treason."

I take a breath and force down nauseous feelings trying to swell up. Fury is familiar, an old friend, but if I let it in, I don't know what else will come up with it. Numbness is my friend now. "Why?"

"Why? Well... There's the unity it will foster, of course I already mentioned that... And then, there are certain arts which you are known to practice. I don't believe in any of that, myself, but my wife -the queen- has a penchant for exploring different... pathways. A voracious mind, she has, and her studies and dealings with those certain types of people... practitioners of so-called dark arts have pointed her squarely in your direction."

A witch. Me. I shut my eyes to keep from rolling them. My curiosity piqued, I dig deep past the numbness to find myself. I open my eyes and stare down the king as I say, "I will not be remarrying. My husband is dead, and I intend to join him in death as soon as possible."

"Preposterous, I won't allow it."

I simmer for a moment. Force down the fury again. "You're used to getting your way. Born with a silver spoon in your mouth. You've probably never had someone tell you 'no' before."

"Correct."

"The answer is no. One of your men will let down their guard, or the maid will leave something sharp lying around, or I'll starve myself if I have to. It might be a long time. You might try to bribe or torture me, but you will never compel me to vow to love and honor any man who isn't my husband. And I don't think any priest would pronounce me married without my consent, even under your orders. You should make a different plan, find someone else to marry into your family, to read the tea leaves and call down the rain. Save us both a lot of trouble. You won't use me."

The king has been watching me with amused eyes while I spoke. He takes a drink of tea. Sets the cup down noisily on the fine china saucer. "First of all, my men are the cream of the crop. They do not let down their guard, under pain of death. Your handmaid, Anita, is the single sharpest woman I have ever met, including even my lovely wife. -Why do you think she was given the task of managing you? Starve yourself if you wish to, but my cooks and staff are more than up to the challenge of holding you down and forcing adequate nutrients down your throat. Bribery, certainly, we'll try that. Torture, too, if a bit of time and bribery can't do the trick. I do not lose, Madam. We can do it the easy way or the hard way, but in the end, I will not lose. What happens next is up to you."

I am recovered enough from the battlefield and the journey after the bath and the meal for a sinking feeling to have begun in my stomach. I am a person, again. Aware of my skin in the warm room, my heart beating a bit harder in my chest, the pain encroaching on me from every direction. More than a person, I am a woman, a sister, a wife. It's going to be unpleasant, I know. The king is no oaf, and I am on my own, now. But I remind myself there is nothing to be afraid of. Nothing he can do to me is worse than what has already happened.

I stand. One of the redcoat guards against the wall flinches, almost moving to step forward and intercept me. But I simply pick up my skirts so that they don't drag, step clear of the chair, and face the king, back straight.

His face brightens, a hint of a smile grows on his lips. He expects me to curtsy, as I have made him believe I am going to.

Instead I grab lower on my dress, taking more of the lilac fabric in my hands, and lift the skirts higher. I spread my legs, squat and urinate on the lovely white and golden rug, a little pool of strong and dark piss. I'm still quite dehydrated and it will leave a nasty stain.

"Good Heavens!" He pounds the table and the china clinks. "Take her away! Lock her in her room, no food for a day for her rudeness. See how she likes that."

They grab my arms and start to drag me, but I walk, throwing my head back and laughing a true witch's cackle. It bursts out of my chest like a bullet, cold and forceful, and I'm sure the king will hear it even as we cross the empty main hall, where it echoes off the stone walls.

Made in the USA
Middletown, DE
17 April 2024